THE
BRIDGE
OF SIGHS

THE
BRIDGE
OF SIGHS

OLEN STEINHAUER

 ST. MARTIN'S MINOTAUR
NEW YORK

www.minotaurbooks.com

Book design by Jonathan Bennett

ISBN 0-312-30245-2

First Edition: February 2003

10   9   8   7   6   5   4   3   2   1

ACKNOWLEDGMENTS

****

A novel's author is inevitably indebted to others for their assistance. This one is no exception.

Much of what I understand of this region of the world was learned during a research trip to Romania, very appreciatively funded by the Fulbright Commission and tirelessly assisted by the fine poet Ioana Ieronim.

For its timely and detailed answers to my questions, I thank the Berlin chapter of the Berlin Airlift Historical Foundation.

Any mistakes, of course, are my own.

For her generosity and encouragement, I warmly thank another poet, the great Gail Mazur.

And for his enthusiasm, good humor and faith, I salute my agent, Matt Williams.

For everything, Krista.

THE
BRIDGE
OF SIGHS

CHAPTER ONE

****

The greeting was in his desk, the center drawer: a piece of fish-stained cardboard with a clumsily drawn stick figure. It had a circular head and an X for each eye. A fat knife separated the head from its stick body. The speech balloon said, *We're on to you.*

His chair wobbled insecurely beneath him.

Emil inhaled slowly, evenly. He sat in the center of the large, stale-smelling office, between two columns, and on the far wall two high, open windows did nothing to freshen the air. His tight suit constricted him as he stared above the others' heads at the clock on the yellow wall. It was the dirty, pale yellow of Austro-Hungarian demise. He had been here only forty-five minutes.

It was Monday, the twenty-third of August, 1948, 9:17 A.M. He still had a whole day to go.

He couldn't match names to their faces yet, but why should that matter? Along the walls, three of the four homicide inspectors grinned at their wide, steel desks, suppressing laughter. They were all to blame. Through the windows, street noises spilled into the hot room: clopping hooves, shouts, the occasional motor car.

His grandmother had starched his suit into a hard crust to celebrate his first day in the People's Militia. He wanted to run his finger between his collar and neck, but knew how it would look.

His exhale finally came.

The fourth inspector wasn't grinning: the stout one at the corner desk with the wide, flat, familiar-looking peasant's face.

Despite the heat wave, he lounged in the leather overcoat of state security. By law, one security inspector was assigned to each Militia department, but no law ordered them to dress like that, like the Russian secret police. Yet they all did. And like their MVD counterparts, they never laughed. This one stared at Emil with the intensity of a scientist waiting for a nerve-provoked response.

In the opposite corner, beside the windows, the largest of them banged slowly at a typewriter. He was a neckless lump of clay with tin rings constricting his thick fingers. The sound of striking keys filled the room.

Emil had spoken to them once when he arrived. A twenty-two-year-old in a stiff suit with a stupid, bashful grin marking his pale features, a blond schoolboy among these dark veterans. "My name is Emil Brod, and this is my first day with Homicide."

A voice he could not put to a face had answered: "Desk's in the center."

Even then, they did not show him their eyes. But he was the only thing they were watching.

Emil settled his small hands on the desk.

At another time and place the sketched decapitation would have provoked violence. But now, here, he separated himself from the anger. He let the cardboard drop into his wastebasket, gingerly shifted the chair beneath himself, and opened the morning's *Spark,* which he had picked up on his way to work. There were grainy images of airplanes in the west, heavy American and British planes over Berlin. Words about remilitarization and effrontery spotted the pages, but he couldn't focus enough to read whole sentences. The typewriter continued snapping. The stuffy room grew hotter.

He had gone dutifully to the desk in the center of the room, just as the voice had commanded, and put down his hat and satchel. Then he rapped timidly on the door with CHIEF painted on the wood. A light curtain covered the dark window beside it. "When does Chief Moska arrive?"

It was an insignificant question, something he almost felt foolish asking, and their agreement was apparent by their silence. He returned to his desk. When he sat down his chair collapsed beneath him.

They had all laughed then, even the security inspector.

He sprang up. The chair was in pieces. The rope that bound its legs together had snapped, or been cut. Their amused faces turned back to their desks as he tied the chair together again with a fishing knot. It wobbled, but held. By the time he was finished, the laughter had been over a long time.

It was then that he had reached for the center drawer, if for no other reason than to look busy.

Maybe it was a joke. He didn't know. They had laughed, so perhaps there was nothing more to this than some gentle hazing. Like in the Academy, when they buried his papers in the middle of the firing range, or when he lay in the mud and they gave him one kick apiece. Certainly this was easier than that.

He set the newspaper aside. In one dusty corner was a brown porcelain heater for wintertime, as tall as a man, and along the walls three desks faced the center—faced *him*. The fourth desk, the state security inspector's, faced the wall.

He settled back into his creaking chair and affected a calm he didn't feel. He arranged the ink bottle on his desk and straightened the blotter, then placed his transfer papers—in triplicate, as required—along the edge. From his burlap satchel he brought out the cigars and the leather-bound notepad his grandfather had been able to unearth in the black market off Heroes' Square. If he focused on these little things he could make it.

The inspectors lounged at their desks, sweating, chewing dried pumpkin seeds, sometimes muttering into telephones, other times writing or smoking. The big one continued typing. Two of them—one scrawny and very dark, the other heavy and limping, spitting out flakes of pumpkin seed—met beside yellowed WANTED notices and joked quietly with one another. The sound of their laughter left small, cold spots in Emil's guts. They left the office together and returned smelling of clear alcohols. The fat one carried a fresh bag of tobacco with nicotine-yellowed fingers.

A man outside was shouting in Russian. Although the rowdy Russian soldiers that still occupied their small capital disturbed him as much as the next person, at that moment he wanted to be with them, under the sun, rather than in this dim, humid room with his own kind.

He stood without knowing why. Then, as he approached the massive typist, he knew. He would start with the largest, if only to instill faith in his courage. Emil rapped on the big man's desk beside an empty paper cup blackened by the morning's grounds. "Where do I get coffee around here?"

He stopped typing and looked at Emil's hand as though his finger were a cockroach. This close, the inspector's face was pocked and misshapen like a battlefield. "No coffee," he said flatly. He crushed the cup in his hand, then tossed it in his wastebasket.

Emil's collar tightened. He smiled involuntarily and stepped back to his desk. He could hear laughter somewhere. It was faint and distant beneath the hot buzzing of his blood. So was the glint of his polished shoes moving across the floor. He was a stiff clown among these wrinkled, dusty brutes. He remembered the Academy director's words: *First District, Homicide. Desk's been open two years since some old poop named Sergei got himself shot after Liberation. They'll take anyone, Brod, why not you?*

Why not, indeed.

The Spark was full of airplanes. It had been full of blockades and planes since June. Muddy newsprint airplanes on cheap, brittle pages, but they were clear enough. Allied airplanes over hills of rubble; airplanes over military convoys; airplanes over the hungry, defeated masses of a crushed Berlin, dropping parachutes with little boxes of food and chocolates and clothing. And—some reports said—guns.

The front page never changed, not even today. A part of him had expected to find the planes replaced by his own face—thin and pale, blond eyebrows almost invisible above his green eyes—beneath the headline: EMIL BROD MOVES INTO THE WORKING WORLD—NO MORE LESSONS FOR HIM! But there they still were, after weeks: airplanes: IMPERIAL UNDERHANDEDNESS IN BERLIN! Comrade Chairman Stalin called the institution of a new German currency a provocation. If the Allies had their way, a reborn, capitalist Germany would consume the workers of the world in fire. General Secretary Mihai, whose office was only a few streets away, reminded all citizens that their own country was small and young. It could easily be divided out of existence again by the republics around it. No one misunderstood his meaning. "Before the Great War, we were only a district of the Dual Monarchy—remember Versailles!" he told a reporter. "The others would claim we are theirs, but we are not pieces of the Ukraine and Czechoslovakia—we're neither Romania nor Hungary nor Poland! We are our own, indivisible nation!" Then: "Up with the Comrade Chairman!"

The second page listed upcoming trials. It was no longer like the days just after the Liberation, when the lists went on for many columns. But there were still some men and women accused of undermining the stability of their socialist state. There were a baker and three politicians and two tram drivers—which proved, according to a certain well-regarded Inspector Brano Sev, the democratic sensibility inherent in the instruments of criminal justice.

Around noon, he tried the smallest one. The wiry, dark inspector who sat beside the cold porcelain stove. He had a face that reminded Emil of the Jews who had appeared at the family dacha in Ruscova during the war. They had come in loose, hungry bands from over the Romanian border, muttering frantically about the Archangel Michael and their villages being burned to the ground. Their families, they said, had been chopped up by the Orthodox. This inspector had that same hungry, war-refugee look.

Emil spoke to him over the hand basins in the empty wash-room. His voice echoed unexpectedly against the tile walls. "How long does this go on?"

The inspector stopped splashing water over the back of his neck. He looked at Emil in the rusting mirror, hungry brow furrowing.

Beneath Emil's feet the decaying floor tiles wobbled. "The silence," he said, trying to make his voice sound light, conversational. "Is this what everyone goes through? I think I know how this works. Initiation?" He twisted his lips into a smile. "Or are you trying to scare me away?" He almost added jokingly that this situation hadn't come up in the Academy lessons, but thought better of it.

The inspector turned away, shook water off his hands and used a towel from a hook. His dark features gave away nothing, his eyes hard and small as he dried his neck. He gave Emil only a passing glance in the mirror as he hung up the towel again. Then he left. The creaking door echoed behind him.

They left the office singly and in pairs and did not return for hours. He assumed they were on cases. The Academy had taught two ways for a homicide inspector to receive a case. Either a switchboard operator sent a message to your telephone line, or the station chief emerged from his office and handed you one. All through the morning the phone on Emil's desk did not ring, and the chief was never in. He got coffee from a workers' café around

the corner, returned, used the toilet twice, read the last pages of
The Spark—all slowly, purposefully.

Around two o'clock, Chief Moska appeared in the doorway.
He was another big man, in his fifties, who hiked up wrinkled,
mud-spotted pants, rolled a cigarette in his lips, and took off his
hat to mop damp, gray hair with a handkerchief. He stopped by
desks and whispered to his men, and when they smiled Emil's
stomach shriveled. These men were tight, had been for years.
They had probably even fought the Germans together—side by
side, without his help.

The chief stopped at Emil's desk and inclined his long, pale
face. The smile was gone. He had the worn features of war veterans who believe they have witnessed everything this life could
ever show them. "So you're the new one?" His voice was no
longer a fraternal whisper; it was deep and swollen for all to
hear.

"Yes, Comrade Chief Moska."

"Emil Brod from the Fourth District?"

"Fifth, Comrade Chief."

"Where did you serve in the Patriotic War?"

"I was too young, Com—"

"Too young my ass!" he bellowed. "You were born in 1926,
which made you of age in—what?—1942, or at the latest '44." He
eyeballed Emil's little hands on the desk. Emil removed them. "I
have a neighbor who fought Germans when he was twelve.
Remember who has your file, Brod."

Emil spoke with as much authority as he could muster. "What
I meant to say was that when I came of age, I was not in the country. I was—"

"You were fishing in Finland!" the chief erupted, his sudden,
broad smile revealing two holes where teeth should have been.
"For little *seals*, no less!"

Their laughter was loud, bouncing off the walls.

"A Finnish company, yes," said Emil, recognizing a slight warble to his voice he hoped was only in his head. "But I hunted in the Arctic Circle."

For an instant he was out of this hot room and back in the icy north, among men so much more dangerous than these.

"You speak Russian, I hear."

"Yes. And German."

"A *scholar*," said the chief. "And now here you are, back at your mother's tit."

"In Homicide," Emil replied, his voice clearing up. "And I'm ready to work. Here are my transfer papers." He held out the folded pages.

The chief suddenly had the expression of a man about to retch. His nostrils, crisscrossed by a drinker's red tributaries, retracted. Then he stuffed the papers into his blazer pocket. "Well, *Comrade Brod*," he said through a heavy sigh, "don't make trouble. If you do that, trouble might stay away from you."

There were sprinkles of weak laughter from corners of the room Emil could not locate, because the blood pumping in his ears obscured their direction.

"I wouldn't consider it, Comrade Chief."

"And don't *comrade* me to death, Brod. Makes my skin crawl. Can you manage that simple task?"

"Yes, Chief."

They were all watching the exchange, their smiles fading in and out until the chief gave him one last miserable look, turned on his heel, and walked into his office. The door latched quietly.

Emil caught their amused faces as they turned away—the big typist, the refugee, the pumpkin-seed eater sweating in the back and the state security inspector with the peasant's features that clicked in Emil's skull, nagging at a memory that would not come.

****

First was the chair. Second, the drawing. Third was the homicide inspector with the face of a refugee who met him on the hot front steps at the end of that fruitless day. Down by the busy street, he smoked with some regular policemen standing in a semicircle around the head of a fly-nagged horse. Red-faced vendors sold wooden spoons and fabrics on the sidewalk, and a butcher hauled a bleating goose into his store. The policemen watched a pair of young women walk by, and hissed admiringly. When the embarrassed girls were no longer in sight, the inspector noticed Emil standing at the top of the steps. He patted the horse's nose, nodded at his friends, and began climbing toward him. The air was perfectly still.

Briefly, Emil felt a surge of the unreasonable hope that had buoyed him most of his life. It had brought him through the deaths of both his parents in the war and his months scraping out a living on the fishing boats of the frozen north. It had brought him through a brief love affair back here in the Capital, and the brutalities of the Academy. It had carried him all the way to these steps, where the concrete was remarkably bright after the gloom of the station. He sucked hot, wet air into his lungs, and blinked.

"Brod."

"Yes," said Emil, feeling the warmth of that hereditary hope. "Terzian, isn't it? Your name? Leonek Terzian?"

Leonek Terzian was two steps down, squinting up at him. "I wanted to tell you something," he said, his voice lacking anything Emil could call emotion.

"Of course."

Terzian glanced at the crowd of smokers, who were not watching, and as he turned back threw a small, hard fist into Emil's testicles.

There was the momentary shock as his body doubled over, just before the tide of gut-pain that ripped through his stomach, intestines, legs, then everywhere. The stink of horses overcame him as he dropped; the stone stairs dug into his ribs. He groaned; his eyes teared. He could smell the vodka but could hardly hear Terzian's voice through the watery pain: "You don't *know* me, understand? You don't know *any* of us."

CHAPTER TWO

****

The walk home should have taken twenty minutes, but he stumbled for over an hour along the dusty, cobbled side streets toward the low-lying sun. Old women with clothes in their hands looked down from balconies, and children fell silent when he passed. The occasional Russian soldier, standing with a pretty local girl in a doorway, was too preoccupied to notice him, but the stray dogs, strewn sleeping on the sidewalks, opened lazy eyes. Veterans with half or missing limbs, some in their frayed, dirty uniforms, tried to sell him rerolled cigarettes. His *no* sounded like a whisper. The pain throbbed through his intestines. When farmers began offering mangled fruits for his inspection, he almost shouted at them. A few policemen in their fresh uniforms watched him crawl past, and he knew, through his blurred vision and muted hearing, that they were all laughing at him. Even the dogs.

The Capital was a shithole. Bullets had scarred the walls along these streets, and most bomb-collapsed roofs had still not been repaired. With all the Russian soldiers, you'd never know that the war had been over for three years—and that their little nation had been on the winning side.

He hadn't been around to hear the air-raid sirens and see the atmosphere filled with stone dust; it was enough to return afterward to find the houses along the Tisa had been cross-sectioned by mortars. Their open floors were a dream for any spy. After the war, upon his return from Finland, he had stood in the middle of the street and watched them cook in these homes, then go to bed like real families in real homes, and when they pulled up the covers he had wanted to run back to Helsinki. He'd seen too many great cities to be impressed by this ignorant, provincial village that just happened to have reached the dimensions of a city.

Heavy lead balls ground between his legs as the street narrowed and rose into the Fifth District, where the ornate Habsburg homes had somehow escaped German and Soviet artillery. Wrought-iron windows and balcony railings appeared; tinted glass still survived. They were once valuable because of their opulence, then because they were still in one piece. The aristocrats had fled long ago, their homes now stuffed with poor families— proles every one—who could prove their loyalties with prewar red cards.

They called us back to help the Liberation, his grandfather liked to boast, but when Emil's grandparents returned to the Capital after the war, waving a faded, creased Party card, the Liberation was long over.

Emil stepped over transients sleeping in the entryway, two black-shawled old women from some other corner of the Empire. They had appeared in the spring—a little younger then, more talkative—looking for two sons they had obviously still not found. They slept on the steps during the day to avoid the apartment supervisor, and the effects of this insufficient bedding showed on their discolored faces. He tried to avoid waking their black, lumpy forms.

By the time he reached the top landing and made it through the heavy door with BROD written in chalk, his testicles had settled into a low, dull throb. Grandfather lay sleeping near the open balcony door, beside a high cabinet filled with dusty books. His pale lips moved soundlessly in the white tufts where wool leaked from the sofa cushions. He was thin these days, sustained by cabbage and potatoes. His pallor was distinctly unhealthy. He blinked rapidly when Emil latched the door. "Boy?" he asked hoarsely, for a moment not seeing far enough. "Boy, you're home!" He struggled up and wiped his face with thick, arthritic fingers.

Emil settled beside him, spreading his knees to give himself room.

"And?" said Grandfather, reverting to the shorthand of his excitement. "*And?*"

Emil shrugged.

"Come on, then."

"Nothing," said Emil, leaning back. The dim, airless room brought on a fresh sweat. "A desk. I sat at a desk for eight, nine hours."

"Nothing?" His voice was vaguely disbelieving.

Except the chair, the cardboard sign and the groin. But he couldn't go into it yet. He wasn't up for the old man's lectures.

"Nothing, Opa."

Grandfather placed a cold, knobby hand on his grandson's cheek. Smiling, he said, "Young. Needing something—what? — to *do*."

"Not so young."

"What? Twenty?"

"Twenty-two."

"A *child.*"

Emil sighed. "Hardly."

Grandfather raised one hand while the other reached discreetly beneath a worn cushion. He produced a brown cardboard box the size of his palm. "Go on."

Inside was a scuffed silver watch on a chain, ticking softly. It took an instant—a brief suspension of memory—then he knew his father's watch. The one the late Lieutenant Valentin Brod would swing impatiently when they lived in the Third District, waiting for his son to return home for dinner. The one he left behind for safekeeping when he marched westward. Emil felt the ticking pulse in his closed hand.

"You like?"

Emil smiled.

"From a hero to a hero," said Grandfather, raising the last syllable in preparation for one of the monologues that were, by now, melancholic compulsions. "Even in great times like this," he said, "we have heroes taking care of the *everyday*. You understand?"

But before Emil could answer, the front door opened, revealing his squat, round grandmother. She shook drops off a hand, gripping a wet-bottomed paper sack with the other. Her white hair was twisted up like a flame.

"Cabbage in town," she hummed melodically, and shut the door with a wide hip. "Stewed for my policeman? *Inspector* Emil?"

His smile became weary. "Let's not make a production."

"Who's making productions? Cabbage for a good price, a bottle of extremely cheap brandy. Some would say I'm out to kill you."

She ran the groceries into the kitchen and emerged again, wiping her hands on a threadbare towel. When she noticed the watch in Emil's hand, her shoulders sank.

"Avram Brod. You were supposed to wait."

Grandfather shrugged theatrically and patted Emil on the back as his wife's expression settled into a whitewashed, momentary fury.

Dinner repaired him in a way he hadn't thought possible, and when they prodded for details, he lied with remarkable vigor. He said they were playful children, those homicide inspectors. They joked and threw paper balls and shared cigarettes. He said they all had nicknames—fun, childish names like Train Wreck and Mouse.

"What's yours?" asked Grandmother.

"They're thinking one up."

"Even in great times like this," Grandfather began again, grinning, then took a quick shot of plum brandy. He blew the heat out of himself. "Even now we're young. It's wonderful to be out of the provinces."

Grandmother's face shifted again. Mention of their return, after the war, from provincial Ruscova back to the Capital always brought on her mute severity.

"We're no farmers," Grandfather reiterated as she disappeared into the kitchen. He smiled at Emil and took a cigarette out of his vest pocket.

As if she could see through walls, Grandmother's voice: "Don't stink up my house!"

He palmed the cigarette and nodded toward the balcony. "Come on."

Lime paint blistered off the gangly chairs, which, at their angle, looked down on Heroes' Square. This was why, according to Grandfather, the Brods had it as their sacred duty to covet this apartment: the view. In the center, a naked bronze boy stood atop a dry fountain, holding garlands and kissing in the direction of the clouds. The fountain hadn't worked since 1918, when a premature Bolshevik bomb ruptured its underground pipes; Grandfather claimed to have known the young man who died placing it. But rather than foment revolution, the bomb had only made the stone boy's kiss eternally dry. Other pipes led to a line of six spigots on the mottled wall of a state bread store, and at any moment of the day, six wide-hipped, kerchiefed women could be found chattering and filling pails and bottles. Grandfather liked to watch this prized view at dusk, lascivious eyes leaping from rump to rump as he smoked. He puffed dramatically, his thin lips spilling smoke over his chin and nose. New electric lights illuminated six draped behinds. He passed the damp, poorly rolled cigarette to Emil, who took a quick drag and handed it back.

"There are numerous heroes. Kinds of heroes," said Grandfather. "Your father, my Valentin. A reluctant hero for sure. Then there are eager heroes. Like Smerdyakov. Correct?"

"I suppose," said Emil. His father, who had loved his family and the Church more than war, had waited until the king's soldiers knocked at the door, demanding he defend his country against the Nazi blitzkriegs. Grandfather had never quite forgiven this ambivalence in the fight against fascism. A stark contrast to the war hero known as Smerdyakov, or the Butcher, whose eagerness had outstretched even the Red Army's. The legend—it could hardly be called anything else—was that he joined the Soviet soldiers when they liberated the Capital, a stranger stepping into history. He went with them into Czechoslovakia, and near Prague rushed ahead to Berlin on his own, with only a pistol. When the Red Army finally caught up with him, he brought the soldiers to the room on the second floor of a crumbling apartment building, where he had kept his tally. Twenty-three dead German soldiers, in a pile. Killed in a mad, single-handed enthusiasm.

The Brods' fighting spirit was more diluted with each generation. Grandfather, the tiger who ran to Moscow to aid the Bolsheviks in their liberation of mankind. Father, the moral soldier. Emil, who had not seen a day of war, only its aftermath. He had killed no one, at least not during war.

"Your father was split," said Grandfather, nodding into his chest. "He had loyalties everywhere. The Church, the king, the land. He was muddled. It was sad to see."

"He was sensible enough."

Grandfather frowned in the shadows and was briefly lit by a streetlight that flashed before hissing out. The women's mutterings came to them on a warm breeze. "You know the last time I sat before the iconostasis and listened to those priests?"

Emil knew, but knowing did no good. He waited for the inevitable, watching two women step past a broken bicycle as they exited the square. Their places were filled by two newcomers and a mangy, spotted dog.

He prepared himself for the anger.

"October," said Grandfather. "Nineteen-seventeen. Your father? The day he died, no doubt." He scratched the back of his hand to tame the arthritis. "No doubt. What did that get him? A grave, if he was lucky." He settled his hands on the loose arms of his chair and looked at Emil. The balls of his eyes were draped in loose-fitting lids. "We lose our adjectives. You're following? When in 'seventeen I heard Ilych in Moscow, I knew this was worth it. Jesus? We're workers. More than Christians. And I don't care who knows." His white, swollen hands were ready to squeeze the chair into kindling, but his voice had a fatherly earnestness. "One man has only so much loyalty. Figure out where yours lies."

It was here. The anger was sweating out of Emil's pores, stiffening his jaw, flushing his cheeks. Down in the square the women filled their bottles and shuffled away, and Emil got up—stiffly because of his clenched muscles. He walked inside.

Mention of his father always brought the heat pouring into his head, making him angry and stupid. He stepped past Grandmother drying the table with a towel, and ignored her questioning look. He hurried through the dark corridor, past the building supervisor snoring in a chair, her wide girth spilling over the edges and a clipboard propped against her ankle. He descended the stairs, watching for loose boards, and when he emerged into the cooling night he walked briskly through the square, past the women at the spigots.

He did not look back at his grandfather. He pushed through the black cobbled paths that led to the water.

Nineteen thirty-nine had been a bad year. He was thirteen when his father was drafted into the king's army, and his mother soon followed as a nurse. Grandfather was an old-time, ranting

Communist, so when the Germans overwhelmed their nation's little army, he took Emil and his wife south to wait out the Occupation. Their train only made it as far as Vynohradiv before collapsing completely. They had to hitch rides in farmers' carts the rest of the way to Ruscova. In that village, the peasants vaguely remembered the Brods, who had migrated to the Capital a generation before. They took over a weathered, cramped dacha abandoned by a family of panicked Magyars.

He heard whispers, and water dripping. Around him, soldiers lounged in black doorways, some with girls, others alone. Russians all. He turned down a wider, lit street.

The war years were spent with a pickax, cutting the hard soil and gazing at the hungry Romanian Jews Grandfather let stay with them. Some had seen things they could not speak of, while others would not stay quiet. There was a madman on a white horse convincing peasants to chop their Jews into pieces, and there was a meat factory in Bucharest that ate Jews alive. One of them—Ester, a girl about Emil's age—was silent; she said nothing even when she sneaked into his bed on cold nights, but her desperation had always been palpable.

He could smell the Tisa up ahead.

When the official letter appeared in Ruscova and told them what they had suspected all along—that Valentin and Maria Brod were dead, their bodies buried somewhere in the snows of Poland—it was the end of 1944. The Red Army had liberated the Capital, and in nearby Sighet young Russian soldiers set up moving pictures to prove the superiority of Soviet society. *See what socialism brings us,* said Grandfather, pointing. Eighteen-year-old Emil gazed at the pulsing lights and shadows projected on the high wall of the municipal prison, and was stunned by what he saw. Not the Soviet ingenuity, the tanks and bombers and troops, but the immaculate, chipped cities they marched through. Prague, Warsaw, Moscow, Budapest. Where were these world capitals? Mute, desperate Ester, after a week of strange love, had moved on with her father long before, and there was nothing to tie him to the countryside. He even had his fare: a German pistol he would trade for a ticket. Only a couple weeks after that newsreel, he was on a train headed north, to Finland.

He reached the Georgian Bridge that led across to the Canal District, and leaned over the railing to stare into the black, silent currents of the Tisa. He felt the waste of years. Nine years since his father, and then his mother, had left him with this old couple—nine years adding up to this one failed day.

He turned around. The homes along the bank had been repaired haphazardly—boarded-up windows, patches of concrete.

The war had been over three months when, back from Finland, he stood in this same spot, hands in his pockets, spying on families. Then he was distracted by a noise. A half-naked woman—hands tied behind her back, a shaved head, bruised face and shoulders—was being dragged forward by a clamoring mob. The citizens led her down the street by a rope leash, with COLLAB-ORATOR in cracked red paint across her breasts. He wondered what he had returned to.

CHAPTER THREE

****

O n the way to the station house he stopped in an alley and scuffed his shoes in the dusty concrete. He twisted his stiff pants in his fists, leaving jagged wrinkles running up from the hem, and swung his jacket hard against a brick wall. He threw himself—and his white shirt—into that same wall a few times, and only after scratching his chin did he brush himself off and continue down the street.

They had abandoned all weapons but the most effective: silence. They attacked with leisure, the hours slowly accumulating, while Emil arranged and rearranged his desk supplies. There were no pranks, no laughter, not even the sense that they were watching him without looking. The big typist was at it again, banging away excruciatingly, and the others either read or ate or mumbled into the telephone.

Emil moved ink bottles to the deep side drawer that moaned when he pulled. Stacked crisp, white sheets on the corner of the desk. Placed department stamps in the accessible wide-top drawer—easily accessible because Grandfather had said that a man with stamps is a man with power.

He was pleased that his father's scuffed watch, which he examined minute by minute, matched his new, weathered look.

From the administrative buildings on the opposite side of the street, sounds of revelry reached them. A celebration, punctuated by shouts and breaking glass. Emil gazed out the open window, but from his angle could only see a top floor of windows, and blue summer sky.

He was becoming adept at using his peripheral vision, seeing what was not directly seen. The chief, again, was nowhere. The state security inspector was making notes in a file. The fat one was eating sunflower seeds this time, the green flecks of yesterday's pumpkin seeds still visible beneath today's black shards. Leonek Terzian read a book—Emil couldn't make out the mysterious, squiggly characters on the cover.

There was no telling what their reasons were. He tried, but came up with nothing of use. Hazing no longer seemed possible. Did they think he was a spy in their midst? A visitor from Moscow? Maybe from a family they disliked—this was still the old world, and family animosities went on and on.

Or maybe it was his face. Unscarred, inexperienced. He stroked his sore, scratched skin. Maybe they hated to see how far they had come from their own honest boyhoods.

It was well into morning when he realized—late, it seemed to him—that he was the only one without a typewriter. His white paper was lined up evenly with the corner of his desk, useless and clean.

"Supply room?" he asked the air. "Anyone tell me where it is?"

The tired answer of bald scalps and messy heads of dense hair. The snap of typewriter keys.

The security officer's stone face turned from the wall to meet his gaze—Emil could read nothing in those heavy, sleepless eyes—and nodded in the direction of the door.

Light reflected in the corridor, footsteps ricocheting, and up ahead a white-scarved woman dragged a damp mop. Uniformed Militia stood in pairs, talking and laughing—their shoulder patches matched the one on his dress uniform at home: the red hawk with head in profile, wings folded, on a field of yellow.

This was another world. Some smiled at him as they passed, and a few even nodded cursorily. He read what was stenciled on each door's translucent glass: ACCOUNTS and EXTERNAL and MUNITIONS and TOILET and INTERVIEW. A mousy secretary coming out of the interview room with a notebook to her chest smiled at him. Her eyes twinkled.

The corridor turned left, then right, and at the far end, upon cracked glass, was SUPPLIES. He rapped with a loose knuckle, then entered.

A thin, tanned man wearing blue coveralls leaned back in a chair, reading *The Spark*—yesterday's afternoon edition—drowsily. His sockless, pale ankles were crossed on the counter, his black shoes polished. Behind him, seven overflowing, gray shelving units led to the dim far wall.

"Comrade," said the thin man as he dropped his feet. "You are to be congratulated. Says right here that the murder rate in the Capital has plummeted fifty percent in the last three months." He slapped the paper with the back of his hand. "It thanks *you.*"

Emil closed the door. "Me?"

His smile was rich with yellow teeth. Emil couldn't place the accent. The man's bloodshot left eye remained trained on the small side window. "You, yes! Figuratively, at least. All the Comrade Inspectors of the People's Militia."

This sudden end to the silence stunned him. He opened his mouth. The end of the silence and its form: a deeply creased, tanned face with a lazy red eye. "Not this inspector," said Emil. "Only my second day."

"Then don't send the rate back up."

Emil propped himself with wide-set arms against the counter. He was acclimating to conversation. "Do you have a typewriter?"

"Your very lucky day." The supply clerk smiled, wiping sweat out of his day-length beard. He wandered back into the dark-ness—his slight limp was apparent beside the hard, vertical lines of the shelves—and returned with an old monstrosity, weaving a little, gasping as he dropped it on the counter. "Beautiful," he said, and swallowed. "No?"

It looked less like a typewriter than a cumbersome piece of steel furniture.

"You can't go wrong with a classic. German. *Weimar,* no less."

Emil touched it timidly. "It works?" It was cold.

"Mostly, sure. Except the J, and the apostrophe. And, if I remember—" He pressed a button that clattered loudly, then squinted his strong eye at the black impression on the black roller. "Yes—the B."

Emil exhaled. "You have something that works?"

A cool look of judgment filled the clerk's features. "I shouldn't do this." He moved with exaggerated labor, his limp almost a stumble, back into the gloom. One hand fondled his chin, and the other held his backside as he frowned at shelves.

Emil wandered to the muddy, face-high window that looked down on a concrete courtyard, thinking again what he'd thought when he returned after the war: *This is a nation of cripples.* Dirty officers' children played soccer in the courtyard, their shouts muted by glass. A cool tickle of sweat drew down his back. Then something hit the counter.

This typewriter was small, virtually new, and all its keys were intact. The clerk tested them with a light finger.

"Is better?"

"Significantly." Emil lifted it easily with two hands.

"Is worth something, no?"

He set it down again, and waited.

"The last one that went out," said the clerk, his brown features paling in the square of light from the window, "went for, I believe, five koronas."

"*Five?*"

"But you're new, right? And, after all, this one used to be at your desk." He talked a quick retreat. "Sergei's replacement, correct? I thought so. Exactly. Must be fair," he said, then gazed at the scratched counter. "Poor Sergei."

The other cadets had eagerly told Emil the rumor of the man he was replacing: Sergei Lvonic had been shot by a 7.62mm Tokarev. A Red officer's pistol. But like most things that occurred just after the Liberation, it was never investigated.

"What about you?" asked Emil. "Can I know who you are?"

The clerk shrugged. "Roberto."

"Spain?"

"Everyone thinks that." He shook his head. "I get points for the Franco martyrs—the girls think I've lost my family to the fascists. But no. Argentinian." He placed a hand over his chest and intoned: "My parents knew the way of their hearts." The hand dropped and he winked.

Emil leaned closer. "So you know who I am?"

"Who doesn't? Brod, Emil. Homicide."

"Then maybe you can explain it to me."

"Explain what, Comrade?"

That word dropped a curtain between them, as though Roberto had suddenly reached the limits of his affability and was backing up again. "The men," said Emil. "They hate me. I don't know why. They don't speak to me, and there's been some violence."

Roberto snorted, impressed. "Violence?" He wiped his damp cheek with a thumb and settled into his chair. "Sergei was loved. You can be sure of that." He took a pack of Czech cigarettes from his pocket and shook one out. "There weren't many like Sergei." He puffed as he lit up. "Don't worry, they'll get over it. What they are are . . . victims of melancholia."

"After two years? This is melancholy? Someone hits me in the balls, and that's just melancholy?"

Roberto shrugged in his tired way; none of this was news to him. "Just wait until you see those men really angry."

****

The typewriter was, Roberto assured him, a steal at only four koronas, and he included *The Spark* as a gift. But when Emil returned with his new possessions, he was deep in the silence again. They could not know it had been broken already, so they persevered, keeping their eyes to their desks as he set the typewriter down. He tested the chair with a hand, then settled down and experimented with a few keys. The silence *had* been broken, whether or not they liked it, and with time it would necessarily dissipate.

Again, that hereditary hope.

He got up and gazed over the big typist's head at the bulletin board. Poorly printed faces of convicts and escapees, letters from appreciative citizens, and memos with stamps that proved they were words sent down from levels as high as the Central Committee. The memos outlined new laws controlling how the inspectors should go about their jobs: which buildings they could enter without authorization and which they could not; the limits of interrogation methodologies; when a case had to be handed over to state security for reassignment.

The typewriter stopped, and the big inspector—whose name, Emil knew from the files, was Ferenc—glanced at the chief, who had just arrived and hurried directly to his office without a word to anyone. Then he looked briefly at Emil before returning to his typing.

Pinned to the corkboard, criminal faces were labeled with names and numbers and lists of murders and dates committed. Some were doubly guilty; frauds or conspiracies were piled upon their homicides. A few faces were obscured by a blue stamp: DECEASED.

Emil smiled at Ferenc. The man's hard, cold stare looked nothing like melancholia.

At three, Leonek Terzian called to Ferenc and the fat one (Stefan, Emil recalled): "It's time."

All three grabbed their hats and jackets and headed for the door, Stefan walking with a barely noticeable limp. The security inspector didn't look up.

Emil followed after a moment, but cautiously, Terzian's small fist still crisp in his mind, and from the top of the steps watched them climb into a black Mercedes. The engine made knocking sounds as they drove away.

The security inspector looked at him when he wandered back in, but by the time Emil nodded, the inspector's face had returned to his papers. He was too busy safeguarding the socialist state to acknowledge anyone. There were volumes stored in his locked files, and Emil felt an overwhelming curiosity. A peek, or just a hint. But not even he was stupid enough to break the concentration of a member of state security.

Emil's desk, tidy and unused, *The Spark* folded loosely beside the smart typewriter, was thoroughly uninviting. He touched the stack of paper with the tips of his fingers.

This, truly, had gone far enough.

He took five firm steps to the chief's door and pounded with the side of his hand. The milky glass rattled.

"Enter."

The office was a mess, papers scattered like seed over the wooden floor, stacks slipping from file cabinets and out of boxes piled in the corner. It stank of stale smoke, and the beige curtains behind the chief were untied so only a single white blade of sunlight made it through. Above, a yellow bulb burned.

"*Christ.*" Chief Moska tossed a pen on the desk, splattering black ink, and settled back into his creaking chair. "What is it?"

Emil shut the door and centered himself. He wanted to do this right. "Chief Moska. I need to work."

"You have your own desk, Brod."

He held himself steady. "I have no cases. If you give me a case, then I can do my job."

"Your job?"

"Exactly," said Emil. "My job, which is to investigate homicides reported to this office."

The chief leaned forward between his spread elbows, and his chiseled face stretched a moment. His shirt was stained at the pits; it was terribly hot in the office. "Your job, *Comrade* Brod, is to do what I say. That's why I have these walls and that door." He nodded at the door as if the movement would push Emil through it. "You follow?"

"Yes, Comrade."

"*Chief.*"

"Yes. Chief."

Moska's chair moaned as he shifted and set his two open hands on the desk. He turned the hands over, palms up, then looked slowly around the room. "I wouldn't want to waste your particular talents, Brod, which are no doubt considerable." Something caught his eye, and he leveled a long finger at three boxes of files stuffed in a corner beside a dismantled radiator. "Some jackass put those files in chronological order. Can you believe it?"

"I'm trying to, Chief."

He peered at Emil, and in the yellow, dusty light his expression was murderous. "I want them in alphabetical order, Brod. You're familiar with the alphabet?"

"Intimately."

"Get to it."

The boxes were unwieldy and heavy, but his stupefied anger sustained him. He lined them beside his desk, ignoring the security inspector's beady gaze, then sat on the floor. From the first box he removed all files in which the family name began with A. Althann, Abajian, Adamów, Annopol. The same with the second box, and the third. He made a pile. Then B. It went on. A sharp ache rooted into his back, but he did not change position. He wanted to give no sign of pain. Street voices came in waves, arguments and the crack of an automobile hitting a wooden cart. The ache grew into his shoulders, and by the time he reached M, it covered his entire back. Outside, the squeal of a pig being butchered. Maslow, Miroslav, Mas. Unstable towers of folders rose all around him.

It was after five-thirty when the chief emerged from his office, stretching into a gray blazer. He nodded at the security inspector, then stood over Emil a moment.

"Don't work so hard, Brod. You want to make this last. Consider it your own five-year plan."

Emil squinted up at him; the light from the windows made a hard silhouette. When he spoke, his throat was dry: "Is this what everyone does?"

"Everyone?" The chief's smile was just visible on his backlit face. He shrugged instead of answering, and walked out.

The security inspector, hands on the file in his lap, turned to him and frowned. His flat face expressed nothing.

"There's something you want to *say?*" called Emil, all good sense gone. "Have some *thoughts* you want to share?"

The security inspector stared a moment more, raised his eyebrows as though about to shrug, and closed the folder in his lap. He stuck it under his arm, grabbed his hat and umbrella, and followed the chief out of the station.

CHAPTER FOUR

****

The war was winding down when he took the train, alone, from Ruscova, through the Capital, and farther north. Through sallow, crumbling cities: Warsaw, Vilnius, Riga, Tallinn. The ferry brought him across the Gulf of Finland. Soviet Russia had only recently stopped bombing, but Helsinki, compared to those others, was still a city in form and structure, waterborn and regal. It took his breath away.

He didn't know the language, so like all foreigners he found his way to the little bars scattered throughout the islands like tiny, intoxicated nations. He found his own nation in the Carp, a dark, fetid place where they posted news of work and warnings to newcomers. A drunk countryman stumbled off his stool and told Emil about the fishing expedition into the Arctic. *This is real money,* he had said, nodding into his vodka. *You come back a rich man.*

That hadn't been quite true, but after four months of splitting open those heavy, gray creatures with his curved knife and washing their scarlet guts from the deck alongside bitter Slavs and Mediterraneans and lost Arabs, using German as their shared language, he returned to the Capital with enough money to take an apartment in the crowded Sixth District, where the proles emerged from their low, rented rooms and squeezed into trams headed for factories and shops in town.

On one of those trams he met Filia, a pale girl married to a soldier not yet back from the war. She was reading a magazine with

Soviet dancers kicking legs high on the cover, and when he looked over her shoulder she asked him if he was always so rude. Thin, bitter lips and straw hair. At a café he explained that his family had recently returned from the southern provinces, he from abroad; her family, she told him, was dead. Her husband, who had marched off to war years before, was a question mark. Emil never saw her apartment, but she moved her clothes into his, and after they made love she told him stories about her childhood in the mountainous northern provinces. She spoke as though it were a paradise of honesty and brotherhood.

Why don't you go back? he had asked her, and she only stared at him, as if he were mad.

She had sudden, unexpected moods, when her eyes became cold, dull stones that looked right through him. The squirming fear this provoked in him was always matched by desire.

They ate their meals on the living room floor—whatever was available at the market—and listened to the radio trials of Nazis and their sympathizers, and the reports of the coordinated rebuilding efforts. Russians and British and Americans, briefly, unified. They were rebuilding the Capital too. Russian engineers filled the city with their measuring equipment and cyrillics, and the Soviet soldiers who had arrived a year earlier did not leave.

Once, when she was in a mood, Filia said she only stayed with him because she was afraid of being raped by the Reds. *You're my protection against the Bolshevik drip.* He looked at her stone eyes, hurt. Her smile came back and she asked why he had come back to the east, when he could have stayed in Helsinki, or gone on to London. Even America. She said *America* like an incantation.

Instead of answering, he told her his father had led a campaign through Warsaw that ended in a hero's death. She didn't believe him.

You're telling the story with pauses and bursts; you're a bad liar. Her own husband was at the Front; she could see right through

Emil. So he admitted he didn't know anything about how Lieutenant Valentin Brod had died, nothing except Warsaw and a bullet, this knowledge culled from a sparely worded telegram addressed to his mother, who was by then dead as well. Was she satisfied? *Hardly,* Filia said, then asked again why he had come back from the west. He said because he needed to meet her. She laughed and said, *Seriously.*

He told her how his mother had died. *Starvation. On the Front.*

War and war. She had heard plenty of it, she said. But he told her anyway.

Maria Brod had been one of those nurses who followed their husbands all the way to the battle lines, then died. Stray bullets or disease or, if, like Maria Brod, they were unfortunate enough to become separated from their staff on those vast mountain ranges, they died of starvation and exposure. The Red Army soldiers who came across her body on a ridge of the Tatras mailed her papers back to the Capital, where a friend at their old address forwarded them on to Ruscova. But there was no word on what they had done to the corpse, and Emil imagined her still lying among the snow-stripped trees in the mountains, missing only her identification papers.

Filia didn't ask anything more—this story, at least, was true. The following Monday morning she left for the factory, and did not return. By then the last of the troops were stumbling back into town, and her husband was no doubt among them. He was alone now, almost out of money, and his grandfather had moved from Ruscova to the Fifth District with a red card and a modicum of prestige.

"Today?" Grandfather asked when the silence of the table had stretched too long. "How was it?"

They were unbearable tonight. Both of them. It was no one thing they said; it was every word, every syllable. He plotted his escape. He would relocate near the water, maybe even the cleaner edges of the Canal District. Over boiled cabbage he did the math, knowing from the start the numbers were doomed, but following them hopefully to their predictable, lacking end. The pittance from the People's Militia would not earn his freedom; bribes, the government assumed, would make up the difference.

He'd had money once, but that had all been frittered away. On that girl.

"A day. Just a day."

Grandmother frowned at Emil's wrinkled, soiled suit. "You really must learn to take care of yourself. What's that on your face?" She wiped the sore on his chin with a spit-damp finger.

He dreamed of seal boats cutting through the ice sheets of the north. A ship of nomads who thought nothing of risking their lives in the miserable cold. They had nothing to lose. They drank heavily and fought on the icy deck; by the time they reached the hunting grounds, the Croat was already dead, having plummeted, drunk, into the black waters. In his dream, when the dissatisfied Bulgarian pulled a knife on him over a card game, his stomach did not sink as it had in reality; it levitated. Then he floated up through the cabin ceiling. He dreamed of little fat bodies, gray and silver bundles sliding down ice slopes into the water, eyes like black coins with a woman's long lashes. Their insides steamed when he cleaned them out; their red organs misted in the white snow. He dreamed of the Bulgarian who was found among the seal guts, facedown in the gore. Gored himself. Gutted and discarded on the ice.

When he woke his conviction of failure was somehow less inevitable. The night's sleep, or the passage of time, had rejuvenated him, and he rushed through the alphabetizing of the chief's files. He ignored its insignificance—the task was something he had to do as quickly and mindlessly as possible. Like the seal carcasses.

A few files fell open, and he scanned their contents. Criminals now locked away in prisons in the provinces, some working in the western swamps, raising land from mud, harvesting reeds. The records went back decades, and the prewar files had stamps with the icon of a crown. All that was over now. Some new files had symbols borrowed from the Soviets, while others—the hawk, primarily—were local. Wings pressed to its sides, its beak in profile, talons extended. Hammers and sickles and stalks of wheat bent like parentheses. Above a star: *1917.*

"Enter."

He pushed the door open with the S-through-Z box and set it in the far corner. The chief watched as he brought in the other two, stacking them on the first. Then Emil stood before his desk. "Now," he said breathily. "You have a case? For me."

The boredom in Chief Moska's eyes was overwhelming. "Those are in order?"

"Absolutely."

"Maybe you should give them another look-over. To be sure."

Emil's face warmed. He closed the door and, after it latched, stood again in front of the chief's desk. He spoke clearly and calmly, his jaw muscles tensed: "I don't know what's been going on here, why you and your men are acting like this. But I came here as a homicide inspector for the People's Militia, and if you refuse to give me a legitimate case, I can't be responsible for what follows."

The chief leaned back and balanced a stubby pencil between his fingers.

Emil hoped his red face and boldness would give the impression of someone who might do anything if provoked, however reckless. It was the look a young man had to cultivate in the Arctic waters.

The chief brought the pencil to his mouth, his lips closing on it, and when he brought it away there was black residue. He spoke slowly, lazily. "Yesterday. Something came through and, well, I don't want to waste my men's time with it." He was talking to the papers on his desk. His hands had given up on the pencil and were flicking through smeared, typewritten sheets. "Fourth District, a singer. No. *Song*writer." He licked his fingers with a fat, lead-blackened tongue as he searched through the pages. Emil made sure he missed nothing.

"This songwriter's dead?"

"That's how they come to us, Brod." He held out a handwritten sheet.

Male, Janos Crowder, 35, dead in apartment, severe trauma to head. Liberation Street 12.

"Called in after hours," the chief muttered. "District police station took pictures, samples, the usual. I'll let them know you're coming."

Emil opened his mouth. He wanted to ask what *the usual* meant, but nothing came out. His feet seemed to disappear from under him. He had his case. So quickly, easily.

"You need mobilization papers? Get going."

Emil found his feet.

On the tram, he held on to a leather strap, a pendulum swinging between a woman taking bites out of a round loaf of bread and two laughing boys repeating *damn* and *shit* to one another. Emil recalled the dead man. At least one of his songs was very famous, something children sang in school. He'd heard them on their marches down the boulevards, looking smart in kerchiefs and buttons, but he couldn't remember the name of the tune. Part of a lyric came to him as they left the First District's mustard-colored administrative centers for the carved entryways and wrought-iron gates of the unbombed, still-prestigious part of the Fourth: *There are White Guards in your heart that must be torn apart.*

There was nothing left of Janos Crowder's face for him to recognize.

The policeman who had been waiting for him—a boy little younger than Emil, with a loose-fitting blue uniform—let him in and nodded at the body. A wrench lay a few feet away, where it had stained the thick, white rug in a brown mess.

The melody would not leave—it revolved in his head. *There are White Guards . . .*

It was a lush, expensive apartment, and it had been ripped to pieces. The humid stench was everywhere. Upturned shelves lay on the floor, atop books and broken vases; the sofa cushions had been sliced open and ripped inside out. A baby grand piano filled a corner. Its lid was propped open, and on the carpet beside it lay framed pictures that had slid off.

It was the stink, Emil realized, of rotting meat. The musk of the country's finest patriotic melody-maker turning to mold.

"Your chief said to leave it as it was." The young cop held his cap in his hands, shaking his head. "Never seen anything like that before."

The body was arched backward over a sturdy, coarse coffee table that looked like it had been made in the provinces. It was cracked and bent in the middle where the body had hit, but was not separated.

That was peasant craftsmanship for you.

. . . must be torn apart.

The wrench had been used to beat the face until it collapsed into pulp, then had been used on the back of the head, leaving tiny pink skull shards sprinkled over the carpet. Emil tried not to breathe through his nose.

He had seen plenty of dead bodies before—on the Arctic ship, in the fields and trains between Finland and here—but nothing quite like this. Not a corpse inside a wealthy man's living room. The location separated it somehow, made it more appalling. Boats were for dead people. Trains and open fields. Not living rooms.

"Get some air in here, will you?"

The policeman opened the French windows. A hot breeze took some of the stink with it. Emil joined him and they looked out over the city, where clay and tin rooftops led into the distance.

Reluctantly, he went back and kneeled by the wrench. The steel was caked with blood, but there were no fingerprints, only gnarled threads. Once white, they were now a crusted brown. Gloves.

He went through the photographs that had slid off the opened piano. Behind framed, cracked glass was the Magyar face—prominent brow, gaping nostrils—he now remembered from clippings in *The Spark*. The dead man smiled broadly at a soiree with none other than General Secretary Mihai. Some of his best songs had been for their dashing partisan leader—now an overfed politician: a "thick Muscovite," as they were called in private. The chubby arm of the interior minister hung over Crowder's shoulders in another picture.

Emil went through the other luminaries on the carpet, who presented the dead songwriter with star-shaped trophies and plaques which, despite the black and white, were plainly gold, their stars a glossy red. He wondered idly where these trophies were stashed, and how much they were worth. Shaking hands surrounded him on the floor, clapping hands and hands presenting valuable awards. And everywhere: big toothy smiles.

Then it came to him. A flush of understanding.

He had walked into a trap.

At first he didn't believe it—the realization was too easy, too sudden. But he thought it through. It made more sense than he would have liked. Moska had given him this case to get rid of him.

He looked at the photo of the General Secretary again.

Janos Crowder was connected; he had friends at the very top. This simple fact made the case, by default, political. In political investigations, nothing was allowed to go wrong. At the first sign of a mistake, Emil would be ripped off his first case, maybe even kicked out of the department. The security inspector with the metallic gaze and peasant's features would be handed the Crowder case. He was probably sitting at his desk now, browsing through files, waiting for it.

His hands went cold, and the General Secretary, smiling, fell with Janos Crowder to the carpet. Emil patted his thighs to get the blood moving again. He stood up.

"Tell me about him," Emil commanded the empty room.

The young policeman came out of the kitchen, licking butter off a finger. His peaked cap was set back on his head. Emil didn't know how anyone could eat with this smell.

"Crowder. Tell me about him."

"Comrade Janos Crowder," the policeman recited from memory. "Songwriter of note, from Budapest originally, moved here just before the Patriotic War. An infantryman on the Front, suffered a shrapnel leg, Royal Medal of Honor. After the Liberation he produced a remarkable variety of songs honoring the country."

"*Remarkable* variety?" asked Emil.

The policeman shrugged. "One hundred thirty-seven songs in two years."

Emil nodded. "Remarkable. Anything else?"

The policeman sighed the last detail: "Married to Lena Hanic in 1945."

"Has she been notified?"

"No, Comrade Inspector."

"Good. I'll do it myself. You've taken photographs?"

The policeman returned to the kitchen and came back with a large, cream-colored folder. It was heavy with prints.

"Who found the body?"

"Building supervisor, Aleksander Tudor. Was bringing up the mail." He nodded at the vanity beside the door, where some envelopes lay. "Decided to leave them inside. This is what greeted him."

Emil surveyed the demolished room, trying to remember what else to ask. In the Academy there had been simple checklists that alleviated the need to think things through, but he had gone blank. "Have the supervisor come up on your way out."

"You're done with me?"

Within the policeman's voice, Emil thought he heard something like surprise. Surprise that the interview was so short. So incomplete, inept. "You have the wife's address?"

The policeman paused, eyes shifting across the floor, deftly bouncing around the corpse.

"Call it into the station," said Emil. "They'll leave it on my desk." Even as he said it, he wasn't sure he believed it.

Three envelopes, all bills. He opened and read each in the vain hope that something would float to the surface, but the first two were nothing but the mundane finances of life. An expensive tailor on Yalta Boulevard had made Janos Crowder a suit and was waiting for his payment. A greengrocer two blocks away was becoming impatient for his fee. The third, though, was from the Aeroflot office down by the Tisa, the itinerary for a flight to Berlin that was leaving this morning. Emil checked his father's watch—12:40. A flight that had just left.

"Comrade Inspector?" A fat man stood in the doorway, his pink arms spilling from a white sleeveless shirt stained by cooking grease and sweat. When he breathed, Emil could hear it across the room.

"Comrade Building Supervisor Aleksander Tudor?"

The supervisor nodded, lips pressed tight as he edged his way inside, peering at the body. His nose flared involuntarily.

"Close the door, will you?"

He did.

Emil held up the envelopes. "Since when do building supervisors deliver mail?"

"Two days. The mail was just sitting there." His voice had a pleading note to it. "They might have been stolen. I *worried*." His eyes fell again on the body, as though gravity pulled him there.

Emil stared at the supervisor's white face until the eyes flickered back.

"Tell me what happened when you discovered the body. Every detail."

Aleksander Tudor tried to breathe steadily. "Yesterday. Night, yes. After dinner."

"So you were in your apartment."

"The dogs."

"Dogs?"

Aleksander Tudor nodded eagerly. "They were barking outside my window. Like always, but this time." He closed his eyes then opened them. "This time I went to shoo them away. That's when I noticed. His box. Comrade Crowder's. Full of letters." His loud exhale sounded choked. "Two days. Very irregular. But there was no answer," he said. "To my knock."

"And you had heard nothing before this?"

"Only the dogs."

"No noise? No sounds of struggle?"

Aleksander Tudor shook his head stiffly.

"And you just came right in?"

"I have the key, Comrade Inspector."

"You couldn't slide them under the door?"

The supervisor turned toward the gaping, drafty space beneath the door. He turned back to Emil, mouth working but forming no words.

"Comrade Supervisor," said Emil, slipping into the authoritarian tone the professors had made him practice for hours. "You seem disturbed. Do I disturb you?"

"I—" he began, then faltered. He leaned his full weight against the vanity; Emil could see the other half of his sweating face in the mirror. He blinked at the corpse, ready to faint.

Emil led him into the hallway, where frying oils obscured the smell of rot. "Try again?"

Tudor steadied himself on the railing, and finally formed

words: "I was curious, Comrade. That's all. I wanted to see if he was gone, or . . . I don't know." He shook his head.

Emil reached into his jacket and retrieved his notepad and a small pencil. *25 Aug 48. Victim: J Crowder. Interview: Apt Super, Aleks Tudor—found body. Delivering mail. Nerves, a wreck.* "Did you suspect this?" he asked. "Before you opened the door."

"This?"

"Murder. You heard *nothing*?"

"No. Oh, not at all." When he shook his head, his flushed, damp cheeks trembled. "I only . . . *wondered*. You see?"

"How long has Comrade Crowder lived here?"

"Six, seven months? I need to look it up."

Emil pointed at the door across from Crowder's. Someone had painted it a garish red. "The neighbor?"

"Polacks," Tudor whispered. Then, with a wry smile and a half-wink: "Genuine *proles.*"

"Comrade," Emil said, his voice now very official again, "this is a nation of proles. The proletarians have succeeded with the generous assistance of our friends to the east. Proles is the name by which we all live."

Aleksander Tudor looked ready to cry.

CHAPTER FIVE

****

The Polish proles included a mother, father, three children and three grandparents. The door opened noisily, the thin, blond father shouting back for one of the children, a Marie, to shut up. But when Emil unfolded his green Militia certificate, a silence dropped over the household, as though even those out of eyeshot had seen an alarm blink in the other rooms.

"Come in," said Tomislaw, the father, wiping a hand on his pants and then waving Emil inside.

There was the dense, familiar smell of boiled cabbage and overused sunflower oil in the fabric of the home. All three grandparents ushered him to a lace-covered dining table and served hot tea, while Tomislaw changed into a clean shirt. The grandparents—two of them women—stood against the stained, floral wallpaper and stared at him, smiling nervously, while the heavy, dark-haired wife herded the children into another room. But the whole time there, Emil could make out the children's shadows beyond the cracked door.

Tomislaw appeared at another door, a fresh, brown shirt hanging from his bones. He smiled as he sat down. "What happened to Master Crowder," he said, using the title a peasant would and simultaneously mauling the language with his accent. He pressed his lips together in a tight frown, shaking his head. "This city, it will get you."

"Tom," warned his wife. Her sturdy face looked unaccustomed to taking chances.

"But you heard something? From next door, I mean."

"In this apartment?" asked Tomislaw, looking to the grandparents for support. All three faces nodded vigorously. "With the dogs outside and the kids in here, how can I hear a thing?"

The whole room was in agreement: it was an unassailable point. When Tomislaw smiled, his high, acne-speckled cheekbones became pronounced.

"Where do you work?"

Tomislaw sat up straight. "I assemble kneading machines. Huge." He opened his arms wide. "For factory bread."

"And how long have you lived here?"

"Two years," the wife said quickly. "We were told to transfer, we have our papers. We were as surprised as you that we ended up in such a place."

"Of course," said Emil. But the inside of this aristocratic house, cluttered by their stout Polish furniture and water stains on the walls, no longer resembled anything aristocratic. He smiled reassuringly and opened his notepad. "I just wondered if you knew your neighbor."

"Sure," said Tomislaw, pointing to the door with an oil-darkened thumb. "Sometimes, we sat out there and had a vodka, maybe some brandy." He used his thumb and forefinger to measure the height of a shot. "Just a little. Or his wine. Bull's Blood. From *Eger.*" He raised his brow proudly. "He told me about his songs. You know his songs? *There's a right in the might of the valley!*" he sang in a tuneless march, but Emil recognized it—again from kerchiefed children's throats. He could hear the little ones in the next room giggling at their father's performance. Their mother shot a silencing look at the door.

"What else did he talk about?"

Tomislaw ran his fingers through a pack of cigarettes, finally coming up with a twisted, loose one. Tobacco peppered the table-

top. "Money, what else? He said he could spend more than anyone he knew. Even with all those songs. Can you imagine? He
always ran out."

"He was broke?"

"Broke? I don't know. To me he lived pretty well."

The two grandmothers crossed themselves, and Tomislaw's
wife shifted in her chair.

"What about visitors?"

"He lived alone," said the wife.

"I saw no one," affirmed Tomislaw.

"No girlfriends?"

Tomislaw shrugged. "Maybe a hooker—one time, twice."

"You saw them?"

He shook his head, almost sadly. "But no steady girlfriend, not
this one. That I'm sure of."

"How do you know?"

"You know," said Tomislaw, smiling again, cheekbones high in
his masculine knowledge, and the others nodded their agreement. "There was that one, though—"

"Girl?"

He shook his head.

"That was nothing," his wife said. She cleared her throat significantly.

Tomislaw shrugged.

"What?" asked Emil.

"A plumber, I think."

"Yes?"

"Is nothing," said the wife.

"Is nothing," he agreed, frowning and shaking his head.

Emil looked between them a moment, knowing that nothing
more would come of the subject, then looked back at his notepad. "Did he say anything about Berlin? That he was flying
there?"

"Berlin?" Tomislaw thought a moment, squinting. "Where

they're . . ." He raised a flat hand over his head and whistled an imitation of a plane flying over. "No," he said finally. "Nothing."

"How about enemies? Anyone who might want to hurt him?"

Tomislaw squinted in memory, and Emil noticed his wife's gray eyes measuring her husband's face, as if by these measurements she could predict, and stop, a mistake. Tomislaw turned his palms toward the ceiling. "But everyone loved him! He was like a prince. A very elegant prince."

Emil turned to the wife—he wanted to include her. "Where are you from? In Poland."

"Not Poland," she muttered. She looked back at him coolly. "We're from Brest."

"That's Polish," said Emil.

She shook her head. "For a long time, yes. Then one day it wasn't. When the war was over someone told us we were living in Belarus." Then she blinked, as though waking up. She raised herself in her chair, back straight, and gave him a tight smile. "We live here now, and that's all that matters."

Tomislaw walked him to the door, and Emil touched his elbow to lure him outside. The thin man glanced back fearfully as he closed the door.

"Tell me," said Emil. He held his pencil like a pointer.

Tomislaw furrowed his brow.

"This plumber. What's the story?"

He shrugged. "Really, she's right. It's *nothing*. Just some fellow. She's crazy—she worries because the plumber had an accent. German. Germans scare her."

"What did he look like?"

"Like a German, what else? Blond, sure. Tall."

"And he was a plumber?"

"I don't know," said Tomislaw, raising his hands as though he had finally learned his wife was right—you give an inch and they'll take a mile. "Plumber, carpenter, how should I know? All I

know is he came a couple times and they argued. Money, I think."
He placed a hand on his doorknob.

"Do you remember anything they said? In particular?"

Tomislaw shrugged, leaning into the door, twisting the handle.
"Really, I don't know anything else." When the door opened, his
wife was standing there, pulling him inside, giving Emil a hard,
suspicious glance before shutting the door and slamming the bolt
into place.

He took a meticulous walk through the mess of the apartment,
looking beneath overturned cabinets and sifting through
smashed dishes for anything. There was a Russian camera in
the corner, a Zorki, empty of film. He pocketed it. In a bureau
full of clothes, he found a gold medal—a circle etched with a
hammer and sickle and rays of sunlight, the words LENIN and
MUSIC in Cyrillic beneath. He lifted it—heavy, pure gold—and
considered it.

This was the beginning of everything. He had a real sense of
this. This was a new start, and it had to begin correctly, or not at
all. But hadn't it already been sabotaged by the chief, by everyone?

He dropped the medal into his pocket.

He found a folded sheet of paper behind the piano with lyric
notes and, under a shredded sofa cushion, a woman's black garter.
The kitchen produced jars of fruit preserves—peach and strawberry—that the police had not yet taken themselves. This could
only mean that there had been a lot more, so much that they had
run out of pockets. Behind the icebox, tied to a thin pipe, was a
short length of twine that had been cut with a knife. He didn't
know why. In the bathroom he found French soap. He pocketed
everything, then wrapped the bloody wrench in a copy of *The
Spark*. That's when he realized he was humming. *There are White
Guards in your heart . . .*

He squeezed the murder weapon under his arm, then returned

Janos Crowder's gold medal to his drawer, buried it among crumpled underwear.

He would start yet again.

He used Janos Crowder's private telephone—white, bulbous—to call the medical examiner's office.

The photographs were overexposed, but clear enough. Janos Crowder bent back over his peasant table, arms spread wide. His legs lay limply, knees together, so that his feet rested on their arches in the plush carpet. His fingers were long and thin and tapered. These were not factory hands. His speckled neck was bloated where it began to curve into the soft mush of jawbone and human pulp that had once been a mouth, nose, eyes.

A German. A German who looked like a German and argued about money. Tidbits filled his pockets: a garter, camera, twine.

The brutality made no sense. Janos Crowder would have been dead long before the abuse was over. A manic rage, perhaps. Or an attempt to hide something. But what? A face wasn't needed to identify a body. A simple thief would have taken the camera. A German with a meticulous eye toward money would have found the medal made of gold.

There was a close-up of the head, where an ear had dislodged.

Emil was on the tram, leaning against a pole, and he heard a gasp. The woman looking over his shoulder had finally realized what she was seeing.

He was surprised and somewhat pleased to find on his desk a slip of paper with Lena Crowder's address. The same childish letters he'd seen his first day. No one claimed responsibility for the note, and no one looked up when he dropped the paper-wrapped wrench loudly beside the typewriter. Some were preparing to leave for the day, shrugging into jackets or loosening ties and unbuttoning collars. The security inspector was eating an apple, and when Emil sat down he came over and, very quietly, wished

Emil luck on his case. "This is your first one, I'm correct?" His voice squeaked unnervingly.

"My first, yes."

"Well, good luck," he repeated, and as he wandered back to his desk, Emil felt a cool, focused hatred for this vulture.

The typewriter worked like a song. Emil's preliminary report noted the details he had learned of the victim's life, his occupation and marital status, his rumored economic situation and Party affiliation. He said nothing of the portraits with General Secretary Mihai. He listed the names of those he had interviewed, and pointed to where he expected to proceed next. Lena Crowder, and the vendor of the murder weapon, for which he had the ten-digit manufacturer's number. He would also talk to the coroner, but didn't expect anything to come of it. No speculations, at this point in the investigation, were warranted.

Emil unwrapped the bloody wrench on the counter beside Roberto's crossed ankles. The Argentinean's lazy eye righted itself as he dropped his feet.

"How do I trace this?" asked Emil.

Roberto settled back into his chair, regaining his composure bit by bit until he was deep within his easy worldliness again. He sighed audibly. "It's a poor nation, no? Bureaucracies are limited, they crawl." He gazed at his thumbs. "Could take, say, weeks to trace this machinery."

"There's a book somewhere? With this information? A file cabinet? I'll do it myself."

"The clearance," said Roberto sadly. He picked at his dry lower lip. "Months, I've no doubt."

Emil was slow sometimes, he knew this. He had been like this with Filia at the beginning, in that bombed café in the Third District. All her advances had gone in one ear and out the other. He was only receptive to those who, like the mute Ester in Ruscova, had no time for indirection.

Emil leaned forward and covered the wrench with the paper again, as if to hide their transaction from it. "To know by tomorrow," he said slowly. "How much?"

Roberto smiled toothily. "Only two!"

"Enter."

The chief was caught in mid-reach, one sweat-stained arm sliding into his jacket sleeve, when Emil dropped the typewritten pages on his desk.

"What's this?"

Emil's hands meeting behind his back was instinct, and once they touched he wished he could control his instinctual subservience. "Daily report, Com—" he began, then: "Chief."

Chief Moska had both his arms in his wrinkled, gray coat, and with one hand he lifted the report and separated the three sheets like cards. "You haven't done anything, Brod. Until you do, there's nothing to report. I don't want this." He held out the pages.

Emil folded his arms. "Regulations. Article fifteen, sections twelve through sixteen—communication between levels of service."

"Don't quote to me, Brod. It's disrespectful and ugly." The chief's face was hard when he said this, but he seemed genuinely surprised by the quotation. Emil accepted the report back. He folded it and creased the edge, but did not leave.

"I need some things."

"Things?"

Emil ignored his look. "An automobile, first of all."

"Why?"

"Interviews."

Chief Moska took a slow step back, as though considering sitting down again. "There are trams, Brod. They're very cheap. You're too good for them?"

"My interview is outside of town. Janos Crowder's wife."

"Talk to the garage." He stepped forward again.

Emil held up a weak hand. "A gun. I haven't been issued one yet."

The chief's brows came together, and the sweat on his forehead, disturbed, rolled down his cheek. He was such a large man, bigger the closer one came to him, and his breath seemed to heat the office. "You need a gun to interview a grieving widow?"

"I'm investigating murder, Chief."

"It's the last thing," Chief Moska began, then paused. "A gun is the last thing you want to touch. It's a dangerous thing to have too soon."

Emil said, "But—" then stopped. The chief was already out the door.

CHAPTER SIX

****

He was on the road, gliding past crowds of proles migrating home from work, their faces suddenly alert to the shiny, immaculate black Mercedes—no doubt a remnant of the German occupation—passing them. A couple of half-built apartment blocks rose on the outskirts, just the beginning of what was called in the papers *equal housing for all.* The professors, it was said, would live alongside the peasants and factory workers in the concrete homes of the future. He shifted gears and felt the anxiety of that miserable station unravel.

He'd only driven one other car in his life, the Academy practice vehicle, a KIM-10 with Rostov plates that spent most of its time on concrete blocks in the shop. When it was let out, it sputtered and jerked like a lame horse. This Mercedes took the corners like a cat. The Tisa flowed to his left, and the sun caught in his rearview.

The construction disappeared into farmland. Small houses and a tiny one-room bar lay on the corners of wheat fields, and when the hills began he saw the first of the huge homes. Some were built-up farmhouses, the land around them either tended by renters or gone fallow. Others were the mansions of the old world. He'd heard in the Academy that General Secretary Mihai kept two houses out here, one for himself and his family, the other for a mistress, but that was the kind of rumor schools produce.

He was anticipating the Crowder interview, his first. As he had learned in the Academy, there was a window of opportunity in the interrogation of widows—just after she has learned of her husband's death, and just before the shock has worn off. In this window any question can be asked and answered with authority and clarity. Its length varies with each widow—for some it is only a minute or two—but it can always be taken advantage of. This was a theory of interviewing that originated in Moscow and had been field-tested repeatedly. He outlined his precise use of this window, his questions and alternate lines of inquiry.

But when he turned up Lena Crowder's poplar-lined drive, the questions slid away as the jealousy caught in his throat. Compared to this big, two-story house covered in brown vines and surrounded by tall, manicured hedges, the puny apartment that Grandfather insisted his family cherish was a pitiful joke.

Another huge Mercedes was parked in front of the house—a white and gleaming 540K—and when he stepped out, his foot sank into the soft grass. The afternoon sun was unforgiving, but the air was easy and clean. He filled himself with it. Pink and violet flowers wilted in the heat. Flat stones formed a walkway to the front door, where he paused and touched its etched glass. It was a spiral, ornate design he had seen a lot of in Helsinki. The door opened before he could find the bell, and a short, stunned woman in a maid's uniform stared up at him, surprised. She held a pail of dirty water.

"Comrade Crowder?" said Emil. "She's in?"

The maid glanced back quickly into the house. "Maybe—"

He opened his Militia certificate. "Now, please."

She retreated a step as he came in, and water sloshed up the sides when she set the pail down. She walked quickly, almost running, past thick-framed portraits, lamps and a broad, curving staircase. At the end of a brief corridor, she disappeared through a side door.

Emil followed. He tried to ignore the chandelier above him, the long marble stand balanced by two porcelain vases, and the enormous bearded faces on the walls. But he couldn't. Finally, he made it to the door—heavy oak polished to a reflective shine—and found the maid in a deep room bent over a long, white-gowned woman stretched on a white sofa.

"Show him in!" called the woman, and the way her words slurred and slid, he knew she was drunk. She waved him forward and fell back, then used an arm to raise herself again. It was cool here. The only light was the orange dusk through the windows, but as he approached, her details became visible. Black hair bobbed around a thin neck, and her wide, pale face was marked by small, dark features. Lena Crowder squinted, trying to make him out. "More police?"

"Militia," he corrected quietly.

"The difference," she said, "is no difference to the rest of us." She sighed loudly. "At least I can see your face this time."

He stood in front of her coffee table—no longer local peasant crafts, but something that belonged to a Paris of the East—and held his hat in his hands. He couldn't manage any other pose. "Comrade Crowder," he began, trying to remember the right words, "I'm afraid I have some bad news."

Her expression fell, and he noticed how thick her lips were, how damp. Then the smile came back as a red, angry thing. Her voice was thick too: "Who died *now*—my mother? No—she's already dead."

The hat slipped from Emil's fingers. "You know? About your husband?"

Her anger was replaced by a stumbling, buoyant prettiness as she tried unsuccessfully to light her cigarette. She held the lighter out to him—a man's silver piece—and as he lit it her face went bright in the sudden flame, her pale cheeks smooth as china beneath coal eyes. She looked up at him and spoke smokily around the cigarette. "You really must get your communication straight." She leaned back. "Is this how you run the security of our socialist utopia?"

He sank into an overstuffed chair. He felt awkward and over-grown, his knees leaning together. She shifted her legs on the sofa beneath her gown, and white, manicured toes appeared briefly, the nails a wet-looking burgundy. "Irma!" she called. "A drink for the inspector!"

"No, thank you."

Lena Crowder's tone dropped: "Don't refuse me in my own house." Then the smile returned. "You were saying?"

He rubbed a temple with the tip of his finger. "I want to apologize for the confusion." He noticed his hat on the rug, a little distance away. The rug was thick and white, like her dead husband's blood-stained one. He looked at her. "Do you mean we already informed you of your husband's death?"

Lena Crowder picked tobacco from her lip. "At least you come in person, yes?" She waved the cigarette. "A telephone call. What's that? When you breed *in* equality, you breed *out* manners. *That's* a scientific fact."

Irma set down a glass of something clear with crushed ice, then left again.

"Drink," said Lena Crowder.

It was cool and lemony and potent. The outside of the glass was slick with condensation, and he had a sudden, irrational fear he was going to drop it. "If you want," he said, "we can talk later. I just have a few questions."

"Just *ask*, Inspector. The quicker we can end this." She threw a hand into the air, and it fell limply to the side of her thigh. "Irma!"

The far door opened immediately.

"For *me*?" She held her hand as if there were a drink in it.

Emil found himself staring at the side of her thigh. When he realized she was looking at him looking at her, he took out his notepad and looked at the scribbles instead. He cleared his throat. "Your husband. Did he have any enemies? Of which you are aware?"

"Only those who knew him."

Emil raised his head.

"That's a *joke*, don't you see?" She laughed, not very convincingly, then took another drag and shot smoke into the room. "He was nasty to be around when he'd been drinking, no doubt about it. But *enemies*? Janos? An infectious little man. He was always that. You *do* know we were separated?"

He shook his head.

"The organs of state security at work. I thought you knew everything."

"I'm not state security," said Emil, "and I'm not with the police. Homicide is a division of the People's Militia, and we only know what people tell us."

She accepted the drink Irma handed her and tested it with a frown. Her voice came out thicker, clotted. "Six months. That's how long we were separated. Maybe a little more. Still married, yes, yes." She waved her hand again. "That kind of thing drags on, but he lived in town, and I lived, well, *here*." She opened her hands to display her world of oak cabinets and framed portraits and French lounge pieces.

"So, no enemies?"

"He had bill collectors, but as far as I know they just disappeared."

"What kinds of bills?"

She shrugged. "*Living*, what else? Food, drink, *women*."

"Women?"

"Suspicion, intuition. Nothing you would call hard *evidence*."

"When did you last hear from him?"

She opened her mouth as if to let another casual remark spill out, something she might find funny and expect him to be amused by as well, or horrified by, but nothing came. She closed her mouth again. "A week ago," she said. "He came to see me."

Emil's pencil was poised above paper.

She took another swill, then set her drink down. "What he said was he wanted to come back. To me." She looked into her empty glass, eyes glazed. "That's what he said. He said six months was much too long, and he knew now what he had always wanted. And that was me." She pointed at herself with a finger that touched her chin. "*Me.*" She smiled thinly.

"Didn't you believe him?"

"Is there a reason I shouldn't have?" Her smile was gone. "You know, there was a time when I mattered to him. Sometimes that's enough, just knowing you matter. He even used to show jealousy. He called me an unredeemable flirt." She paused. "But then not even that mattered to him."

"I—" began Emil.

She dropped the glass and threw her face behind her thin fingers, instantly sobbing. There was no transition, no warning, just a sudden plummet into tears.

Inexplicably, he almost cried as well.

Irma appeared out of nowhere, arm around her mistress, and whispered things Emil could not make out. But he was already standing and retreating to the door. He could think of nothing else to do; the Academy's limits were becoming more apparent by the second. "I'll be in touch later." His voice sounded weak. "When it's better."

Lena Crowder did not look up.

Irma met him at the front door with his hat. The walls had muted the weeping. "Be easy on her," she whispered, and Emil recognized her accent—the southern provinces, maybe near Ruscova. She had ruddy, loyal features.

"Where are you from, Irma?"

She held out the hat and blushed marginally. "You wouldn't know. It's south of Sighet. Vadu Izei. Just a village."

"Of course I know Vadu Izei," he said. "My family came from Ruscova."

She blinked at him.

"See?" he said. "You think *you* come from a small village." He accepted his hat and slid the brim in a circular motion with the tips of his fingers. "When did they call Comrade Crowder?"

Her face went serious again. "About Master Crowder? Yesterday."

"Early? Late?"

She thought a moment. "Before dinner."

He placed the hat on his head and nodded thanks before going out into what had quickly become a purple, breezy night. His hand in his pocket came up with his father's watch and its soft, soothing tick. The other hand held the black garter he had forgotten to show the widow. His hands, he noticed, were trembling.

CHAPTER SEVEN

****

Instead of returning the Mercedes to the station, he delivered peach and strawberry preserves to his grandmother. Her pink face flushed deeply as she turned the jars over, looking for clues. He placed the Zorki camera on a shelf. "How did you . . . ?" she began. He told them he was taking them for a ride.

"A what?" Grandfather cupped his ears in a mockery of old age.

Children were standing around the car, touching the fender and pressing noses to the windshield. Emil waved them off and opened the back door. Grandfather's emotions raced unconcealed across his face and through his shaking hands, but Grandmother fell into a somber sobriety as she climbed inside. To bring out a smile, Emil explained: "A special car for a special case." It worked.

Grandfather sat in the front, hands flat on his thighs, and gazed through the breezy open windows at the town passing by. His face lit up through the government center, past the Militia station steps that Emil tried to ignore, and the Central Committee building on busy Victory Square. They looked across to the Canal District's gas-lit perimeter that cast an unreal glow, and Emil could sense the speech building inside the old Marxist humming beside him. Tonight, Emil felt generous—let the old man talk.

From the backseat, Grandmother said, almost to herself, "You remember," and Grandfather nodded.

They drove along the Tisa to the unlit city limits and turned north into the half-built residential blocks.

"I heard Ivan Ilych even here," said Grandfather suddenly. "Even then, you know?"

The speech was upon him.

"They said in the Party newspaper that Comrade Lenin was going by train," he explained, rapping knuckles on the doorframe. "All the way to Moscow. But no one knew when. It was illegal, you know. The newspaper." He opened his mouth and gulped the breeze. "The Petrograd strikers, they were my heroes. And Ivan Ilych, well, he was everything. So I told Mara. I said I was going to take part in a workers' uprising in Russia. She didn't believe me."

"I believed you," came her soft voice. "I just said you were out of your mind."

"There was nothing to lose." He flapped a knobbed hand in the rushing air. "What did we have then? We had *nothing*. We shared a room with two other families, and we had nothing to eat. We had education—the Brods always educated—but it's worse for an educated man to be without space. Without *necessities*. He knows better." Grandfather paused, and Emil turned the big steering wheel counterclockwise. They were on Union Street. "You've seen the Sixth District—they have so much more now than when we were there."

"True enough," said Grandmother. But she didn't sound convinced.

"I remember," said Emil.

Grandfather nodded. "And I knew that this was a piece of History I was living through."

So in late October 1917, he and two other husbands from the neighborhood climbed on a livestock train heading east. When the stationmaster swung his lamp into the car, they crawled back and hid among the boars.

"The stink. It's *still* in me."

"Truly," came the backseat voice.

"*Woman.*"

They changed trains in L'viv, then again in Minsk, and crossed into Soviet Russia at Krasnoe, a little west of Smolensk. When they arrived at the outskirts of Moscow three weeks later, they were just cold, hungry foreigners. The other two men depended on Avram Brod for his smattering of Russian as they begged off the kindness of the already starving peasantry.

In the city, they fell in with crowds that choked the grand avenues and chiseled away at the czar's façades. Statues were pulled down with ropes and sweat, and People's commissars in greatcoats directed the workers. Really, though, the Revolution had run its course before they even entered Russia. They saw peasants dragging crates of potatoes through the streets, and for a long time this was their picture of revolution. Crates and sacks of potatoes. No one heard or saw Lenin anywhere. Then he was on the balconies again. "Once a criminal in hiding," Grandfather said, his voice quivering, "now surrounded by generals who looked like dock workers. You hear him speak." He tapped his ear. "It doesn't matter what the words are. I couldn't understand his accent. But no matter. Just him moving his arms, shouting in the cold. Foggy words in his mouth. A man."

He wiped his eyes unabashedly with his too-large knuckles because thirty years ago was like yesterday. He had returned to the Capital with a red card in his bag and orders to foment revolution. He and his two friends already constituted a cell. But then the rigors of life set in again. Food and money. There was a war still tearing apart the rest of Europe, and food was scarce for everyone. All he could do was eke out a living selling withered vegetables to women in the Sixth District who couldn't afford them, trying to support his wife and boy. Years passed, a world depression struck, and their cell consisted of three men who drank together, commiserating over their failures. War came again, and the king sent their boy Valentin—a father himself now—to Poland to defend the monarchy against fascists; then Valentin's wife followed into oblivion. When the Germans marched into the Capital, they fled south with their insolent teenage grandson. Avram Brod had thought it could get no worse than the slums they had come from, but he had never been a farmer before, had never met the Romanian Jews who wore the terrors of the world on their faces.

By the time they returned to the Capital, the Brod clan was decimated, but in the chaos of the Liberation, that weathered, muddy red card earned them an apartment with a view. It was a miserable tradeoff—a family for a home—but Grandfather did everything in his power to justify what he could.

"The 'thick Muscovites' were everywhere," said Grandmother.

"Be kind, Mara."

The "thick Muscovites" were those men who, after spending the 1930s throwing rocks and shooting politicians, had escaped to Moscow during the war, where they camped out in hotels. General Secretary Mihai had been among them. They appeared again just behind the Red Army to set up the interim government, and with the 1946 elections had the remarkable good fortune of being voted immediately into power.

They were called "thick" because when they returned from Moscow they were, almost without exception, so plump their own families had trouble recognizing them.

In no time they were setting up tribunals, sentencing old comrades—primarily those who had chosen to stay in the country and fight the Nazis—to work camps and prisons, some to the firing squad. *The Spark,* the revived Party daily, gave notice of those old communists who no longer carried the torch, and would pay for their lack of enthusiasm. Finally the handsome Mihai—handsome despite the fresh rolls of fat—who before the war had styled himself as a partisan fighter against the monarchy before fleeing to Moscow, found himself with the title, first, of Prime Minister; then, in addition, General Secretary. His portrait began appearing everywhere.

Grandfather was settling into his emotions, ignoring the passing city. Emil noticed the glint of tears on the old man's cheeks.

For Avram Brod, there were two events in history: the Russian

Revolution and the Patriotic War, which resulted in his country's proletarian liberation. In both these events he had been close enough to smell the dead, but too late to make a difference.

"This is the problem with History," he said after the tears had dried and they were turning back toward home. He had regained his liveliness, and kept turning to look at passing shop windows. "When you're living in the midst of it, you don't even realize. You're preoccupied by money and food and the appointment you're late for. But look around yourself, boy. We're living through it now."

Emil slowed behind a delivery truck unloading heavy, unmarked steel barrels. The workers paused in their work to watch the Mercedes drive past.

"What happened in 'seventeen was just the start. There are so many of us now. Poland, Hungary, Romania, Bulgaria, Yugoslavia, Albania, the Baltics and even the Czechs. It's just the beginning. You may not believe it, but in ten years we'll look back with nostalgia. We'll forget how hard it was to get a little meat, or to repair the pipes. We'll wonder how we were so lucky to live through these times. Helping to shape the great experiment."

He was out of words again, and turned to the window. They were back in the Fifth District, moving slowly through dark, narrow side streets.

Emil concentrated on the functional details of driving. Shift, turn, accelerate.

"You glorify so much," said Grandmother. When Emil looked in the rearview, he saw a face obscured by shadows. "The Russians are pigs."

Emil kept his eyes on the road and the families wandering the cracked sidewalks. He'd seldom heard her contradict him like that. Finally, Grandfather's voice came briskly: "Mara, you don't know. *I* was in Russia. They fed me. They were good and true. I was the one who saw them in their own country."

Her voice was hard. "Don't tell me what I don't know." She

shifted in the darkness. "I've seen enough Russians to last me a lifetime."

Just before their building, in the reflection of a passing street-light, Emil saw that she, too, had been crying.

He watched the others work. Leonek Terzian leaned into his tele-phone on the other side of the room, mumbling and nodding. He stared back at Emil with an indecipherable expression as he wrote in his notepad. Big Ferenc, beneath the bulletin board, typed slowly. Stefan, still unshaven, spat pumpkin seed shells that missed his wastebasket, and the security inspector—still, remark-ably, in leather—arranged stacks of files on the floor beside his desk, which faced the blank wall.

This was manageable. This tenuous silence. Each person work-ing on his own business.

He read over the notes from Lena Crowder's interview. So little, he'd have to talk with her again. Part of him dreaded it, while another was eager for the chance to revisit her in that mansion. There was something beyond his prole jealousy that wanted to touch those expensive things. To see those legs folded beneath her.

He looked up as Terzian cradled the telephone and went to the chief's door. When he knocked, Emil could hear the faint "Enter."

He called the Fourth District police station, which had origi-nally reported Crowder's body, and recognized the voice of the bored young policeman who was able to eat butter near a bashed-in skull. "Comrade Inspector?"

"You remember me?" asked Emil.

"Of course."

"Do you remember telling me that Lena Crowder was not informed of her husband's death?"

There was a brief pause, the hiss of wires. "Sure."

"You know why I'm asking this?"

No reply.

"I'm asking because she already knew."

A crackling exhale. "Maybe she read it in the paper."

"She learned it from a phone call," said Emil.

"I said nothing, Comrade Inspector." His words were short, abrupt. "I spoke to no reporters. I did not call Lena Crowder."

There was a small, warm anger inside him. By the time he had shown up, Lena Crowder's window of interrogation had been open, then slammed shut and bolted. And now, no one was taking responsibility.

"Then *who* made the phone call?"

"I don't know. Perhaps you should ask Comrade Crowder."

"I—"

"*Brod.*"

It was Chief Moska, filling his doorway. As he stepped back into the office, Emil hung up and followed.

Terzian was stretched out in a chair across from the chief's desk, one leg tossed over a padded arm. The chief settled, grunting, into his own chair. Emil glanced around for a free seat that wasn't there. He stood finally with his hands clasped behind his back, Academy-style. "Comrade Chief?"

Moska didn't notice the slip. He looked at Terzian, who was focused on some point beyond the beige curtains, and said to Emil, "How's the Crowder case coming?"

It was cooler in the office today. "The wife has been interviewed. But preliminarily. Someone informed her of her husband's death before I could."

"Someone?" asked the chief. "Meaning *us*?"

"The district police, I imagine."

"Go on."

Terzian did not shift his gaze from the curtains.

"I have the murder weapon."

The chief squinted. "The wrench?"

"It's being traced."

"Any fingerprints?"

He shook his head. "Gloves."

Terzian glanced at him, and Emil wished he could read something, anything, in his tanned, hungry face.

"Other interviews?" asked Moska.

"Neighbors on the same floor, Poles. They couldn't tell me much. And the apartment supervisor. I was planning to see the coroner this afternoon."

Terzian looked away from the curtains. He laid his eyes on Emil and said in a quiet voice: "The supervisor's name?"

"Aleksander Tudor."

"When did you last see him?"

"Yesterday," said Emil firmly, wanting no indecision to get in his way. "Three in the afternoon."

Chief Moska raised his eyebrows, and Terzian's head swiveled slowly back to the window, his face a passive mask. The chief said, "Tell him, Leon."

Terzian's head shook incrementally, and he spoke without looking at Emil. "This morning a citizen found Aleksander Tudor floating in the Tisa with two bullet holes in the back of his head." He placed two fingers on the back of his scalp to demonstrate. "His face had been struck struck repeatedly so that identification had to be made by fingerprints."

"Like—" Emil began, but stopped himself from stating the obvious.

"Exactly, Comrade Brod," Terzian murmured.

The chief had another pencil point in his mouth that he pulled out. Again, there was a mark of lead on his lips, and he pursed them before speaking. "My personal inclinations take a backseat to protocol. We understand?"

No one made a move to suggest they didn't.

"There are two bodies," he said. "In the interests of the state, both of you will take the case. The interests of the *state*. Right, Brod?"

They were both staring at Emil, their faces expectant, as if waiting for an answer. But Emil didn't understand the question.

CHAPTER EIGHT

****

L eonek Terzian was plainly uncomfortable with Emil driving,
so Emil drove recklessly. He swerved around wagons loaded
with sweaty farmers sleeping off their predawn chores and made
sudden hard stops at intersections. Terzian's face was awash in
shades of red.

The Unity Medical Complex—a fresh, concrete model of
modern uniformity, built on the foundations of a bombed-out,
fourteenth-century church—lay where the First District sank to
meet the Second. Terzian led the way inside, through institutional
glass doors and gray corridors with moaning peasants covering
the dirty floors beside gaunt chain-smokers in robes and slippers.
They stepped around a dry pool of brown blood. There were no
doctors in sight.

On the far side of the empty nurse's station, they went through
another door and down a stairwell to the medical examiner's
floor. He was a short Uzbek who smoked in the corner of his
examining room, ashing in the sink, while around him four low
steel tables with wheels held bodies covered by white sheets.
"Leon," he said. The coroner's shoulders, Emil noticed, were mis-
aligned, so that in all his movements he looked ready to sit down.
He turned on the faucet to extinguish his cigarette and wiped his
hands on his soiled smock. "You're the new one?"

Emil stuck out a hand and the Uzbek shook it. Cool and dry.

The nails had been pared meticulously, and the room stank of medicinal alcohol. "Emil Brod."

The coroner rubbed his hands together in mock appetite. "Let's take a look, shall we? The freshest first."

They followed him to the mound on a table beside three ice-boxes, and Emil noticed how the absence of windows, more than the medical equipment scattered around, gave this concrete room an antiseptic feel.

The Uzbek drew back the sheet. Aleksander Tudor lay puffed up like an overfed seal. His wide, naked girth was colorless, his genitals sucked inside his groin. His toes and neck were blue, and across his marbled, egglike chest and stomach was a wide, Y-shaped autopsy slice that had been roughly sutured shut.

Again, the face that was no longer a face. But this one had been washed clean by the Tisa, the red remnants drained to a white pulp.

This was yet another kind of corpse—different than a body in a home, or on a boat. The antiseptic smells, the Uzbek casually pressing a finger into the half-mouth to see inside, the post-mortem stitches—he again felt the instinct to vomit, but brought it under control when he heard Terzian choking down his own convulsions near the door.

"The bullet holes?" Emil managed.

The Uzbek lifted the head, his clean fingers holding the back of the skull, where there was still some structure. He nodded at two black-and-blue holes on the round, hairless scalp. "Shots one and two." He let the head drop. A soft thud. He pointed to where a chin had once been. "Exit here. The second got stuck in his jaw."

In the far corner, Terzian breathed loudly through his mouth, echoing glassily.

"Make?" asked Emil.

The coroner picked up a typewritten ballistics report from the counter. "PPK, Walther. German officer's gun. The continent's littered with them these days."

Emil had owned one also. Briefly, in Ruscova. They were cheap and efficient, like most things German. Small and light, easy to conceal. But he'd never shot one—he'd hidden his, and finally bartered it for train fare to Helsinki. "What was he wearing when he came in?"

The little man crossed his arms, which was a peculiar look at his slant, like a poorly constructed building on the verge of collapse. "Low-quality fabrics, worker materials. Empty pockets. No money, ID, nothing. Leon," he said, cracking a smile at the other side of the room. "You ever going to find a better line of work?"

Terzian looked up suddenly, pale, his bloodshot eyes glistening, and stumbled out of the room.

The Uzbek's laugh was high and thin, and as he wiped the faint sweat from his cheek Emil made a connection. "What about Janos Crowder's body? Slugs?"

The Uzbek's smile held as the amusement turned into pride. He tapped his skull. "Didn't see any the first time around, but we weren't looking, were we? Saw no need for an autopsy. One finely obliterated head. But after this one, I went back." He held up an index finger. "One slug, same direction. Slanting down from the rear of the cranium. No word yet, but I'll bet my bone saw it's a PPK."

The bloated navel bulged out, a knot of blue flesh. Emil stared at it, then the battered head. There was still half a face to it. "Somebody wanted to hide the gunshot."

"But ran out of time," said the Uzbek, finishing his thought.

"Or someone interrupted."

He looked at the Uzbek's bright eyes. This was a smart man who had chosen to hole himself up in a gray bunker where he talked only to dead men and militiamen. It was a strange, incomprehensible choice, but maybe no stranger than his own decisions. The little man covered the body and loped back toward the door. "Tell that Armenian slob to quit eating before he comes here. He's a good guy, Leon, but a little stupid." He tapped his forehead again, and the movement that once signified his own powers of perception now stood for another's ignorance.

The Polish children were in the entryway with a wooden ball, and they recognized Emil right away. The small, dark girl smiled at him.

"Marie?"

She nodded, blushing, and he squatted beside her.

"Did you know you've got the same name as my mother?"

She didn't.

He winked at her. "Can you tell me where the supervisor's apartment is?"

"The dead one?" Marie asked, then pointed to the second floor.

Terzian made a huffing sound that might have been amusement.

There was an official notice nailed to the door, warning away the curious, but the wood frame around the lock was splintered and split, as if kicked in. Terzian instinctively took a pistol from a shoulder holster and pushed the door with his foot, exposing a demolished living room. The sofa cushions had been cut open and the books torn from their shelves. Cabinets had been upturned and rugs pulled and tossed over a small table near the kitchen door.

"This is almost a surprise," said Emil, then nodded at Terzian's hand. "How do I get one of those?"

Terzian followed his gaze and made the connection, then grunted noncommittally. He holstered the pistol.

Emil concentrated on the kitchen, where dishes had been pulled from their shelves; shards cracked beneath his shoes. The cutlery had been tossed in a pile against the wall and the drawers pulled out until they had dropped to the floor. When he opened the ice-box, water spilled out over his feet, and he cursed, jumping back. There was nothing inside that told him a thing—except, perhaps, Tudor's final meal: a half-eaten bowl of borscht moldering on the center rack.

He found nutmeg in the cabinet alongside three matches in an unmarked box, and beneath the sink a dirty tin of sunflower oil. He reached into the cabinets, feeling with his fingertips, but only came up with dirt and rat turds.

Then he remembered the twine.

He tugged at the icebox until it scratched across the tile. He looked behind it. Again, twine. It bound two pieces of cardboard together like a sandwich, and tied it all to the iron pipes. Emil used a knife from the floor to cut it loose, and when the sand-wich dropped into his waiting hand several small photographs slipped out.

He glanced at the empty doorway. Terzian was still out there, in another room, moving things around.

The photographs were each the size of his palm, white-bordered. They were taken from a fair distance, at night. In each, two men stood in an empty street, talking, shaking hands, putting hands on their chins in thought. He recognized neither of them. Some pictures were blurred because of the photographer's shak-ing hand, but the simple story the pictures told was clear: Two men meet in an empty street, talk and agree to something, then leave separately. A ten-picture tale.

Glass crashed in the apartment, just before Terzian's "*Shit!*"

Emil slipped the photos into his breast pocket. It was an unconscious movement, but, once completed, he knew he would keep them hidden from his reluctant partner.

Terzian was in the bathroom, standing in front of the shattered mirror over the sink. Shards of reflection lay on the floor, throw-ing light everywhere, and Terzian was gazing at where the mirror had been. He reached into the wall. "What is it?"

Terzian's hand came back with a cardboard box from a hole dug into the plaster. Through an open flap he saw rows of large bills.

They brought it back to the living room, where Terzian settled on the ripped sofa and began to count, laying the bills on the righted coffee table.

"Aha," said Terzian, but Emil was staring at the stacks of money, a slow, leisurely fantasy building inside him; it included train tickets and hotels and places far away from here. He looked up finally at Terzian, who held up the empty box to show the address typed on the outside, topped by J. CROWDER. The fantasy slipped away.

Deliver the mail, indeed.

"That fat, thieving corpse," said Terzian. A big, broad smile emerged despite all his considerable efforts.

No one answered at the red Polish door. The children had been cleared from the entryway, though their scuffed wooden ball remained, lodged in a corner. Emil imagined their fear—or at least the mother's—when little Marie told them about the homicide inspector who had asked where the dead supervisor was. He felt the mother's worry—Germans, police, relocations—and could imagine her low whisper as she told the children and grandparents to hurry, they were going out to the park.

He wanted to talk out the details of the case, but once they reached the Mercedes, Terzian remembered that Emil was anathema, and closed himself into the silence again. So Emil spoke silently to himself as he cruised the narrow streets choked with sweaty horses and workers and the occasional broken-down automobile; disabled Russian models were slowly filling the city.

Someone had sent Janos Crowder over fifteen thousand koronas (accounting for some of Aleks Tudor's inevitable expenditures since the August 18 postmark, and some bills probably in

Terzian's pocket). The money was then intercepted by the building inspector. About August 24, a week later, someone killed Janos Crowder and searched his apartment. Two days after that, someone—presumably the same person—killed Aleksander Tudor. Again, a search. For the money? An imperfect search, if that was the object. And why was Crowder receiving the equivalent of a year's salary in a box? Why too—this was perhaps most important—were photos of two men hidden behind the icebox?

There was a German, maybe a plumber. He could have nothing to do with any of this, but he was the only other person to come up—at least until these photos.

A simple theory would be that Aleksander Tudor had killed Crowder for the money. Someone else—maybe the German—had learned of the money, killed Tudor, and bungled the search for the box. Most crimes, a lecturer had once said, were committed by idiots. Stupidity is a tool of the trade.

But this was more than stupidity; it didn't quite make sense. Emil had seen Tudor standing in the same room as Crowder's corpse. He wasn't the kind of man who could throttle a skull like that.

"Watch out!" Terzian shouted as Emil swerved around three Gypsy children who showed him their fat, red tongues.

"What do you make of it?"

"What?" Terzian squinted at the noon light and brought down his visor.

"This. Our case."

"It's your case, not mine."

"But you have some thoughts."

"I have nothing," said Terzian, still squinting. He turned to his side window. "I'm a man completely devoid of ideas. You can report that."

There was a scribbled note lying beside the paper-wrapped wrench on his desk. Roberto was quick—Emil didn't know how men like him made their ways so smoothly—and beneath the wrench's distributor address he had signed his name with a flourish to the *t* that, in some circles, would have been considered positively decadent.

Leonek Terzian, sinking into his chair on the other side of the room, watched. Emil read the note, looked around, then wandered over to Terzian, waving the paper. "The wrench. You want to come?"

Terzian opened his desk drawer and rummaged until he had found a half-smoked pack of cigarettes. He pocketed it and got up. His words were preceded by a low belch. "I'm driving."

The equipment distributor's shop lay on a back street in the northern Sixth District. It was a hectic prole area that had been severely damaged during the war, leaving brick shells and partially demolished blocks. The Brods had lived here before the Occupation, barely making ends meet.

They drove past the building many times before finding it, Terzian growing progressively more furious at the irregular street numbers. The top floor had been razed off completely. The white door that said in stencils THIRD STATE EQUIPMENT VENDORS, SA was set low into the sidewalk, so they had to descend five steps to reach it. The clerk was a ghost—milky, translucent flesh hanging from his skull, his eyes invisible behind the reflection of fluorescent lights on his round glasses. He stood behind a long counter that was empty, save his pale fingertips, as if he had been expecting them all afternoon. His quiet *Good afternoon* was delivered with an indistinct nod, and his hands sank into the pockets of his white coat. His nostrils expanded pleasurably as he sniffed the lemony air—some new disinfectant—and waited.

Emil unwrapped the wrench and placed it on the counter. Roberto had cleaned it off well. "Can you tell us who you sold this to?"

"Perhaps," came the quiet answer. The beginnings of a smile

creased his lips. Then he looked past Emil's shoulder and his smile faded. Terzian was holding out his Militia certificate. "Comrade Inspectors," he began again, louder. He squatted behind the counter and pulled out a thick book filled with writing: dates, names, numbers. When he spoke, his uneven teeth flashed. "Do we know when the tool was purchased?"

"Before the twenty-fourth," said Emil.

"Of this month?" He sounded vaguely disbelieving. "Between sometime and the twenty-fourth of August? *Any* time?"

Emil shrugged.

The ghost sighed and bent over the book, lining up the wrench so he could read the raised ten-digit number on its handle. He used a long fingernail to scrape part of the number clear.

Terzian leaned close. "I see there's still blood on that thing."

He withdrew his finger as if burned, breathing shallowly through his mouth. But he wiped his hand on the side of his coat and went back to it. Another nail drew down the page, checking sales, one by one. Terzian lit a cigarette and wandered to the far wall beneath a framed picture of General Secretary Mihai, colored lightly by fading paint. It was an older portrait, pre-1945. Back when he was still thin and handsome, thick eyebrows and romantic stare—one of the early Moscow portraits.

"I do know some things," the clerk whispered after a while. He turned a page.

Emil was leaning on the counter. "You know something?"

He raised his head and rested on his elbows, then took off his glasses. Even his tiny eyes had a translucence about them, the lids pink. "In a store, you hear talk. Not that you're listening, but this is a small place. It's unavoidable. Then it becomes a duty. You follow?"

"Spit it out," said Emil.

"Counterrevolutionary talk." His voice gained volume as he straightened, hands on either side of the book. "They come in here, buy pipes. Metal pipes. What for? They don't tell me." He put the glasses back on. "Then they make a joke about the Comrade General Secretary. A joke once about Smerdyakov."

"The Butcher?" asked Emil.

"Not very funny jokes, if you understand me. Even a joke or two about the Comrade Chairman." He shrugged sadly. "I have names."

Emil didn't know what to say. It had occurred to him that he might receive reports like this—half the neighbors in town, one suspected, had such information and were willing to give it out. But even his own family had had some fun at Mihai's expense— Grandfather still had his humor about him. This was not his area. Emil had joined Homicide in order to deal with the clearest and least ambiguous issue of social conscience: murder.

Terzian put out his cigarette on the floor, and Emil noticed the smoke had overpowered the lemon in the air. He could feel the other inspector's eyes on him. He felt the expectation, but didn't know what he was expecting.

"Talk to state security," Emil said finally. "There's one in our station." He turned back to Terzian. "What's his name?"

The dark face stared through the smoky gloom, and Emil had no idea what would come out of his mouth. Leonek Terzian blinked. "Sev," he said quietly, then raised his voice. "Brano Sev." He gave the phone number.

"Inspector Brano Sev?" The clerk was fidgeting now; he glowed. Emil recognized the name too: from *The Spark,* the inspector commenting on the democracy of socialist justice.

The round peasant's face, little black eyes, thinning hair. The vulture. That nagging familiarity finally had a name.

"You mean the German hunter?" asked the ghost.

Famous, even. Brano Sev, named a Hero of Socialist Endeavor a year ago for his part in the arrest of a band of ex-SS hiding out in the Canal District. Nine men had been rounded up at once, accused of horrible war crimes, given speedy trials, prisons and executions. This moderately famous man sat across from Emil's desk, waiting to pluck the Crowder case from him.

Terzian was unimpressed by the clerk's knowledge. He pointed at the book. "Get the name of our fucking suspect, or I'll take you in for destruction of state property."

Another smile: thin, yellow teeth separated by shadows. "But I've destroyed nothing."

Terzian walked back to the wall, where the portrait of the General Secretary made Mihai's eyes too blue to be true. He took it down, walked back, and smashed it against the counter, shouting, red-faced: "That's fifteen years in the *swamps*, comrade! Do you need any help getting my information?"

The clerk dropped to his book and rattled through the numbers at an alarming speed. Terzian returned to his post by the door and lit another cigarette. Emil remembered the small, hard fist. The groin.

Then the clerk was nodding, his eager smile trembling. "Yes, yes," he said. "Here it is, here's your man. Janos Crowder. Yes, Crowder." He took off his glasses again, his voice hysterical. "That's your man, comrades. It's your man!"

CHAPTER NINE

****

"Goes against my best judgment, but here it is, an inch of advice."

Terzian's words came with the smoke that was whisked out the open window. He turned left, south toward the station, and raised a brown index finger from the wheel.

"You're an inspector now, you don't have to be a sweetheart. You break something. You put the fear of the state into them. It's how you get results." He squinted at the road ahead and took another drag. "You kiss them and treat them like equals, they'll shit in your mouth." He made another turn and craned his head at a beautiful young woman in a summer dress emerging from a pharmacy. "It may not be your socialism, but it's the only thing that works."

This was the most he had ever heard from Leonek Terzian's lips. It was not what he had hoped for—some dictate on tough-guy tactics—but he accepted it as a small, fetal victory and smiled into his collar.

Brano Sev's poverty-stricken face nodded passively as Emil explained that an equipment merchant might call with some information. It was probably nothing, he said, but you never know.

Brano Sev's cheeks were marked by three brown moles. Emil now clearly remembered his grainy newsprint features beside a headline: LABOR WITH VALOR! SEV BRINGS IN THE COWARDS.

"What kind of information?"

Emil's stomach tensed. "The man was vague. Counterrevolutionary, he said. Jokes? Yes, offensive jokes."

Brano Sev leaned into the edge of his desk, looking nothing like a Hero of Socialist Anything. The apple cheeks made it wrong. Emil wondered if those boy's cheeks had made it difficult for him to be taken seriously in this most serious of all professions.

Sev held up a finger for Emil to wait. Then he unlocked a deep side drawer. He hefted it open and revealed hanging files stuffed with papers and photographs. He motioned with an open hand. "Do you see these, Comrade Inspector?"

Emil hesitated, then nodded.

"Each of these files," said Brano Sev, "represents an individual living in our city whose central aim is to undermine our way of life. Do you understand what I mean by that?" Tension built beneath his calm voice. "For example—a simple example—there is a man living in the Fourth District who receives regular payments from the Queen of England. These come wrapped in brown paper, hidden behind a loose brick on the rear wall of the Lenin Gymnasium. Once a month he receives these payments. What for?" His flat, round face turned up toward Emil, and he opened his hands. "He passes information about his munitions factory. Do you know how we came to discover this man?"

Emil didn't, and his immobility signified this.

"A neighbor saw this man throw away a volume of Comrade Chairman Stalin's collected speeches." Sev's cheeks puffed as his lips widened into a smile. "Who knows why he did it? Maybe the book was old, or the dog urinated on it. But this old grandmother was disturbed enough to have us look into it, and we learned that our secrets were being sold to the British. You know where I'm going with this?"

Sweat had formed along Sev's upper lip, clear little beads that joined and slipped into his mouth. Emil imagined the saltiness, then little old women burrowing through trash, then he imagined prisons run by state security devotees like this one. He started to answer, to say, *Yes, Comrade,* but Sev's loud voice boomed through the station.

"There's a *war* on, Comrade Brod! You don't see it in the streets, and you certainly may not care about it, but despite your ignorance it goes on! Haven't you heard of Berlin? The capitalists are barking at the gates. An entire world is out to crush us!" He breathed loudly, cheeks red and damp.

A finger pointed at Emil's chest. "These are not just platitudes! Each day people die, trying to keep this great experiment running!"

He stopped, his small eyes swimming in their sockets, flashing at other corners of the room. They steadied gradually, focusing, settling finally on Emil. When he spoke, it was again with control.

"People have to take responsibility for their freedom. You understand?" He waved a hand at the files. Casual. The shouting was over. "These are only suspects from the last three months; the rest are on file in the Central Committee. Do you really think I can follow all these people myself?" He threaded his fingers on the desk.

Emil had to answer now. "Of course you can't, Comrade Sev." His face flushed. "I just—" He started to raise his hands—they were like ice—then let them drop.

Brano Sev picked up his lecture where he had left off. The Allies trying to force us out of Berlin, the tenuous victory of the working class here at home, the martyrs of the Liberation, the insidious influence of opportunists and the apathetic.

The eyes of the whole office were on Emil. They were waiting. For an explosion, maybe. Or a final folding. The lecture went on. The humiliation was a numbing thing, and he felt as though he were standing outside of himself, and he had to force his body to do simple things. Nod. Say *I understand* and *I apologize.*

The numbness kept him distanced from the anger forming in his gut. Hard, dense. He was distracted by the humiliation that saturated his body.

Nod.

Part of him thought: This is a lecture by Brano Sev on the necessity of Brano Sev.

Stand straight. Do not look away.

Another part: You're not getting my case. Just try. I'll kill you.

The thrashing was over. He only knew because Sev, livid again, threw himself into his chair and picked up the telephone to call Third State Equipment Supply, SA.

Turn around. Walk back—balance, now—to your desk. Sit down.

Stefan was on cherries today, tossing white, sucked pits into the wastebasket. He used his tongue to clear residue from his incisors, and raised an eyebrow when Emil looked.

Take out your watch. Five P.M.

Ferenc spoke into his own telephone quietly, shooting brief, clandestine glances, as if he were talking about Emil. But maybe that was the paranoia again. He put the watch away. Terzian was nowhere to be seen. His jacket and leather satchel were gone, and the light in the chief's office was out.

Stand up. Take your jacket. Don't look at *him*. Ahead, through the door.

Emil appeared on the front steps where the angled, late afternoon sunlight glowed on the windows opposite.

He told himself to look around, for safety.

The heat was thick with animal smells, and shouts rang out down below. The humiliation still blocked up his ears, so the vendors' shouts were whispers. The lounging district cops didn't look up as he passed.

Two streets down he bought a bottle of cheap plum brandy from a state store. The tall woman behind the counter with so much black hair looked at him suspiciously. Then he went to an empty state restaurant. More black hair, white smocks, suspicious and slow service. He almost walked out before the pork cutlet arrived. The potatoes had gone cold. After a while he started drinking from his brandy at the table, straight from the bottle, and the waitresses, chain-smoking in the corner, conferred worriedly. He returned to the garage as the sun was setting. He took another coarse swig just before starting the engine, another before nodding to the attendant in his glassed-in box. But the teenager's eyes were already closed, dozing.

The Capital was behind him. It was black out here, farther west than the city's lights could reach, and all he could hear were the wind and the roaring engine. The Tisa's stone and concrete banks had become mud and grass a mile back. His speeding headlights lit the flat sides of long grass, the occasional fence post or discarded plank of wood and, once, a broken-down and stripped Soviet jeep. All around were flat fields.

Another mile, he would reach Lena Crowder's house.

This was the blackness of provincial nights. He remembered those first weeks in Ruscova, the terror it had provoked in him, a teenager in fields that were as dark as closed eyes.

To the north, the land rose from plains to an omen of the Carpathians. He pulled to the side of the road, climbed down a muddy slope, and pissed in the river.

When he got back to the car, a little dizzy, he wondered if he should go forward or back. Westward, farther than Lena Crowder's, were Czechoslovakia and Hungary. His imagination could see Prague. Budapest. He saw them as he had in those Soviet moving pictures on the prison wall in Sighet—as cities of fantastic possibility, as an end to the drudgery of daily existence. Despite Helsinki, that enthusiasm for the great cities still trickled in his veins. He could drive on to the edge of the known world—everything was ahead of him.

Behind was home. A dull, continual humiliation. Ignorance and pain.

****

On the outskirts again, just before the unfinished workers' blocks, he noticed a small shack on the side of the road. The one-room bar he'd seen before. A few carts were outside, some horses resting in the night, and when Emil pulled in he could clearly see BAR painted sloppily over the open door, where light spilled out.

It was barely a room. Short tree stumps had been arranged as unstable stools around three small tables, and, at one, four stout farmers drank from shot glasses and played cards. The bar itself was a plank in front of a fat woman holding a bottle of clear, basement-distilled brandy. Behind her, along a single shelf, were three more bottles of the same poison. The place stank of sour liquor. He bought a glass and settled at a table in the dim back corner.

He tried to focus. On the case, the Crowder case. But he kept coming up with that round peasant's face with three moles. Apple cheeks and propaganda mouth. He tried to evoke Lena Crowder's face instead, those intense, elegant features. The product of another world.

She—yes—*she* could hold his attention.

There was a point in his life where his relationship with women had changed. As a boy growing up in the Capital, or even loitering in the Canal District, he saw women who struck him in a certain way. These women were in abundance. They had details that thrilled him: a face, a walk or the way a dress hung from their shoulders. In the summers between the wars he looked forward to the promenade of girls along the Tisa. They walked as if showing off their glory to the heavens.

It was enough on those hot days to see them pleased with themselves. Sometimes they gave him a smile. Not flirtation—not completely. Just an understanding that, for an instant on a perfect day, they could have the intimacy of eyes. Of a smile.

The effect was always devastating.

When the war came, the summers meant, instead, the sweating

mothers of Ruscova. Women like his grandmother and her friend Irina Kula. Their smiles were obligatory: They meant nothing but the pleasure of seeing youth. Life, suddenly, had lost all sensuality.

The farmers shouted and he jumped, looking around as if waking. But then they were laughing—large mouths missing half their teeth—tossing cards on the table. He bought another shot from the barmaid—she gave it to him with a frown—and looked at the card players on the way back to his table.

In Ruscova the farmers were like that, men who worked like cattle and focused their pleasure into brief, intense games of luck. He sat down and closed his eyes.

Then the Jews came to Ruscova. They spoke Romanian or Hungarian, and French, and communicated as best they could. At first there was no need to hide them. Ruscova had not seen a single German since the beginning of the Occupation, so these immigrants wandered the village, taking work where they could get it, sometimes sleeping in the fields or renting a room from the locals. They were always planning far-fetched escapes to Paris. When the Germans took Paris, they wept and planned for London. For New York.

Then the Germans decided they could take Russia.

This brought convoys through the countryside. Fresh troops to replace veterans, bright-eyed Wehrmacht boys stopping in Ruscova for bread and pork on the way to Kiev, to Minsk, to Stalingrad. Sometimes German officers filled the dusty main square, smoking and joking, and the Jews had to be hidden. A few families latched their gates and shook their heads, but most, once they heard stories of the Bucharest meat factories, gave what space they had.

The convoys filled the center with heady fumes, and the closets and basements and cupboards of Ruscova were filled with Romanian Jewry. Even the Brod dacha kept its transients, and for a single week it held the tiny Caras family—a father and daughter. Each night they were there, the eighteen-year-old girl, Ester, sneaked into his bedroom.

She was one year older, but small and slight and mute. She had not spoken, her father said, since the day she saw her mother dragged by the hair down the main street in Iași. *It was terrible,* the father told them, then shook his head and said nothing more.

Ester never spoke as she slipped out of her nightshirt and drew back his sheets. During that week, she kissed him only once, on the shoulder, then clutched at him in desperation. She made grunting noises when they made love. She did not look into his face until she felt him coming, then she held his head in her hands and stared into him. Black eyes. Burgundy lips. A brown mole on her chin. Afterward, she held him close for a few seconds and, weeping, grabbed her nightshirt and ran out of the room.

Each night, the same stunning performance.

Their meals together were miserable affairs. Grandfather dominated the table, talking expansively about all his opinions on the Fascists and the Soviets, while Mr. Caras, not willing to risk his and his daughter's safety, agreed with everything meekly. Grandfather seemed utterly unaware, and Grandmother said nothing, but Emil felt the pressure of embarrassment as he listened to those endless, useless words, and tried to get Ester to look at him, so he could show with his eyes that he was different. But she did not look anywhere but at her plate, and when, after a week, they moved on, she did not give him anything more. No words, no wishes for the future. Nothing. Then they were gone. To London. Or New York.

It was different after that. First in Helsinki, where he had gone to escape the boredom of provincial life, then back in the Capital, he noticed the change. It surprised him at first, then it offended him. He could not look at women as he had before. It was no longer enough to see that a woman was beautiful; he wanted to know how she was when she was frightened, what her face looked like in the dark. He was desperate to know what had made each woman who she was. It was perverse—he was perverse—but he was drawn to stutterers, and to women with limps; there were many after the war. Women who were injured, brutalized by life. Filia, he learned very quickly, had the basic inability to be happy. Lena Crowder was a bitter drunk. And he wanted her that much more.

He heard the engine, but didn't look up until the soldiers stepped inside. He was going through the photographs of the two men in a nighttime street. He would not figure out anything tonight, not in this state—he knew this—but he examined them anyway: meeting, talking, shaking hands, separating. He thought of spies and secrets being traded. Propaganda mouths.

There was a noisiness about the soldiers, as though their clothes were made to announce them by rustling loudly along the thighs and arms. The farmers' abrupt silence accentuated this effect. The three soldiers surveyed the room from the doorway, sniffed the sour air, then wandered to the bar and asked for vodkas. The barmaid shook her head and showed them the brandy. One of them—a young Russian with pimples along his cheeks—sucked on her bottle, then spat the liquor out on the counter.

The barmaid wiped spray from her arms. Her face went white as she moved back into the corner.

A second Russian continually unholstered and reholstered his sidearm—a nervous movement—and stumbled to the wall to peer closely at a poster advertising a French apéritif. He said to the others, in Russian, "You want this? For the latrine."

He was fiercely drunk, and his friends—one still in the doorway, the other leaning back against the counter—peered around the room that was going in and out of focus. The farmers had put away their cards and stared nervously at their empty hands on the table, and into their laps.

"Hey, sweetheart," said one of the soldiers, and Emil had to squint to realize he was being addressed. "That your car outside?"

Emil answered in Russian: "It belongs to the state."

"And are you the state, Blondie?"

They were all looking at him. The soldiers, the farmers, the barmaid. Emil was not drunk enough to be suicidal. He said, "I'm a servant of the state."

The locals understood none of this exchange, and the soldiers knew it. The one by the advertisement said, "You think we should fuck the woman? Use your car. You can come along if you like." His pistol was in his hand, then it was on his hip.

He did not answer at first. The anger was spilling back into his blood. He'd seen them before, the Russian soldiers who loitered around train stations and bars. They waited for pretty women, or just women, then followed them down the street. Rape was common enough; they picked up venereal diseases and spread them like evangelists.

Emil said, "She's got the clap. Better leave her alone."

All three began laughing, and the short one at the bar turned to her. His language skills were surprisingly good. "Is it true you've got the clap?"

She didn't need to look at Emil to know he was nodding incrementally, trying to give her the answer. "It's very bad," she said, then started to cry.

"Come on," said the youngest, still standing in the doorway. "Let's get a bottle in town. Come *on*." He was the weak one; he pleaded.

The one with the pistol ripped down the French poster and rolled it carefully into a tube. He tapped it on Emil's shoulder and smiled. "Come along?" His expression lacked anything like anger or real human comprehension, just a boyish desire to share his enjoyment. "We're going to have a good time."

Emil shook his head no.

They sang on their way out, some Russian folk song with bawdy verses. They yelled and kicked gravel. Glass was smashed, horses whinnied nervously. They had problems starting their jeep, shouted curses, then roared off into the night.

The barmaid regained control of herself and wiped off the counter with a towel, then told them to excuse her. The farmers nodded sympathetically. Before stepping outside, she told Emil to take a bottle home if he wanted. Please.

He finished his shot and placed the glass on the counter. He didn't want a bottle, but knew it would mean a lot to her. The farmers gave him severe, respectful nods, and the barmaid almost ran into him on his way out. She looked pleased to see the bottle in his hand. She was wearing a different skirt. He realized she had wet herself.

He started the Mercedes, but the headlights would not come on. He got out under the gazes of the nervous workhorses. The lights had been smashed to pieces.

It was still dark that morning when he arrived home, having worked his way through the rest of his first bottle and the unlit back roads of the Capital. He had kept his eye out for the Russians, wondering without decision what he'd do if he saw them again, then stumbled drowsily up the dusty steps, where the supervisor still snored in her chair. Grandfather was in a robe and slippers in the kitchen. Emil wobbled over and sat across from him. He wanted to tell the pouting old man about the soldiers and his small act of courage, but the only thing that came out was, "I'm leaving the Militia. I've had enough."

Grandfather pressed his hands on his knees, standing slowly, and stepped over to Emil. Then slapped him once, sharply. The arthritic bulges struck like stones and left his cheek burning. "Don't tell me that."

So Emil rose, the chair scratching the floor, and left again. He edged around the supervisor and made it out the front door before the old man caught up with him. They sat together on the front steps, but did not talk for a while. Grandfather produced two cigarettes and lit them both. He handed one to Emil. The dark city was almost silent. They ashed on the cobblestones.

"Men are different," Grandfather said after a while. "They're made different. Your father, he was ... *unchanging.* Truly. Him and that god of his. But he could walk out onto the battlefield. He had that in him. He was loyal. Loyal to his country." He took three quick drags, trying to keep his cigarette lit; it glowed. "Not me. I was never loyal to my country. I stayed out of their so-called Great War. But I went to Moscow. I was in their war because I loved the workers. My loyalty was that I loved anything that wasn't a king. And when the Fascists arrived, I supported that fight, though I was too old to pick up a gun myself. You follow?"

Despite the heavy, sleepy end to his drunkenness that muted everything and kept his throbbing eyes from focusing clearly on a family of Gypsies passing on the other side of the street, he was following everything because he knew where it all was going. His grandfather had said nothing new in a decade.

"And there's you," Grandfather said wearily. "I don't think you're a coward, but maybe ... maybe I'm too old to want to think that. Not of my flesh and blood. You could have gone to the Front. Yes," he said, raising a hand against Emil's lazy attempt to debate. "You could have. They would've allowed it. Gone with your father. Maybe even saved him from that bullet. But you decided to leave, go on a trip. To where you weren't needed. To make money you wasted on some *girl.* I never understood why." He shrugged as though the effort of understanding had exhausted him. "When you leave your family—*if* you leave your family—it should be for a reason. I don't know yours." His cigarette had gone out, and he flicked it into the street. "Why did you go?"

A boy detached himself from the family and snatched the cigarette butt.

"Get away, rat," snapped Grandfather.

The Gypsy boy scurried back to his parents, sucking on it, and Emil watched them turn the next corner. He wondered if it was age, if the old bastard was too far along to remember what it was like to be a teenager, to want to have nothing to do with war, with these vast movements of people, to want only to find your own way, even if that meant cutting a path through the Arctic waters and risking your neck over dead seals and violent Bulgarians. Maybe Emil had been a coward, maybe that was why he had decided it was impossible to join his father's military unit or his mother's medical regiment. But his grandparents had not been around that day in Ruscova when he saw how crowds can turn inhuman, or later, the other mob here in the Capital that led the woman to her death. And was there no room in the old man's heart for insolence and confusion and the simple fear of death?

"When you told us," Grandfather said, his wavering voice still even-tempered, "that you were joining the Militia—well, I can tell you we were very proud. And I thought, This is the day he finally becomes a man. No more fear." He turned his heavy eyes on Emil, his lids half-drawn. "Now here you are, only—how many? *Four* days! And now, here you are, quitting." He shook his head. "It makes me sick."

Emil opened his mouth, half stunned, half preparing to defend himself. But all the words drained from him, and he was left with only the impotent fussings of a child. *You don't understand. Leave me alone. I don't need to listen to this.* A frightened child with nothing show for all the miles he has traveled.

CHAPTER TEN

****

Leonek Terzian was not at his desk when Emil sauntered in, though his jacket was draped over the chair and his worn leather bag lay on the floor. Emil waited at his own desk. Despite the aching muscles and joints, the burning forehead and throat, and the fact that he'd gotten no sleep, he wanted to get moving. He wanted to see Lena Crowder again. He wanted to hear what she had to say when she wasn't a drunk, grief-stricken widow.

He went through his sparse case notes, trying to assemble facts. Two bodies. Money. Ten photographs. A German. A Walther PPK.

The speculations . . . he had them, but this wasn't the morning his sleepy head would put them together.

A half-hour later, Terzian still hadn't appeared. The others had been doing an admirable job ignoring Emil, even Brano Sev, who was back in his files, making occasional phone calls and glancing everywhere but at him. Emil said to the room, "Where's Inspector Terzian gone?" The only reply was a squealing pig and the smell of sawdust from outside.

He went through the notes again, slowly.

The money in Janos Crowder's cardboard box, found in Aleks Tudor's apartment. Fifteen thousand . . . payment . . . for *what*?

A possibility floated to the surface.

It helped that he was feeling terrible. He could concentrate on the pain that rippled up and down his body with each step toward

Brano Sev's desk. He stopped beside it, a shoulder against the wall, then squatted so his face was just above its edge. Sev looked up blankly.

"Comrade Inspector," said Emil. "I was wondering." A sharp pain trembled behind his eye, then went away. "Do you have a file on Janos Crowder?"

Sev looked down at the open side drawer. "Your dead man?" His voice squawked. "*That* Janos Crowder?"

Emil nodded. "I'd like to rule something out."

"His loyalty?" The question was snapped back. No hesitation.

Emil opened his mouth to say yes, his loyalty and patriotism were in question, but couldn't spit out those kinds of words. "Do you have a file on him?"

Brano Sev closed the files on his desk, one at a time, and leaned close. He had a mouth of half-digested garlic that fumigated the air between them. "These files are for suspected traitors."

"You've told me. Thus my question."

The flat face puffed as he chewed the insides of his cheeks. He leaned back and spoke firmly. "A public figure such as Comrade Crowder is by necessity examined very closely. We have no evidence of his involvement in traitorous activities. Do you?"

Emil stood up, his knees cracking. He had at least ruled out the Queen of England from his list of suspects. "Thank you, Comrade Inspector." He paused. "Do you happen to know where Terzian is?"

The small eyes blinked up at him. "Try the interview room."

It felt like weeks had passed since he had wandered these corridors looking for a typewriter. The room he wanted was beside the toilet, its scratched wooden door the only one without a glass panel. He leaned his head against the stenciled INTERVIEW and listened. Voices—two men, words unclear—then laughter that dissipated when he knocked. The handle wouldn't budge. The sound of his knuckle striking wood provoked the beginnings of a full-fledged hangover. The lock was fooled with, and the door opened a fraction. Leonek Terzian's dark features appeared: "What is it, Brod?"

He could see nothing past his face except hazy walls covered by more scratches. He hadn't thought through his words. "What are you doing? On the case. Let's compare notes." Emil took out his notepad to make his intentions clear.

"Not now," said Terzian. "Later. Maybe."

"Who are you interviewing?"

"It's nothing."

"It's something."

Terzian sighed heavily and opened the door enough to slip out into the busy corridor. His voice was a high whisper: "*Never* interrupt me when I'm interviewing. Understand?"

"Who is it?"

"No one. An informer." Terzian's hard, weathered face would not give Emil anything but eyes, nose and mouth.

"For our case?"

"*Your* case, Brod."

"Well?"

Terzian nodded at a pair of Militia in dress uniform. They muttered a familiar greeting back at him. Once they were gone, he said, "A witness. He may have come across Aleksander Tudor's killer."

"Let me talk to him."

Terzian's features became harder, the bags under his eyes deeper. Anger was easy to read. "You don't talk to him, Brod. And the fact that I hate you has nothing to do with it. He's a regular. He's my boy. No one else ever talks to him."

"It's my case."

"*It's my case,*" Terzian whined back. "You're a fucking infant, Brod." He said, "This is the way."

Emil remembered the last time he had heard that phrase, on an icy boat in the Arctic, a drunk Bulgarian accent making a mess of the words. He felt the chill of that hard deck, and when he returned, the door to the interview room was closing again. He heard the lock drawn into place, and felt the hangover come upon him like an animal: fully, hungrily.

He drove first to Liberation Street to find out if Tomislaw recognized anyone in the photographs. But the family, the new building supervisor—a severe, forty-year-old spinster—told him, had left for their summer holiday. So he went where he truly wanted to go: westward. Past the one-room bar—in the morning light, it was more dilapidated than it had looked last evening—and past the low, muddy riverbanks to where the driveways led back over small hills. The morning lit Lena Crowder's home particularly, and the windows glowed like those in the Canal District, reflecting sharply into his aching skull.

Irma made him wait in the entryway, where he cradled his head in his hands and gazed up at the painted men with thick white Tolstoian beards, echoes of some family fortune that predated everything he knew. Grandfather had, with the blush of joy, described invading abandoned mansions with the Russian hordes, turning over expensive vases and crapping on portraits. Emil picked up a long, blue vase covered in angular, gold etchings. Grandfather said that these people held an ax over the heads of the working classes. Equality was a blade away. The vase was heavy in his hands.

"Don't break it," Lena Crowder commanded. She stood in the doorway with her hands joined in front of her white nightgown. Its draped form accentuated rather than hid the easy lines of her body. She seemed never to dress. "My dead father's in there."

Emil put the vase back, using both hands to keep it stable.

She placed a cigarette in her mouth and waited for him to stumble over and light it. She sniffed at his face, her small nose wrinkling. "The Comrade Inspector's been drinking this early?"

"Last night," he admitted.

Her eyes roamed his face, hair, shoulders, his hand that held the lighter. "Too bad," she said. "I admire early drinkers. It's a rare honesty." She smiled suddenly. "But last night? That makes you unclean. You want a bath?"

"No," he said, hesitated, then repeated: "No." He wasn't quite convincing himself. "I just have some more questions."

She turned up her cigarette hand—a kind of shrug—then led him back into the lounge. Long sofa against tissue-thin curtains. The chair where he had watched her slide to the floor in a widow's intoxication. Now she was tall and lithe, and the billowing hem of her gown made her seem to float as she swooped to the sofa and settled down. She was a different woman, almost, but no less impure.

"How are you?" he began.

She stopped in mid-drag to frown at him. "This is part of the investigation?"

"Could be."

She completed the drag. "Then I'm fine, my dear Comrade Inspector." She placed the ashtray on her bony knee, where it wobbled. "Today I've been thinking of my poor father and his weak heart. Do you realize that in the space of a month I've lost both my father and my husband?"

She had a look of surprise on her face, as if only now, while saying it, she had learned the news. "I," he said, "I didn't know."

She wiped a thumb beneath her eyelid and sat up. "You don't want to listen to a rich girl's blubbering. No," she said, "you want to know about my husband. You want to know, for example, that Janos and I were not very close in the end. You want to know that he used his little apartment in town for his girls, and I did what I pleased out here. A marriage in name, but more of a business proposition."

Emil's notepad was on his own knee, but he couldn't bring himself to open it. "I don't understand. You were with Janos for money?"

"Me?" she said in disbelief. "Did you see those men in the hall? With all the hair? My great- and granduncles. Industrialists living off the wage slaves. *Coal.* All the time. Coal and coal," she said, echoing *War and war* in Emil's head. "That songwriting ponce came from a long line of mud-eaters. Peasants, all. Everything he has he got from me."

"Had," corrected Emil involuntarily, and she looked at him as though she didn't understand. Then she did, and the look became unkind. Emil said, "This apartment in town. With your money?"

"Why should I pay for his lifestyle when he treats me like a prole? No offense to our comrade workers," she added, flashing a nervous smile. "When we married, I gave Janos a modest allowance. When it became clear I wouldn't give him more, or less, he had no reason to speak to me anymore." She looked around. "It's a big house; you can miss each other if you try." She was smiling at him again, but with Lena Crowder, he didn't know what a smile really meant. "Seven months ago the bastard moved out. Are you thirsty?"

His mouth was a ball of cotton.

Irma brought big iced scotches, and Lena made sure he drank his. "Don't go around smelling like a drunk unless you actually are."

"But your husband," said Emil, setting his half-empty glass aside. "How did he get money? If he wasn't assigned his apartment, he had to pay for it. It wasn't cheap."

"Maybe he was writing songs. That *was* his business."

Even Emil knew melodies never earned boxes of cash. "What about these women you mentioned?"

"His whores?"

"Were they really that?"

This smile seemed to be a weary apathy. "I've no idea. I never saw one, he never talked about them, but I'm still enough of a woman to see through a man."

He finally opened his notepad and leaned back.

"Your drink," she said, and pulled her feet up beneath herself again. Her toes were as white and the nails as polished as before.

His ice was melting. "You said before that you last saw him a week ago. What happened?"

She moved her tongue quickly inside her mouth. "He had come back a week before then, two weeks before . . . *it*. He tried to patch things up. He'd heard my father had died. Wanted to *console* me." She gave a small, tight smile.

"Your father?"

"My father. Elias Hanic. Heart attack, I don't know. While riding a horse." She nodded, muttering, "The last Hanic." Then: "I still need to take his urn out of here. To Stryy."

Emil waited while she mulled over that trip with her father's ashes. Then he prodded: "Janos came back."

She woke up. "Yes. Janos got word of my father, and he came like a prince. What should I have done? I was still angry about the women, and how he treated me—like some money tree—*everything*. I kicked him out. But he came back the next day, apologetic. And he came back the next. This is the dumb persistence that makes the weak inherit the Earth." She took another swill, and even in this dim room Emil could see the wet glaze over her eyes. "He had the key, he'd always had it. He could come and go as he pleased. On the fifth day I gave in. Women get stupid for the men they've married, it's a fact. I think one of our Comrade Soviet scientists proved it."

When she smiled at him his scalp tingled pleasantly.

She gazed into her glass and drank the last of it. "Irma!" She looked at him. "But something was clear to me after, I don't know, the second day we were back together. According to the inheritance laws, everything of my father's was supposed to go to the state. But Elias Hanic was no imbecile. He had found a way to give most everything to me. The house, the land, the money from the old coal shares." A grim smile. "This is what Janos had learned, the little mud-eater. That's why he came back. That much money was so good that even staying with *me* was worth it."

Emil was genuinely surprised—not by Janos Crowder's behavior, but by the Hanic estate. "You can *do* that? Pass your money on?"

She leaned forward and put a cool hand on his hand, the one that held the notepad on his knee. "Dear, with money you can do *anything.*"

"And you," he began, hesitation stalling him. "You kicked him out?"

"Like a White Guard," she said, leaning back and flicking her fingers in a swatting motion. "Right out of my heart."

Irma arrived with two more drinks. He finished his first quickly—it chilled his teeth and made a cavity ache—and handed the empty glass back. Irma was silent and efficient and soon gone. Emil reached into his inside pocket. First, his fingers touched the garter, then moved on to the photographs. She looked interested as he handed them over.

"Do you know these men?"

"Sit over here." She touched the sofa with her thin hand. "We'll see."

He brought his drink with him and sat so he could look over her shoulder at the pictures, but it was awkward. His arm was in the way. So he stretched it over the back of the sofa, behind her head. She didn't notice, or pretended not to. She went through the ten shots, the simple story of the meeting. He was surprised that she didn't smell of liquor. She smelled fresh.

"I want to apologize," he said under his breath.

"For what?" She was also whispering. Their proximity demanded it. Her eyes were very big, their brown speckled details clear.

"Your father, first of all. I didn't know about him."

"We don't mourn the rich," she said, and he couldn't find the sarcasm that should have been in her voice. "Second of all?"

"The phone call. I told our people not to call you; I'd wanted to deliver the news in person. They're a bunch of fools."

"But you're not, are you?"

She had said this softly, her eyes very serious, and he couldn't answer.

"It's all right," she shrugged, and he finally caught a whiff of the morning's scotch. "Though they were surprisingly rude about it."

"Rude?"

"Abrupt. The man said, *This is the Militia. Your husband's been killed; we'll be there soon.* That was it. I thought it was a joke. This is the level of humor in the country now. But then I was sure someone was watching me. You know the feeling. Eyes in the windows. It was frightening. It made me think of my uncles—my father's brothers. They were shot in Vienna in 'forty-two. Executed in the street. They were rich too, all the brothers were. But that didn't save them." She frowned and shook her head. "At first I was scared, but by the time you arrived I was just angry." A pause. "I'm sorry about that."

He was filled with a sudden, hard hatred for the entirety of the police division, the People's Militia, the state.

"You're all right?"

"What about the pictures?"

She pointed at the taller of the two men. "I don't know him, but this one, the shorter one," she said, shifting her manicured finger. "He's a friend of Janos. *Was.*" She brought the finger to her lower lip, tapping. "Well, I don't know about *friend.* Acquaintance. They met when we went to his house for a dinner party. Hateful stuff," she said. "Those people are all bravado and ass-kissing. They both spoke Hungarian, I remember, Janos and him, so they got along. A *politicos*, that's what he was. An untouchable in a society built on equality. *Nice.*" She smiled, and her finger—he was watching it closely—came away from her lips damp. "What's his name? Jerzy. Yes. Jerzy Michalec. Lives not too far away, a few miles farther west. Did you know he was Smerdyakov?"

He thought he hadn't heard her right. "Smerdyakov? The war hero?"

"I'd never met a hero in my life," she said. "Janos told me. Michalec doesn't advertise it. A politicos likes to be quiet, not raise too many heads on his way to the top. He'll only use his nom de guerre when he needs it."

He opened his mouth, not knowing what to say. The man was almost a figment of his imagination by now. He hardly believed he existed. Now he was celluloid in a dead man's apartment.

She was looking at him, and when she spoke all levity had disappeared. "I wasn't just thinking about my father today, Inspector. I was thinking about you."

He started to say *Me?* but didn't.

"I've lost two men, and I've never been without one. And when I look around at all the men I know, there's only one I can see clearly. It's funny, I don't understand it. There's only one man I want to trust." Their foreheads almost touched, and her face emanated warmth. "Are you sure," she whispered, "you don't want a bath?"

He did. He wanted that bath more than anything in his life. A bath and a thick, fresh towel on the upper floors of this magnificent house. He wanted her most of all. He didn't know what to make of Lena Crowder, if he should be ashamed of his desire for this widow or this unexpected desire for him. No—he knew. He should feel shame and self-hatred—she was weakened now by all her losses, and he was just an animal—but he only felt the pleasure of her coarse, broken life beside his.

"I'd like to," he began, then pursed his lips and shook his head, trying still to convince himself. "Another time."

"Maybe there won't be another time." She smiled and touched his cheek with her cool fingertips.

CHAPTER ELEVEN

****

He was feeling unofficial, unkept. He didn't want to fill out paperwork that would be tossed aside by that lumbering fool of a chief, and he didn't want to put up with the station's leers at his intoxication, or Terzian's indifference. Instead, he drove across the Georgian Bridge and parked in the small gravel lot at the edge of the Canal District. He pulled the brake and rolled down the window. There were two other cars—eastern models coated with the dust of the provinces—and a farmer tying feedbags to five horses and talking loudly to them. He noticed Emil, tied the last bag, and wandered over an arched, stone bridge into the labyrinth.

Emil brought his hand to his face and rubbed, thinking of Lena Crowder's lighter-than-air gowns and Jerzy Michalec: Smerdyakov: the Butcher. Grandfather's vision of the perfect grandson.

It was hot. Gravel crunched beneath his shoes.

The buildings ahead were piled upon one another, centuries covering swamp gasses and filth. Not even fire trucks could attack the tiny, winding footpaths of this city in miniature, and when fires sprang up, sparks shot across the narrow canals and slowly ate the Canal District. It was only a matter of time before heat and decay wiped out all of it.

He crossed the arched bridge and glanced up at high, curtained windows and mossy stone walls. He emerged onto small squares where children shared cigarettes and threw yellow wooden balls against the buildings, the *thump* echoing down the footpaths. Some squares were wide, dominated by flat-faced, cracked churches where old women in black congregated and chatted among themselves. He smelled piss. This was the unsocialized part of the Capital, where each corner hid some illicit entrepreneur or a moment of spiritual reverie. He saw a grandmother on her knees, praying to a hole in a stucco wall that held a rough, childlike portrait of the Virgin.

He could still hear the *thump*, streets back, of wooden balls, and the lapping of water on stone. The wet air was very cool in the shadows. The narrow walkways could not accommodate anything except a noontime sun, and it was still only morning. It was what he imagined Venice to be like, as the Croat had described it before he tumbled overboard, drunk, to his Arctic death. He had been a refugee from Split and, after crossing the Adriatic, had hidden in a friend of a friend's wet Venetian palazzo. He called the city a stone angel and described in awed, exaggerated detail the porticoes and canals and piazzas and arched footbridges. He held his hands close together to show the narrowness of the passageways. Everyone in that small, cramped cabin nodded.

The Bulgarian had already stormed out; he didn't believe a word. The Croat, he said, loved to be the center of attention and would make up anything. *Who could walk through a passage like that?* It was true, but no one else cared.

Arched bridges? Emil had asked, thinking of this place in his own country.

They were all sweating from the heat of the boiler room next door, and there were too many of them, sprawled on the floor and the table, the wind hissing over the deck above them.

The Croat described the walk from his friend's palazzo to a canal that was overlooked, high up, by a covered bridge that connected two stone walls. *The doomed,* he told them. *They crossed here on the way to the prisons. They call it the Bridge of Sighs.* The Arab asked why. *Because the prisoner had been convicted, and this was where he saw that, at the end of that short walk across the bridge, his life would be lived behind a stone wall. Behind iron bars. He would live and die in the dark.*

A bleak silence fell over the cabin. No one spoke. Each man remembered his own bridge, but Emil, still so young, only knew he was missing the power of the moment, and said nothing.

At one corner a thin man offered black-market socks—"Good price, good price." Emil took a swig of the barmaid's rotgut brandy, adding to Lena Crowder's morning cocktail, and shook his head. He thought of Smerdyakov, the happy butcher, piling up dead Germans for his own private gallery in a bombed-out Berlin. Was that really the kind of boy Grandfather wanted?

But a butcher, remembered Emil, was just what he was.

Cold water dripped on his ear. Above, a mother hung lines of heavy laundry between the buildings. The ground was covered by black spots. He crossed another bridge.

Jerzy Michalec, a politicos. But he was also known as Smerdyakov, the Butcher. Grandfather called it courage, but Emil wasn't sure that courage was the right word for butchery.

There were two benches in the square, one with only a single, uneven plank, the second with all three. Emil settled on the good one and propped the bottle on his thigh. Ahead, where the walls opened onto a larger canal, a group of pensioners lounged on the bridge, eating pumpkin seeds and pointing at trash floating in the water, just like children.

There had been an editorial in *The Spark* last month calling for the demolition of the Canal District. The writer claimed—and not without evidence—that it was a breeding ground for crime and disease, and any attempt to repair its crumbling infrastructure of water pipes and collapsing walls would bankrupt the nation. It would be the symbolic extension of the Liberation:

Wipe away the wormy, decayed past, and build up the future. The writer predicted high block apartments checkered atop the wet, fractured foundations, the swamp drained and its water managed into small brooks running water wheels to light the city. He had been to Moscow, he said, and had seen what great heights unity and resolve could achieve. Later, the rumors swept through the Capital more quickly than *The Spark*: The Comrade Chairman himself wanted to funnel funds into the city's coffers to put the idea into action. Under the condition, the rumor added, that it be called New Stalingrad.

The pensioners had moved on and been replaced by three prostitutes. Two heavy matriarchs and a young, pretty girl. All three looked at him, then began talking among themselves.

It was true, the Canal District was a cesspool. Here Emil had come when he was a boy, with friends, sneaking into the dark passages where they could disappear. It was here he had first sowed his dreams of leaving the country. They were planted here, and had bloomed through the Soviet window of moving pictures in the provinces. The Canal District had that effect on him, on most people, and if anything was to blame for him boarding that train headed toward the icy north, it was this swamp-born city within the city.

He took another long, burning swig.

In the Arctic, the Bulgarian refused to lose at cards.

He swallowed.

They were stuffed in the hull of the boat—ten men in a cabin built for three, choked with smoke and sweat—and when Emil showed his winning kalookie hand to the limp-cheeked Bulgarian, the shouts almost shattered the walls. The big man pushed the money over with a look of hatred.

Smerdyakov was a war hero. Grandfather called him the greatest ever, a testament to the nation. Emil had never known war. Not the war of armies and soldiering.

The Bulgarian followed him afterward, pestering with his

blunt, hard hands, grabbing him by his shoulders and shaking. He followed Emil across the icy deck, using Bulgarian curses no one could understand, and swung fists. Emil left with bruises and a bloody nose. The next night was no better, nor the next, and finally Emil just bolted when he saw the Bulgarian approach. In his cot each night he fingered the curved work blade he held beneath the blankets.

The pretty whore balanced on the single board spanning the bad bench. It wobbled beneath her, and she smiled at him, amused. He nodded an invitation toward the corner of his own bench. He knew what he was doing; any man who had grown up in the Capital knew. But all he wanted now was her physical presence, her proximity. When she settled down, the violet folds of her skirt collected behind the bend of her knee. Her lipstick and rouge were bright and fresh. But in his head he saw the Bulgarian with the baggy cheeks who attacked him that fourth night on the cold deck.

"You're very handsome," she said quietly, near his cheek, her breath warm.

The other hookers, the veterans with rough cheeks and black eyes, watched from the water's edge. One stood with her hands on the small of her back, as if stretching after washing clothes.

The Bulgarian had stood like that when he caught sight of Emil. Then he leapt.

"You'd like to go somewhere, love? I know an alley."

She was very young, he now saw, her soft red lips muddied around the edges, her eyes very big. Her accent was definitely out-of-town, and from the way she crossed her legs and moved with a stuttering motion closer to him, he could tell this was new to her. She was maybe thirteen. There was a fine coating of freckles the white powder on her cheeks did not cover.

Eat this, the Bulgarian had said, using their shared Russian, throwing a drunken fist at Emil's teeth. A mouthful of Bulgarian knuckles.

"Where are you from?" he asked the girl.

"From here." She spoke as though she hadn't heard the question. "The alley's very close. It's very cheap." Then, as an afterthought: "Because I like you."

Cheater, the sagging cheeks had said. His knees held down Emil's arms, and he bounced on Emil's belly. The deck was cold and ice-dry against the back of his head. The fear turned his blood to sand.

"What's your name?" he asked her.

"Livia," she lied.

He touched her fine, child's hair. "Do you like this? Your work." He didn't know what he was saying.

"I like to make money." She smiled. He caught sight of her teeth, rounded and small, a few missing. Milk teeth. The teeth of a five-year-old in a teenager. "And this way—who doesn't like it? It's what people like."

This is the way, the Bulgarian had said when he pulled a fat, purple cock out of his pants. Emil's pinned hand had found the curved blade in his pocket.

The older hookers were leaning from foot to foot, impatient, watching every move he made. He should have called one of them over; there would have been no worries, no nagging conscience, nor that claustrophobic sense that all eyes were on him.

The thick pants slowed it, but the blade broke through. It glided into the Bulgarian's thigh, struck a vein, and when he removed it, the warm, black fountain began to flow. He pushed the blade in again. The Bulgarian said *Uhh* and fell back, holding himself.

The girl smelled of rosewater; she had been prepared. This must be her first time.

Jerzy Michalec, Smerdyakov. A hero. And Emil Brod, a murderer leaning over a child.

He had squeezed out from under the baying Bulgarian, then

went about it with the efficiency of his craft. His seal's blade found quick ways to silence the squeals, his movements by now instinct—a seal-butcher's instincts. And only when the job was done and he leaned on the railing, gasping, his blind fever passing, did he think to push the carcass over the edge onto the ice below. He watched it drop silently beneath the wind, and felt as if he were standing on a bridge, watching everything end.

He sighed and, with closed eyes, leaned toward the girl, breathing in her fresh scent. She turned to accept a kiss, but he whispered, "I'm a policeman."

He heard her feet move, the boards shifting as she rose. The quick jogging across cobblestones. Voices. When he opened his eyes finally, the square was empty and silent, save the sound of dirty water lapping on stone walls.

CHAPTER TWELVE

****

Jerzy Michalec's address was even further out of town than Lena Crowder's. When Emil turned down the long, poplar-lined drive, he couldn't see the house. Then, from behind a grassy rise, there was a bearded peasant swinging a scythe a few inches above the earth. Then the house. It spread wide and high, a long porch wrapping around half of it. Another swig of brandy steadied him and held his headache at bay. It was one.

The young man with a wide green tie who opened the door was the second butler Emil had met in his life. The first had been at the home of the Academy director, who invited all the graduating cadets to a celebration of their entrance into the world. That butler had been reserved yet always smiling; this one was reserved and disdainful. He made no effort to conceal his instant distaste for Emil's stench as he gazed down on him—a trick, since he was shorter than Emil.

"Comrade Michalec," said Emil, tense. "Tell him a homicide inspector from the People's Militia is here to see him."

"He's expecting you?"

"No."

The butler shut the door in his face.

The peasant in the distance had stopped, leaning on his scythe to stare back. The blade glistened. Beyond him were stalks of wheat. In Ruscova they worked in groups of five and ten, cutting swaths over the low hills, down to the winding creeks, and dozed after lunch in the shade of a haystack, waiting for the sun to become merciful. He'd done some of it himself—hateful, hot work he'd never gotten used to. A cool breeze ruffled the stalks around the peasant, who now sharpened his blade with a stone. The scraping sound came faintly on the wind. Emil was very thirsty. He banged the door with a fist. It was jerked open.

"Comrade Michalec is attending to other matters," said the butler, a stiff, anxious grin on his face. "You may return later."

"I'll wait inside." Emil inserted his foot in the closing door, then leaned into it.

The marble entryway was cool and dark, and ahead rose a wide, spiraling staircase. He had seen this before, or something like it, in a picture show. A melodrama on the aristocracy. "Tell Comrade Michalec I've come on urgent state business. I'll wait for him here."

The butler was visibly angry, but controlled himself. Emil found it vaguely disappointing. He wanted a reason to put his fist in the man's face. Anything. But the butler only unfolded an arm in the direction of a chair beside a rack of coats and umbrellas. Then he disappeared up the staircase with a soft *pat pat* of feet.

It was like Lena Crowder's house in its absolute distance from anything Emil could ever imagine calling home, but even he could see that its scale was far more grandiose. There were no family portraits crowding the walls, no framed Orders of Lenin, nothing personal at all. The scarlet drapes covering the high windows looked foreign—Oriental—and new. The chair beneath him was modern, angular. Uncomfortable. Not made for human forms.

He shouldn't have come here, not in this mood. All mood, no facts. He had no idea why a politicos—a war hero, no less—was in the photographs of a dead man, or why those photos were hidden behind an icebox. Whoever tore apart the dead men's apartments—were they looking for these pictures? For the money? Jerzy Michalec, at least, had no need for money.

He paced, soles clicking on marble, his nerves slowly unraveling. Through the front window, the peasant swung his scythe again—slowly, ploddingly. You could put a peasant on a machine and know that, barring mechanical failure, that machine would go on for eternity. For nothing.

In place of family heirlooms was a sculpture centered along the wall, on a white pedestal. It was a long, vertical sliver of metal, curved slightly, thicker in the middle, pointed at the top and bottom. Perfectly smooth. He'd never seen anything like it in his life. And in the mist of the morning's drinks, he hated it.

Pat pat.

The butler trotted down the staircase with a worried eye measuring the distance between Emil and the sculpture. "I'm sorry, Comrade Inspector," he said, raising his voice dryly. "Comrade Michalec cannot make exceptions when he's working on his own state business. I'm sure you understand."

Emil smelled the tonic lotion in the butler's hair as he pushed past and started up the staircase.

"Did you hear what I said?" called the butler, close behind. "The Comrade is exceedingly busy; he'll get in touch when he's able. Inspector!"

Emil was running now, skipping steps, reaching the second floor, where the long red rug slid and buckled beneath his feet, past closed doors toward the sound of a man's voice ahead. On the dark oak walls paintings appeared, but they were nothing like people. They were splashes of color, unidentifiable shapes. Unformed. Disturbing.

"Inspector! Inspector!"

The heavy door at the end of the hallway was half-open, spilling light, and he struck it with his palm. An office, vast walls covered with book spines. He stopped to catch his breath. A marble-topped desk in the center, where the shorter man from the photograph talked loudly into a black telephone.

"Yes, of course, yes," he was saying, not looking at Emil. His face was pitted by old acne scars, their shadows lengthening as he nodded, smiling into the telephone. He even ignored the butler's whispered protests about the inspector he could not control. Jerzy Michalec waved his butler into silence with the back of his hand.

He looked nothing like a war hero. Certainly not a Smerdyakov. He was fatter than the pictures suggested, and his dark suit hung on him poorly, wrinkled at the joints. He rested his neutral gaze on Emil and said into the receiver, "Of course, we'll do that then. Give her my best. Until later." He hung up and gave Emil a cool smile. "So you're the impatient inspector?" He had a voice of so many accents that it was untraceable.

"I tried—"

"Radu. Tell the trade commissar I'll be with him in a moment."

Radu bowed and withdrew.

Michalec's eyes were a cool blue, surrounded by wrinkled, blackened sockets. He sniffed. "I assume you don't need anything more to drink." He reached into a pocket and removed a small red booklet emblazoned with a gold, five-pointed star inside a ring of golden laurel. Above it was a hawk at rest, its head in profile. "Comrade Inspector, do you know what this is?"

Emil stepped from one corner of the desk to the other, ready to snap, but he spoke clearly: "Proof of membership in the Party."

"Yes, and no." Michalec settled into his chair. His gravelly voice had a way of communicating in each syllable his disregard for Emil. He held the booklet out for him to read. "What does it say beneath the star?"

Black block print: POLITICAL SECTION.

"I'd heard," said Emil.

"Maybe you're unfamiliar with the terminology. Many people are unclear. Times change quickly, and you have to pay attention to everything in order to survive. Believe me." Michalec leaned back in his chair and tossed a foot on the edge of his neat desk, folding the red card into his shirt pocket. "It's not simply a word.

Politicos has meaning. We, as members of the Political Section, have very specific duties. And these duties confer upon us specific *rights*. You're following?"

He felt like he was back in the Academy. It was a hateful feeling.

"For example," said Michalec, "a politicos cannot be imposed upon in the normal course of his duties. Not even by members of the Security Section. Unless, of course, there's some specific piece of evidence making this necessary. Is there, Comrade Inspector?"

Emil tossed the ten photographs on the desk. They scattered. "Tell me who you're talking with."

"Maybe you're as deaf as you are stupid," said Michalec, only half-glancing at the images. "I knew a politicos once who walked into a Militia station, pulled out a pistol, and shot the station chief." He raised his arm and used his hand to shoot Emil, then dropped it and shrugged. "The chief had made him angry. Today that man is a member of the Central Committee inner circle, the Politburo." His smile became wider, more convincing. "I, Comrade Inspector, am very close to the Politburo myself."

"Look at the photographs."

The smile disappeared, and Michalec pressed his fingers to his cheeks. "I'm giving you good advice, Inspector." His voice had lowered an octave. "We don't make the rules. Others make the rules. We can only try to live by them."

Emil tapped the desk. "The photographs."

Michalec put up his other foot and crossed his ankles.

Emil picked up the photos, one at a time, his impotence burning inside him. He saw everything at once, like a mystic: the two dead men in the city morgue and the dead soldiers in Berlin, twenty-three in a pile; he saw the hatred and suspicion and ignorance, the wars and the marching little children singing their inane political lullabies; a Bulgarian on the ice. He put nine photos back into his pocket. Busted bodies, bodies kicked in the mud. The tenth photo remained in his left hand. Hookers and pension-

ers and soldiers and Jews—and Lena—all nothing to the fero-
cious gears of this world.

With his right hand, he snatched an ankle and threw it high, so
that Michalec spilled back with his chair. He rolled on the rug,
stunned and silent, then Emil was on his chest. He wanted fear. A
little terror. But there was only dull shock in Smerdyakov's eyes,
then contempt.

Emil slapped him hard, three times. Both cheeks were red, the
eyes wet.

"Again," said Emil, forcing the words through his teeth. He
held the photo to Michalec's face. "The name."

Michalec's blinking eyes focused on Emil's, then past them. He
trembled; his eyeballs shivered. Emil drew back. Michalec's head
jerked sideways; his eyes rolled back into his skull. White eyes rid-
dled with fat, red veins.

A sputtering groan came from Michalec's throat, and his
whole body seized up, shaking, blue cords rising from his neck.

A hand on Emil's shoulder tugged him back, and he saw a flash
of Radu's furious face, then a black stick coming down.

Pain snapping in his head and neck, trickling like cold water,
reverberating.

It did not put him out, but made him briefly senseless. Radu
was over his master, stuffing something into his mouth, holding
an arm over his chest.

Emil closed his sore eyes and saw bright lights.

When he opened them again, Michalec was wiping his forehead with a hand, eyes closed, and Radu was returning to Emil,
swinging the club. He threw up a hand, wanting the strength of
his anger back, but it was too late. The club hit the side of his
head, burning bright sparks in his skull.

Pulled to his feet. Heard *come on* as he was pushed forward,
stumbling. *Get out* came through the hazy noise in his head, and
he wanted to stop and turn around and throttle someone, but

couldn't make it happen. There was another thump on the back of his head halfway down the staircase, and it felt like something had cracked.

For a moment he was still awake—suddenly clear-headed and thinking—and then he wasn't.

He was lying in the hot front seat of the Mercedes. His skull felt shattered. Eyes open. Eyes closed. Open. He sat up. The low sun burned his brain. There was blood on his hands, on the passenger's seat, and in the mirror his tender mouth was crusted with blood. He could smell his own bile and sweat in the stuffy car. He was parked at the beginning of that long drive, by the main road. The light spiked his eyeballs. Poplar trees led up to the rise, and off to the right the bearded peasant swung his scythe in long, low arcs.

They were staring. His right eye was already puffing up, and he had patted down his hair in an unsuccessful attempt to cover the red scratches around his neck and ears. His head was about to explode. They all could see plainly what had happened, could read everything in his wounds, but he didn't care. He was as loathed here as he was in Smerdyakov's house. But it no longer mattered. Nor did his grandfather, not even Lena. For the moment, there was no one else in the world. The beating and the shame were nothing; he would be willing to suffer so much more if there were some sense to it all. But there was no sense. There was nothing here for him.

No hidden gazes now.

They watched him stop at his desk and sit down, swivel, and shake his head. It was difficult to ignore them. Pain rippled behind his eyes and throbbed across his skull. From the drawer he took the pen tips, ink and cigars, and found pockets to hold them. He moved his father's watch to his breast pocket. He left the stamps behind.

Leonek Terzian was standing in front of Emil's desk, fingertips spread on the surface. His face showed something approximating compassion—or was it a trick of the light? It was certainly the buzzing in his skull that added compassion to Terzian's voice: "Michalec called. Angry." He shook his head. "You attacked *Smerdyakov*?"

It wasn't compassion. It was amusement. Hilarious bruises. Funny, broken boy.

He tapped the chief's door, and before he could say *enter*, Emil was in, closing the door with his backside. The air seemed to compress in that hot, small room.

"There you are." Moska hung up the telephone.

Emil took out his Militia certificate. Not much different than Michalec's, only green instead of red, with the word MILITIA. He tossed it in front of the chief.

"What's this?"

"Resignation."

The word contained within its syllables so much relief that he almost dropped to the concrete floor and cried. But he wanted to make it out in one piece.

"Now wait, Brod."

But Emil was already back in the station house. There was nothing else to take with him, so he passed the inspectors—it was strange, even after only a week, to no longer call himself one. They looked surprised, even big Ferenc, hovering over his typewriter, but Emil didn't know why they should feel surprise. This moment had been preordained from the very start. Terzian was calling something to him. Asking him to wait. Emil had waited too long already.

He passed into the corridor that echoed his footsteps and Terzian's voice behind him—"Hold on, Brod, wait!" Emil stepped onto the bright concrete steps. He wondered if Terzian wanted a repeat of that first day.

By God, he'd give it to him. He was in just that sort of mood.

"Brod!"

A car at the corner laid on the horn to get some horses moving, and a band of Gypsies carried heavy sacks on the opposite side of the street. People shouted, but the buzzing was so loud that their shouts were like whispers. He was on the hot, cracked sidewalk, walking nowhere. Some uniforms looked up—more laughers, no doubt. What a funny town.

He wanted to take a bath at Lena Crowder's grand house, among those paintings. Long beards of history. He wanted Lena Crowder to use her white, intoxicated fingers on his back and his bruised eye. He would go see her. Yes. Get a ride. A taxi.

"Brod!" Terzian whispered back there.

Another car, blue, driving beside him—a small, sleek make he didn't know—honked. It was like a whisper too. The buzzing was a river in his head.

But when he longed for Lena Crowder he remembered her husband's crushed skull. It was all sickness and disease anyway, and he might as well search for a hooker with stubby workers' fingers and a low price. Young, old—it no longer mattered.

The blue car moved ahead a short distance and stopped. A tall man in a light-colored overcoat stepped out. Another familiar face, but from where? Over the noise of his skull he could hear the man's accented voice saying, "Comrade Emil Brod?"

The man had curved smile lines that connected his lips to his eyes. Emil stopped. "Yes?"

The smile lines deepened as the man pulled out a pistol with his white-gloved hand. There was an instant in which Emil's mind did the work very quickly and identified it as a Walther. Probably a PPK. Officer's gun, German—German, like his accent. But as soon as the identification was made, it fled his mind.

The man emptied three rounds into Emil, jumped back into the car, and swerved away.

CHAPTER THIRTEEN

****

It was a sharp connection: his head against concrete. His hands wobbled out to the sides, somewhere, his knuckles scratched. Tires burned against the road. Carbon monoxide and hot rubber. The sky fuzzed over and was visible again, and his thumping heart obscured all sounds. The buzzing was gone; only the back-beat of his blood remained. He could not even hear the yell shaped mouth of the dark, hungry face bent over him. The name came to him in a flash: Leonek. Leonek's mouth made long ovals as he yelled at the crowd forming around them. Wide-brimmed fedoras and women's shoes, vivid, red-painted nails emerging from white leather straps. Breathing was forced labor; there was soon nothing in him. He tried to raise his head to swallow the air, but something was sitting on his chest, maybe Leonek, or the Bulgarian, but he couldn't know. He couldn't see a thing except blue sky, then nothing. He was sinking in a warm, watery pain, an angry bathwater covering him in blackness.

A mountain range, high grass above the treeline, tired soldiers poking through the underbrush, looking. They evaporated to white and faded into an angry, violent crowd with large, flat rocks in their hands. They threw in silence. Then came the hard-edged ache behind his eyelids. He opened them to let it out, but light spilled in, cutting into his brain. His thoughts were porridge. The light would not form into shapes. The smell of human sweat and warm decay was inescapable. Voices hummed around him like flies, louder, and when he tried to swat them, fresh pain erupted and he gasped, gripped by it, his whole body seizing up, crying. He saw the calm, everyday expression on that face, but the details, the features, were unclear—*Comrade Emil Brod?*—then the pistol emerging slowly, more slowly than possible. He could almost make out the slow bullet in the air pocket that burned around it, hot waves rippling along the slug. Then the moment of impact, cracking through ribs, soft tissue, organs. The pain was terrible. Through it a woman's voice said *there was* and *Comrade Brod*. But he was already out again, warm rivulets filling mouth, nose, eyes.

The hospital room was high-ceilinged and airy, and when he shifted his head, sore neck creaking, he saw a plain-looking nurse in the corner, knitting. She looked up from her needles to his bloodshot eyes, and he thought that in the midday light she was beautiful.

"You're up?" She set the needles aside.

The pain returned when he tried to move. It scratched through his guts and chest. He opened his mouth, but all that came out was a whisper: *"Water."*

She shook her head. He said it again, trying to wet the inside of his mouth with a dry, heavy tongue. But she was firm. The doctor forbade it. "You have holes down there. We don't need you leaking all over the sheets." He saw the knitting in her hand. Something blue and small and soft, for a baby. "You've been out a week, you know?" She put the knitting in her pocket and felt his face for fever. "We almost thought," she began, then smiled and left the room.

The windows were covered by a translucent white drape so thin he could see the crowns of leafy trees and white-spotted sky. The walls hummed like a machine.

So he was alive.

It surprised him that he couldn't think it with more enthusiasm. All he could imagine were innumerable days ahead forming a long line to his eventual death. Days of working and fighting, or days of inertia. He didn't even have a job now. He wasn't even an inspector.

It was almost funny, but not enough to test his body with laughter. Only a week into his job, and someone had blown a hole in him. Three holes.

A young doctor with a buzzed head looked into his eyes while holding the lids open with his thumbs, then removed the bandages that covered his chest and stomach. Emil almost screamed. The doctor winced with him, as though he could feel his patient's misery. Then the bandages were off, and Emil—with an extra pillow behind his head—looked down on the white expanse of sickly flesh and sewn holes. It was as if he were looking down on a different body, one uncovered by the gleeful Uzbek coroner. Only the pain reminded him it was his own, each time the doctor touched the puckering, swollen seams stitched by black thread. There were three gashes: one along the edge of his right breast, another just below his left breast and heart, and the last in the center of his soft gut. The doctor affirmed that his survival was a miracle.

"A scientific miracle," the doctor specified. He looked at a watch while he held Emil's wrist. "Feeling up for visitors?"

He felt up for nothing. The doctor's hand was covered by a thin mask of black hair.

"Inspector?"

"Sure," Emil croaked. "Of course. Watch?"

"Pardon?"

Emil pointed at the doctor's wristwatch, then at himself. "My watch?"

The doctor settled his patient's hand back in the sheets and rummaged through the things on the bureau. Pushed past the photos, lifted the garter with a wink. Then he found the chain, and lowered the watch into Emil's hand. "We'll wait a few hours for water."

He felt the ticking in his palm. Steady and even.

"They've been calling every day."

"My grandparents?"

"Yes," the doctor nodded. "Them too."

Chief Moska came as sun was falling and the tree outside was just black silhouette. Holding a copy of *The Spark* in one big hand, he rapped on the doorframe with the other. Emil felt an urge to mutter *enter* in the chief's resolute way, but words were making his thirst a desperation. The chief had a lumpy expression of bafflement, and when he pulled a squeaky wooden chair beside the bed, he left his jacket on. He sweated the whole time.

"Brod. You're feeling well." It was almost a command.

"I'm awake."

"That's something," Moska agreed. "We made sure you got your own room, a ward didn't seem right." He looked at the sheets. "They say it's a remarkable recovery."

"Scientific miracle."

The big man's hat was in his hands, squeezed and released repeatedly. He settled back in the chair and blew through pursed lips. His eyes focused on the far wall, the bedside table, the framed amateur painting of the Georgian Bridge at twilight, then back to the sheets. Emil's hands lay there, beside the newspaper. The chief cocked his head to the side. "I wanted to talk to you. About the case," he said. "Your case."

Emil's voice lowered. "No case. For me."

"We agree there," the chief said quickly. "But we both know, don't we? Who did this to you."

He nodded.

Moska looked at the sheets, then his hat in his lap, the light fixture in the ceiling, and squinted. "You've been treated unfairly, Brod. We know this now. There were . . . *misunderstandings.*"

Emil waited.

The chief's squint tired. He blinked and wiped his cheek with a hand. "This is the nature of bureaucracies. *Large* bureaucracies. Lack of trust. Before the war it was different." His voice wavered slightly, as if he were about to cry. But he wasn't. "Before the war we didn't even need a homicide department, you remember? We were all just *police.* Then it grew. Everything grew. The Militia, the divisions, state security. I don't know anyone outside my little department anymore."

He seemed genuinely saddened by this, but Emil was still unable to understand. He almost asked for clarification, but the chief was on his feet again.

"It's insidious, this situation. Yet we have to make it work." His large, long features twisted as they forced out the words. "Apologies all around, Brod. It's what I've come to say. I'd prefer you didn't resign. The others too. They feel the same. We've all been shamed by this."

Emil opened his mouth to ask for something more, some detail he knew he was missing—some *why*—but the chief was already out the door.

The tree had gone indistinct against the night sky by the time his grandparents arrived. She patted her tear-stained cheeks with a musty handkerchief, and the old man stood in various corners of the room, as though ascertaining all possible avenues of escape. She opened a package of bread and hard cheese and told him to eat it slowly, because that was what the doctor had told her, that the hole in Emil's stomach would require slow eating. "Slow," she repeated, patting his head like a dog's.

"Water?" he whispered.

"Will they let you?"

"I've had nothing all day."

She frowned. "That can't be good." She set the cheese and bread on top of the newspaper. "Let me find out." She was gone.

Grandfather emerged from one of his corners and informed Emil again that he'd been unconscious for a week. "We thought," he began, but like the nurse he couldn't finish.

"I'm all right now."

The light made Grandfather's flesh pink and more healthy-looking than it really was. "You're a hero," he said earnestly, but Emil didn't answer. The silence between them was awkward, so after a while Grandfather cleared his throat. "This is a *great* pride. For you. Serving your country this way."

"Serving the great collective," said Emil, finally smiling. But Grandfather didn't smile. Emil felt the old man's loose fingers in his hand, squeezing, kneading his palm. The door opened. Grandmother stood, like an angel, holding a glass of cool water.

Clarity came with Leonek Terzian. Emil had slept off and on, and in the morning, after breakfast, he read the paper. There were trials beginning to unravel in the east, in Moscow, and airplanes still flying in the west. On the second page was brief coverage of Palestine; there was more fighting in the Holy Land. Only at home was everything ideal: record crops and the lowest crime rate in memory. Then Leonek arrived with the lunch. He slouched in the chair beside the bed to better reach Emil's tray. He took a bite of bread and dragged an index finger across the wide block of margarine, white wrinkles collecting over his print, and sucked it with his small, dark mouth. Emil ate mashed potatoes and waited.

Leonek swallowed. "Chief talked to you. Didn't he?"

Emil nodded.

Leonek seemed satisfied. He took another bite of bread. "He's right, you know. About everything. It's been a mistake, and I'm not the only one who's sorry. There are—do you mind?" He took a slice of red apple from Emil's tray. "You have to understand."

"Bureaucracy," offered Emil.

Leonek shook his head. "Rumors. *That's* the problem. We get them in the office every day." He pursed his lips in reflection, and Emil found his easy manner annoying. Maybe he hadn't noticed, but Emil had almost died. Leonek shrugged. "Sometimes the rumors catch, sometimes not. We heard a rumor once that Sergei, the man you replaced, was going to be killed. That rumor didn't catch. Then he was dead." Leonek finished the apple slice and shrugged, as though Sergei's story was commonplace. "Then, a month ago, a rumor did catch. From this guy, an informer I keep down in the Canal District. The one I was talking to when you came by that day, the interview room. A weasel named Dora."

"*Dora?*"

"A man with a woman's name," said Leonek, nodding. He took another wedge. "I met him years ago, some nasty business." He stopped, as if he had lost his thread, then began again: "Anyway, that's when he started informing. But three months ago, the district police picked him up for black-market pork. You know the stuff. Rotting right through, covered in flies. Real shit." He waved a hand. "So when they brought him in, he said he had information for Homicide—for me, since I'm the one he always deals with."

Emil shifted his arms painfully and brought water to his lips. He was still so parched.

"Dora told us that sometime soon—he didn't know when—a spy would be brought into Homicide." He paused. "Preparation for a shake-up."

Leonek watched closely, but Emil was not reacting yet. He was waiting. Leonek finally gave some more:

"Come on, you know how things are. Berlin. And Vienna and Italy, I hear. We'll be fighting the Americans soon—even the Big

Comrade in Moscow is uneasy. He's seeing enemies everywhere. It's like the thirties all over again."

"How would Dora know this?"

Leonek took Emil's water to rinse out his mouth. "He knows everything and everyone. He gets jobs out of town, in the mansions, or the bars here in the First District. He listens. We never ask where it comes from because he wouldn't tell us. Eighty percent of the time Dora tells us the truth."

Hearing it explained made it made it no less incomprehensible. "You thought I was a spy."

"Right out of the Academy. Why wouldn't we?"

In the Academy he had been taught that informing on a fellow officer who chose to disregard the tenets of Marxist justice in favor of opportunism was a duty. But he knew no one who believed that outside the classroom.

"And your Opa. Yes, we know about him. Old-time lefty. Privilege home in the Fifth District. You know what happened last year? Three policemen were put away for life. A snitch working right beside them."

"And Brano Sev? What's he?"

Leonek frowned suddenly. "Take a look—no one talks to him. He's nobody's friend."

He had finished the whole apple and was now picking at the potatoes. Emil doubted this oaf's regret went nearly as deep as his stomach. He'd known men like this in the Arctic, men with consciences the size of sunflower seeds. Little more than dogs. "What about the case?"

He took a moment to swallow. "What case? It's dead."

"Not for me, it isn't. Tell me what Dora told you."

Leonek's tongue cleared food from his palate. "Listen, Brod. Jerzy Michalec is a member of the Central Committee. He has friends *everywhere*. Why do you think you're lying in here? We know about limits in the People's Militia." He gave a final swallow. "Don't worry about your record. We'll erase the whole case."

The banality came over him: the erasure of two men's murders, as though Janos Crowder and Aleksander Tudor had never existed. "You can't do that."

"It's why they give us erasers."

"Tell me," said Emil. "Dora."

Leonek leveled his gaze. "Twenty percent."

"What?"

"What I told you," Leonek explained patiently: "Eighty percent of the time Dora tells the truth. Twenty percent . . ." He shrugged. "The story about you was made up. After you were shot I tracked him down. He didn't know anything about you, not even your name. All he knew was he needed to come up with a story to save his ass."

"What did he say about the case?"

"Nothing. He told me he'd heard a gunshot near the water, in the Canal District. On his way he tripped, made some noise— probably because he was scared—and then heard something being rolled into the water, then someone running away."

"That's something," said Emil.

"It's nothing," Leonek repeated. "Nothing, no identification, no clues beyond what we already know, and it's all for a case that doesn't exist. Got it?"

The nurse came for the tray and complimented Emil on his healthy appetite. Leonek followed her out with his eyes.

Emil knew he would go back—it was the only thing left to him—but right now he wanted nothing to do with the People's Militia.

CHAPTER FOURTEEN

****

The nurse's name was Katka, and she hovered over Emil through the daylight hours, provoking brief erotic fantasies to accompany his naps. The doctor finally appeared again after a week to remove the stitches from his chest; the ones in his stomach would have to wait. They left behind a dull, throbbing ache that settled into his ribs and back, particularly when he struggled to the corner of the room in his soiled, gray robe, practicing the art of walking.

Katka told him about her family. Mountain shepherds from the north. She said her grandfather was famous for breeding the loveliest sheep in the Tatras. He wondered how close they lived to the spot where Maria Brod had starved to death, somewhere, perhaps, above the treeline. He asked when he would be released, and as she took his bedpan she said she would find out.

His father's watch had been chipped along the edge of the glass. Its ticking filled the hours.

The photographs were still on the bureau, and he asked Grandmother to bring them to him when she visited. She turned them over in her hands. "What's this?"

"Nothing."

Two men, a street, night.

She handed them over and smiled before turning to go.

He wished for Lena Crowder all the time.

****

It was a little embarrassing when the roses and daffodils arrived with a card that said in typed capitals: HOMICIDE, FIRST DISTRICT. He imagined those gorillas fumbling through a flower store. They'd probably sent a woman from Accounts, or one of their wives. He wanted to like the bouquet, the way it lit up the room in reds and yellows, but couldn't escape the feeling that the flowers were a trick. Something to humiliate him, or to lure him.

At the end of two weeks, Katka brought him a damp bag of baked apples and said he was free to go. He was helped into his clothes—Grandmother had left behind a fresh change when she incinerated the bullet-and-blood scarred suit—and given a worn, wooden cane. He hobbled around the room a few times—clumsy, shaky. Leonek was waiting in the corridor. He looked Emil over approvingly. "Let's get you out of here."

In the Mercedes, each small bump ripping through Emil's insides, Leonek asked about the broken headlights.

"We didn't know. We thought maybe you went crazy and broke them."

"Yes," Emil grunted. "I went crazy. I took a piece of wood and I beat the hell out of them."

He spent two miserable weeks at home, in bed. It was difficult holding in the frustration. There were so many hours in each day, and during most of them he tottered on the verge of shouting at his grandparents to leave him alone. Grandfather beamed, reveling in his newfound pride—he had a hero in the house, after all—and Grandmother pestered him with food. Grandfather read the paper to him, using his most urgent voice to say that General Secretary Mihai had announced his distaste for the corruption being practiced in some corners of the state security division. It was an urgent matter—the stability of the nation was at risk—and would be looked into. Grandfather smiled when he said that the General Secretary's standing ovation had lasted seven full minutes. Sometime during those two weeks the refugee mothers who slept on the staircase disappeared. No one knew if they had found their sons, or if the supervisor had had them shipped away. Grandmother appeared with a bowl of cabbage soup and a crust of stale bread. Emil was beginning to hate all leafy vegetables.

On his second Thursday, he used his cane to reach the communal telephone on the landing. A Militia operator patched him through.

"Terzian."

"It's Emil."

"You're ready to come in?"

"I think so. You have something I can help with? Some work?"

"Sure . . ." He made clicking sounds with his tongue. "Two bodies. In Republic Park. *Coitus interruptus*."

"Can I help?"

"I'll bring the file by."

As he hung up he heard movement behind him—the building supervisor, on her blue-veined, tree-trunk legs, puffy hands folded on her wide hips, stared suspiciously. He was the first one to use the phone in over a week, and her sweat-sealed brow said she would brook no nonsense on her landing.

True to his word, Leonek arrived a little after five with a folder under his arm. Hungry face, hungry eyes. Grandfather asked if he was called Mouse.

"Mouse?" He frowned at her.

"No," Emil said quickly. "Not this one."

"Dinner," said Grandmother, her soft, lined cheeks flushed from the heat of the kitchen. "You should eat. With us."

"My mother's expecting me," said Leonek. "I live with her."

"*That's* a good boy."

Grandfather plied him with his bad cigarettes. "Come on, have one on me. Rolled myself."

They withdrew to the bedroom and opened the file. Emil supported himself against the headboard, and Leonek sat at the foot of the bed, passing individual pages on to him.

"Here it is. Two kids, teenagers." Leonek produced photographs of a boy and girl, both blond and half-naked, bent among the overgrown bushes along the eastern edge of Republic Park. Near the bush was a small splash of white vomit, also photographed. Then, a map of the park with the location of the bodies marked by two overlapping Xs.

The girl, Alana Yoskovich, had been strangled with her scarf. The boy, Ion Hansson, had been struck with an ax where his shoulder met his neck. The ax had not been found at the scene.

"You've done some work on this?" asked Emil, setting the photographs aside.

Leonek lit one of Grandfather's cigarettes. "Of course. The evidence points to the girl's father." He took a drag and gave the cigarette an abrupt, fearful look. He jumped up and tossed it out the window. "Christ!" He blinked, recovering, and waved away the black smoke, then was back. "It's simple: The old man finds young Hansson molesting his only daughter, and proceeds to kill him. Then strangles the girl—out of rage, shame, whatever."

"And you've followed up on it?"

He settled on the bed again. The shifting mattress shot sparks through Emil's sewn gut. "He's in the holding cell. Hasn't admitted to anything yet. We searched his home and a small dacha out of town they share with another family. But listen to this: not a single ax."

Emil understood immediately. "With winter coming on? No ax?"

"Exactly," said Leonek. "And rows of firewood up to my chin."

"There's another boyfriend?"

"No one knows of any."

"And a mother?"

"Died. Back in 'forty."

"Boy's parents?"

"Live in Cisna. He stays with an uncle, who's been on business in Prague for the last three weeks."

Emil let this settle in. He tried to see it from different angles in his head. It was a simple mental exercise, but something. Finally something after these empty weeks. "You've talked to the friends?"

Leonek smiled. "School's out until next week."

"I'll come with you."

"You're sure?"

Grandfather stuck his head in and asked how the cigarette was.

"Terrific," smiled Leonek.

Grandfather waved, grinning, as he withdrew.

"I am," said Emil. "I'm very sure."

The next day—Friday, the first of October—he came by the station. It took a lot of effort, hobbling down the stairs, then along the insecure cobblestones to the main street—he couldn't move faster than a steady walk, nor raise his hands over his head. He didn't know why the pedestrians looked at him—his wounds were hidden beneath his shirt, and there were so many real amputees and maimed citizens in the Capital that a pale young man waiting for a bus could not have deserved much attention. But they did watch him as they passed, and on the bus a woman offered him a seat, but he refused. Each bump and turn ripped through him. In the station, his shaky form limping toward his desk was the only thing to look at. He was the youngest in the room, but he looked like a pensioner. Leonek appeared next to him. "You aren't up for this."

"Change of scenery," said Emil. He settled into his desk and again took the pens and ink out of his pockets. He took out Grandfather's still-unlit cigars and the notepad filled with scribblings about his dead case. Everything into the drawer. His eye kept wandering the desk for telephone messages from her he knew wouldn't be there.

The chief stood in his doorway, hesitant, as if preparing to tell Emil to come to him, then realizing his mistake. He said something under his breath and lumbered forward. Emil leaned back in his chair to look up at him. "Chief?"

Moska reached into his jacket pocket and placed Emil's Militia certificate on the desk. He left his index finger on it. "This is yours, Brod."

Emil looked at the chief's finger, at the green, glazed cover with the imprint of the hawk, its head turned aside as though trying to ignore something.

The chief was plainly uncomfortable having an invalid in the station. But the others, after a few minutes, were relieved to have a chance to express their self-loathing. Big Ferenc said it outright as he brought Emil a cup of coffee: "I must apologize for the way I've acted. It's unforgivable. I can only try to repair what's come before." His tight, sympathetic smile and eloquence were unexpected, and Emil, stunned, accepted the coffee.

Stefan brought a potato casserole his wife had made, his limp a little more noticeable today. "Russian recipe, but filling." It was the first time he had spoken to Emil. He smiled then, winking. "Now I'm not the only cripple."

Brano Sev did not approach him directly, but gave him a knowing nod and smile from his desk. Leonek shot Emil a wide-eyed look of warning.

The holding cells were right beneath their feet, reached by a long walk down the corridor, deeper into the building, through an unmarked door and down metal stairs into the blackness. The air was humid and stank of sweat. The bare lightbulbs gave a hard, contrasty light. The walls became vertical steel bars, and in the gloom behind them Emil saw faces buried in shadow. Gaunt expressions, hungry. He thought again of refugees. Leonek looked positively regal beside them. Cornelius Yoskovich was at the end, on the right; his bald head hung below his shoulder blades. When

Leonek tapped the bar with a knuckle, the man looked up quickly, then stood. He was tall, his grimy, sleeveless shirt too short, exposing his navel. "Are you letting me go?" He had a voice like a radio announcer, like someone speaking to a crowd.

"This is him," Leonek said to Emil.

Yoskovich came to the bars and held them in his fists. His beard was coming in, and his eyes were desperate.

"Where's your ax?" asked Emil.

"I told them." He looked at Leonek. "I told you, didn't I?"

"Tell me," said Emil.

Yoskovich released the bars so he could open his hands to them. "I don't know. Disappeared. *Stolen*, I guess."

"When did it go missing?"

"I've *been* through all this."

Emil turned to Leonek—slowly, because the motion shot hot threads up his spine. "Is there a reason he's giving me trouble?"

"I—" began Yoskovich. "I didn't know it was missing until the police came. I used the ax last week. Saturday. For wood."

"Witnesses?"

Yoskovich shook his head and whispered, "Only my Alana."

At first, Emil didn't recognize the expression that covered his face. Then he did. He'd seen it on the train, on his way back from Helsinki, on the faces of German villagers following Germany's new borders out of Poland: heavy eyes finding nothing to focus on, mouth hanging loosely open, wordless and useless. The expression of someone who once had something and now has nothing. The look of someone who is staring into the abyss and can find no reason to keep on going.

No, he hadn't killed his girl. But he'd done something. Emil would bet his fresh Militia certificate on it.

Leonek, Stefan and Ferenc took him out for drinks. It was Ferenc's idea, but the big man didn't know until they reached the bar that Emil couldn't drink anything but water and some fruit juices. He couldn't even drink the coffee Ferenc had brought earlier. The bartender unearthed tins of pineapple juice taken from a shipment, he said, of abandoned American army rations. Very expensive stuff. Ferenc bought three glasses of it, and Emil drank out of kindness. It was sticky, and tasted of the steel it had come in.

"Who did it?" asked Stefan. He'd found a bowl of pumpkin seeds on the bar and was shoving his fingers deep into them. "Your holes."

"We know who," said Leonek. "But our hands are tied."

Emil nodded. "Smerdyakov."

Stefan wasn't surprised. "You did throttle him, after all."

"But I didn't." He tried to lean back on his stool, but it was more painful than sitting straight, which was also becoming unbearable. He grabbed his cane and pointed with it. "Can we sit over there? My back."

They moved to a low table near the splintery wood wall, where the chairs could support him, and for their patience Emil took out Grandfather's cigars. Leonek at first was wary, but Emil assured him they had been bought, not rolled, by the old man. The cigars were rough on the throat, dry from sitting around for so long, but tasty. Soon their corner was thick with smoke. Stefan waved his cigar when he picked up the thread again: "You said you didn't do what? Didn't throttle Smerdyakov?"

"I only knocked him over." Emil shrugged. "I was going to hit him, but all I got in were a few slaps. Then, he—I don't know. He *shook*."

"Shook?" asked Stefan.

"You mean a seizure," offered Ferenc, puffing smoke.

Emil thought about that. "Maybe."

"You don't know your literature." Ferenc leaned into the table. "The name Smerdyakov comes from Dostoyevsky. A fool stricken by the falling sickness. The Russians love their epileptics—turn them all into holy fools." He rolled ash into a small saucer. "Nicknames don't come out of nowhere. They come from *Karamazov.*"

Emil remembered eyes rolling to whiteness, arms and chest trembling.

"Yes," muttered Stefan, understanding now.

Understanding, Emil thought, made the experience no less disturbing.

The others became drunk surprisingly fast, and Emil, stone sober, watched their steady decline. Their words became weak and over-lapped; their bodies slid deeper into their chairs. Stupid grins popped into their faces unannounced, and there were sudden, unpredictable silences. Leonek, distracted by his own thoughts, fell quiet and did not really recover. Emil asked about Chief Moska.

"What about him? Where's he from? Why is he . . ."

"The goddamn way he is?" asked Ferenc.

Emil nodded.

Ferenc and Stefan looked at each other, as though waiting for the other to begin, and finally Ferenc blurted it out: "The old guy's wife is leaving him. What else?"

Stefan puffed three quick times on his cigar. "Not everyone has the perfect marriage." He nodded at Ferenc, who shrugged.

"You get what you put into it," he explained. "The chief has no time to put into his."

"And me?" asked Stefan. "What the hell don't I put into mine?"

Emil felt the tension rise between them, and tried to redirect: "What about my drunk fool over here?"

Leonek, deep in his silence, didn't stir.

"He'll be a bachelor until the end," said Stefan. "What woman would live with his mother?"

Leonek finally stirred. He looked up, blinking himself into focus, and smiled.

"That's right, eh?" said Stefan, patting him on the arm. "Isn't that right? The boy, the devoted son!"

Leonek's smile slipped away again, and he faded.

"I'll bet you're not married," said Ferenc.

Emil shook his head.

"But you want it. I can see that."

Emil said he didn't know—he hadn't thought of it—but Ferenc didn't believe him.

"Kid like you, it's all you really want."

Once the cigars had burned down, Ferenc stood up—his own wife and daughter (that was a surprise to Emil) were waiting for him, and Stefan, also standing, teased him. "Tell your old bitch to sit down and wait, for once in her life."

Ferenc laid an arm over his shoulder. "You've just proven my point."

They gave Emil a comical salute and pronounced him the finest cadet they'd ever met. Stefan thought the rhyme was funny, and laughed the whole way out.

Leonek's silence was hard to ignore.

Emil looked past him to the short bar, where men just off of work sat in their blue coveralls, drinking silently. The bartender, a man with blue-veined features, knew them all.

"Where were you?" asked Leonek, and Emil turned to him again. His dark face was covered in black spots where blood beneath the surface had collected.

"When?"

"The war—wait!" He raised a finger. *"Finland."*

Emil hadn't realized how drunk Leonek was.

"The *ovens*. Did you see them? In your travels?"

He shook his head. "I was in the south. Ruscova, a village."

"So you didn't see it. Nothing."

Emil drank the metallic pineapple juice. He was still, after three weeks, thirsty. "We saw some refugees," he remembered. "From Romania. They said it was some kind of mania. Whole villages turned on them. Some stayed at our dacha."

Leonek spoke loudly: "*My* people. They did it to *my* people first." He took another swill and banged the glass on the table. Beer spilled over.

Armenian, Emil remembered the Uzbek saying. Terzian was an Armenian name.

"In my family's village the Turks took a whole family. Ten, I think. Yes. I was seven, and there were ten of them. The soldiers tied them together with rope. You know, from the back. Hands back here," he said as he demonstrated with his own hands behind his back. "All of them connected so they couldn't see each other. Their faces." His hands were in front again, clutching his glass. "I watched from a ditch. They tied them so they couldn't move, then pushed the family into a lake. One whole family. Sunk like a rock. First they screamed, then they were underwater." He took another drink.

"And you?" asked Emil.

"Look at me!" He opened his arms and let them fall by his sides. "I'm here, right? They tattooed my father and took him away with the other fathers. We thought they were going to prison, but as soon as they were out of sight we heard gunshots. On our way out of Armenia we saw Turkish soldiers using knives. You know. *Casually.* Like cutting fruit."

He slipped back into his silence. There were voices building in the front of the bar, jokes and sporadic laughter. Leonek's black face was sweating.

"You all right?" asked Emil, leaning closer.

A tight, glistening smile. "What are *you* doing here? This job will eat you up."

Emil opened his mouth, groping for an answer. Then he realized—with cool shock that drained into his arms and legs—that he had been let into this man's head.

This story was the basis of Leonek Terzian. It was the root of all the choices he had made since that day when he was seven and watched a family drown, or saw his father grimace at the burn of a tattoo. It was the same as Ester watching her mother be dragged through the streets of Iași. It colored everything that followed. It was why Leonek was devotedly living with his mother, and why he worked in Homicide, where the stink of death and the misery of humanity was thickest.

"Come on, then," said Leonek. "Out with it." His smile had become loose, more convincing.

Then he knew. For the first time. He had known it when he was in Finland and felt that need to return, when he saw the mauled woman on the street and knew it was too late to leave. He had felt it in all his love and hate for this city. He saw it in Lena Crowder's wonderful eyes when he closed his own. He tapped the table with his knuckles. "Because I want to be devoted."

Leonek looked into his empty glass, then back at Emil. "What?"

He knew it all now, and the realization was a rush of pleasure like a clean, warm bath. "I want to believe in one place," he said. "I want it in my blood."

Leonek looked again into his glass, and smiled. "It'll get into your blood, all right." Then he did the unexpected. He leaned over the table and pinched Emil's cheek, like a Ruscova grandmother wanting to make sure the sweet vision of boyhood in front of her was actually there, in the flesh.

CHAPTER FIFTEEN

****

Over the weekend, Emil went to a film alone. It was an old Soviet comedy, and he went in order to make himself enthusiastic. He thought that by looking at the pictures flickering on the screen, he might get a touch of that mania he had once known through those Soviet newsreels. But he couldn't concentrate on the shadows shifting and talking on the screen, the man with the ludicrous mustache whose monocle kept dropping from his eye. And when the audience laughed, he lost track of the Russian dialogue. He left halfway through.

That Monday Leonek picked him up. Rather than the office, they went directly to the Sixth District and parked outside the newly named "Rosa Luxembourg" High School, and Emil waited behind the wheel, his cane between his knees, while Leonek sauntered inside. He watched the clouds through the windshield collect in the west in preparation for a storm, and almost jumped when Leonek popped open the back door and shoved in a fifteen-year-old girl. He slid in beside her. Although it hurt terribly, Emil turned to face her.

"Meet Liv Popescu," said Leonek.

She was small and pretty with a round, bright face. "You know about your friend?" asked Emil.

She didn't say anything. Her gaze was fixed outside the car, on the houses lining the street, at the sky.

"Liv?" he tried again. "Do you know?"

"Alana?" she asked, and looked at him. Her cheeks were smooth and unblemished.

"That's the one."

Liv shrugged and looked at clouds.

"There's someone out there killing your friends," said Leonek, his voice softened by a transparent attempt to soothe the girl. "You understand? This person kills them, maybe vomits on them, and tosses them in the bushes."

At the mention of vomit, Liv Popescu looked at him.

"But the problem," he continued, "is that when we talk to you there's not an ounce of worry on your face. Nothing. Which leads us to believe . . . Emil? What does it lead us to believe?"

The handoff was unexpected, but easily taken. "It leads us to believe that you, Liv, are involved in your friends' demise. Both Alana and Ion." His left lung was burning badly at this angle; each word was a little fire inside him. "That you know something, or you did something. Is that what you imagine, Leon?"

Leonek nodded and placed an arm on the seat behind Liv's head. The cushion squeaked as he settled. "I imagine this has something to do with Ion Hansson," he said. "The handsome young man with the ax in his neck. I'm not too far from the truth. Am I, Liv?"

Liv Popescu made no move, no sound. Her hands were wedged between her knees.

"Do you know what a crime against the state is?" asked Emil. "It is something which interferes with the smooth operations of the federal and legislative bodies that govern our workers' state. Would withholding information about her friend's murder rank as a crime against the state, Leon?"

"Absolutely."

Emil looked away momentarily to ease the pain—just a brief instant—and when he looked back she was crying. At some point the fear had dissolved her confidence in her own silence. Emil had doubted she would have much to give them, but teenagers had a way of saying either nothing or everything. Some small lead, perhaps, would come out of badgering her. But now her twisted face fell into the bowl of her hands, and she blubbered what she knew in wet stutters: Alana's father was to blame.

Over her head, Leonek nodded knowingly at Emil.

"He's a brute, you understand? A long time—*years*. He'd been doing things to Alana. His own daughter. *It*, you understand?" She couldn't say the word.

Leonek's proud face hesitated.

Alana had been too ashamed to tell anyone other than Liv, her best friend. For a long time, only her. Then, later, she decided to tell the boy who had fallen in love with her: Ion Hansson. But she didn't tell him at first. She wanted to, but then she couldn't. She went back and forth daily. Then one afternoon she told Liv she would reveal everything to him that night. But she would only confess after she had let Ion do *it*.

"She was confused," Liv insisted. "She didn't know how he would react. He might be angry, you know? Or disgusted. Or just shocked. She thought if she gave herself to him, it would be easier for him to accept."

The ax was Alana's idea. It was the only weapon her father owned. She asked Liv to hold on to it and hide in the shrubs. In case her father burst onto the scene.

"She wanted *you*," said Leonek. "In the bushes. *Watching?*"

"Protection," said Liv, her tears under control now. "After that night, Ion could protect her. But until then, I would look over her."

"And you were willing to do this?"

Liv looked at him with complete scorn. "You've never loved anybody, have you?"

Leonek opened his mouth, but could say nothing.

"Why in the park?" asked Emil. "Ion's uncle was out of town. There was a bed, right?"

The scorn remained on her bright face as she showed her teeth. "*Neighbors.* Why else?"

Emil started the car and began to drive around the block to avoid prying eyes. He looked at her in the rearview. "Go on."

It was a dark night, but she had been able to see it all from the bushes. She saw them have sex, and was surprised by how quiet it was, how calm. Afterward, they lay beside each other in the grass, and Alana told him everything. Liv couldn't hear it all, but she had a clear view of Ion's face as it settled into an expressionless, frozen look. He seemed to be taking it calmly. Alana was still speaking when he rolled over and vomited into the grass. Alana got up to see if he was all right, and he grabbed her scarf and strangled her with it.

"I couldn't tell," said Liv, the tears back with her. "Not at first. She wasn't fighting at all. I didn't know what he was doing. She just lay there and accepted it. I still don't understand."

But then, in the flash of passing automobile lights, she saw Alana's head: it hung at an awkward angle, lips thick, her eyes bulging from their sockets. Ion was crying over her body.

Emil parked again in front of the school. Spots of rain appeared on the windshield.

"That's when I did it," she said, her voice cool once more, and measured. All her tears were gone now. "I watched myself do it. I walked up and raised it over my head and brought it down on him." She looked at Leonek hovering over her, and his face was lost in a rare fear—complete terror. It was more than simple repulsion, and Emil found himself turning to start the car just to avoid seeing his face. Liv's voice floated through the car: "It was like cutting wood. But softer."

They brought in the girl because there was nothing else to do. On the way she told them she had thrown the ax into the Tisa, which swallowed everything. She was arraigned by a thin woman in uniform who seemed proud of the line of six stamps she had at her disposal. She stamped PROCESSED on Liv's paperwork, and handed her off to another woman, who took Liv to the cells.

Emil stopped Leonek just outside their own office. A crowd of policemen swerved to avoid running into them. "What was that?" he asked. "Back in the car. You were . . . I don't know. What was it?"

Leonek peered, frowning, into Emil's eyes, then looked away. Everyone else in the building was going about his business. "It's nothing," he said finally. "Weren't you bothered?"

"Not like that," said Emil. "Not like you."

Leonek held his hands up. "Can't we have our moments?"

They let the father go. Cornelius kept tugging at his spotted, stretched collar, as if he couldn't breathe. Leonek led him up from the cells and through the corridor to the broad front doors. But once he was on the front steps, where the drops were beginning to fall in earnest, he dropped his hands and smiled. He breathed the fresh air through his nose and looked back at Leonek and Emil. "Is the People's Militia going to pay my taxi home?"

"You're lucky I don't break your neck," called Leonek. "You worthless shit."

Emil opened the door, and they left Cornelius Yoskovich to the rain.

There were two notes on his desk. One from Roberto, who said that if Emil stayed out of his equipment shop any longer, he would die of poverty; the second in an unknown hand: a phone message. A woman who would not leave her name. But he knew the number. He turned the yellow slip over to its blank side. Leonek was typing up the report. He turned Lena's number over again—it felt like electricity on his finger.

He asked the operator for the extension and, after a moment, recognized the southern tones on the line.

"Irma? This is Inspector Brod. Comrade Crowder called?"

"Right away," Irma whispered, then was gone.

Leonek yelled an elaborate curse as he ripped paper from his typewriter, crushed it and threw it at his wastebasket. It missed. He rolled in a new sheet.

Through the phone he could hear her faintly, shouting in another room: *But how do you* know *it's him?* Then footsteps echoed along the marble floors—he imagined the grain of the marble, the black, sharp heel striking it. A breathless voice: "Emil—is it really you?"

"Yes, Com—" he began.

There was only the sound of her breath against the receiver, and rain pelting the station windows. He noticed that his hand was sweating freely, then passed the phone to his other hand and wiped his wet palm on a knee. Typing began again in earnest.

"We have to talk," she said finally. "To meet. Somewhere."

"I'll come over."

"Not here!" She sounded desperate. He wondered if she'd been drinking. "Can you go to Victory Square?"

"It's raining."

"You won't *drown.*"

When he hung up, Leonek was throwing away his second draft. "You're going somewhere?" he asked as Emil slipped into his coat.

"I'll be back soon."

"Need company?" Leonek opened his jacket, pointing at the wide pocket sagging from a heavy metal flask. "Your first completed case, after all. God knows I could use a drink."

Again he felt the incongruity: his life before and after the gunshot. A month ago, this man was shoving his fist deeply between Emil's legs. But Leonek—and the others too—had fallen quickly into their new roles, almost without reflection.

"Another time," said Emil, his cane ticking on the floor as he limped away. "When I'm allowed."

"Dr. Terzian says tomorrow." He winked, and closed the jacket.

CHAPTER SIXTEEN

****

On the edge of the Fourth District, just east of the old administrative center, Victory Square had been built in the midst of defeat. Luftwaffe bombs had decimated this northern bank of the Tisa, then Soviet bombs expelled the Germans and turned the rubble into dust. By Liberation, it was a vast square of negation, a noncity inside the Capital. But General Secretary Mihai, with the financial backing of Comrade Chairman Stalin, had other ideas. He repaved the roads and began building. He crisscrossed the area with wide boulevards, their names reflecting the names in every other city under the Empire's shepherd eye. Liberty, Gorky, October, Progress. And from the rubble that had symbolized the nation's history of inevitable military defeats, a huge concrete intersection had been constructed around the statue of a strong man and woman with rolled sleeves sharing a torch held aloft. The intersection had been named Victory.

Gazing past the spastic windshield wipers, Emil realized with some dread that they hadn't agreed on a corner. He left the car in Victory Park and used his cane unsteadily along the wet concrete. He had no umbrella, and his hat quickly flooded as the gusting rain came at a sharp angle into his face. Between two light poles, a wind-tossed banner proclaimed: UNITY INDUSTRY COLLECTIVIZATION—ONWARD THE FUTURE!

He moved gradually around the endless edge of the roundabout, stopping when the traffic blared before him. His cane splashed in puddles as he crossed each of the eight roads. He passed the wide steps leading up to the one government building here, topped by the sculpture of a hawk at rest—the Central Committee chambers, its rear facing the river. The wet, cold air was hard on his weak lungs, and when he finally saw Lena stepping out of a taxi on the far corner of the square, he was out of breath.

She was in a crisp, rain-speckled overcoat that looked like it had never been worn before. A wide-brimmed hat and sunglasses hid her face. She tensed visibly beneath her black umbrella when she saw him making his way back across the streets, then crossed one in order to meet him sooner.

"I have a car," he gasped. She followed him silently toward the park. Despite the glasses, he could feel her gaze locked on his cane, on his limping form. He opened the door and made sure her head didn't hit the roof, then got in on his side, throwing the cane in first. She had taken off the hat and glasses. Tasseled hair and brilliant, bloodshot eyes.

He started the engine to obscure the sound of his labored breaths. The car became hot, stuffy. "You want to tell me?" he finally managed.

She leaned forward, quickly, and placed a small, warm kiss on his cheek. Then she pulled abruptly back. "Drive, please." He was driving before he had decided to.

He took them westward along the Tisa. He checked the mirror a number of times, and forced himself to twist around to point. "See? We're not being followed."

Her eyes followed the line of his finger out the back window and down past the Georgian Bridge. During rainstorms the city's dust settled and you could see the empty outbound boulevard for miles.

When she spoke, it was a whisper: "You've been hurt."

It sounded good to Emil. Soft, concerned. "It's nothing."

"You're using a cane."

"Nothing," he repeated. "What about you?"

She turned to look out the back again, then sank into her seat. The hot car was unbearable now, and she cracked her window. The wet air hissed. He almost didn't hear her say, "They're trying to kill me."

Although he could not have admitted it to himself, he knew she was going to say this, or something like it. It was the inevitable end point of her behavior. It was no small part of his adoration. He could smell the alcohol on her breath, and her paranoia was apparent. He turned north into the maze of medieval Fifth District houses and parked at the curb. He shut off the engine, then painfully faced her. *"They?"*

"Him, they—*I* don't know." She opened her silver cigarette case and waited for him to light the one she put in her mouth. She exhaled toward her open window, but the smoke rolled back inside. "They, *he*, broke into the house. Tore apart the second floor, looking for I-don't-know-what."

"When was this?"

"A week ago. Well, we *found* it a week ago. After I saw you last, Irma and I went to Stryy."

"Stryy?"

"Up north," she said. "I told you. I took my father's ashes back home. Then, when we came back a week ago, the house was a wreck. I called you. Immediately. But a rude woman said you were on leave. *Where were you?*"

He was uncontrollably pleased that the reason she hadn't called him before was that she hadn't been in town, and that as soon as she returned she had tried—but he only said, "Go on."

"The woman patched us through to the district police, and they poked around. A bunch of *imbeciles,* of course." She clutched her cigarette, filling the car with her smoky breath.

She shot him a nervous smile, and he felt a tremor of pain in his side. She was really very beautiful. "What did they take?"

"*Nothing.*" She stared at the dashboard. "Not that we could find. No jewelry, money, nothing. Irma spent the whole week cleaning up, such a job she did. Then the phone call came." She took another drag, but forgot to even try for the window. A cloud hung between them until Emil opened his own window and the cross-draft sucked the air clean. Water dripped from the window frame to her overcoat, but she didn't notice.

"A call?"

"Same as before. The same voice. The same one who called when Janos was dead. It wasn't your people after all."

Figures passed in the rain, women and men wrapped against it, jogging from doorway to doorway. The storm was beginning to let up. He noticed a clear drip forming on the tip of her pale nose, and fought the urge to wipe it.

"*It,* he said. He knew I had *it.* He said that *it* didn't belong to me. Said I should hand *it* over before I ended up like Janos. *That's* what he said."

Emil started the car and took them around cracked walls and wet pedestrians. He didn't know how much to trust. He wanted to trust it all, but she was drunk and frightened and maybe a little manipulative. Even so, he wanted to believe every word that came from her lips.

"And you don't know what *it* is?"

"If I did, I'd hand it over, wouldn't I?"

"That would depend on what it was."

She crossed her arms over her chest and looked out the window.

"When did the call come?"

"Last night," she said to the window, and when she brought the cigarette to her lips her hand shook. "I need a drink."

They were beside the Tisa again, driving west. "You said Janos came back to you before he died."

She nodded.

"And he didn't give you anything? No gifts? Nothing?"

When she looked at him, a familiar, ironic smile had appeared. "Janos thought *he* was gift enough."

They were passing half-built blocks that gave way to large, open plains.

"You're taking me back!"

He wasn't sure what he was going to do. He could ask someone to stay at her place. Leonek, maybe. He owed Emil at least that. Someone who could fight back if necessary—not an invalid.

"This person wants something. Right?"

"That's what he said."

"If he kills you he won't have it."

She closed the window. "That didn't help Janos, my dear inspector."

The rain had let up, but the long driveway to the Crowder house was marked by black puddles and long tire tracks. The stone walkway was dark with wetness as his cane tapped along it. He could hear birds, but couldn't see them in the low trees surrounding the house. She walked ahead of him, and all he could think of were the dreams he'd had of her while lying in the hospital.

"You're going to have to tell me about that cane, you know."

"I thought as much."

The door opened by only the pressure of her hand. She stopped and stared. When her eyes focused, she caught her breath and bolted inside. He hobbled up to join her.

Irma was lying at the foot of the staircase, arms hanging out like logs beside her, trying to breathe through a smashed nose and swelling cheeks. She blinked behind blood-stained strands of hair, and they could barely hear her whisper as Lena lifted her head into her lap: *"He's still here."*

Then they heard it: the bark of an engine outside, a high whine, tires spinning in mud.

Emil moved as fast as possible, jumping into each step, ignoring the pain, and saw a short, blue car—a make he wasn't familiar with—spraying mud as it rocked through the driveway, laboring over lumps and puddles toward the road. Emil dropped his cane and ran after it. The pain ground inside him, but he pushed it down. The car slid sideways, then caught again. He was sprinting now, and the engine whined in his ears. Dark blue, no license. He was close enough for the mud to spit across his face as the tires climbed forward. Then the pain jumped again, into his chest, suffocating him. He opened his mouth, but all that came was mud. He was almost at the fender. Then he wasn't. There was something on his chest, squeezing the air out of it. The car dwindled in the distance, turning onto the main road, and his vision dimmed. He dropped into the mud, unable to move, gasping, his lungs two useless bags heaving inside his bullet-scarred chest.

Lena helped raise him, her narrow shoulder under his. She didn't notice the mud smeared all over her coat, or that her shoes—her feet, now that her shoes had become stuck a few paces back—were deep in it. Nor did she mind the tracks they made across the marble, the sitting-room rug, and all over the sofa she dropped him in. She was remarkably strong for her size.

"You're bleeding!" Lena kneeled beside him and unbuttoned his shirt.

He'd already known it; he could feel the bite where each suture in his belly had ripped loose. She pressed a soft white towel to him, and it came up red. He took the towel from her hands and used it on his face.

"You need a doctor."

"Irma needs a doctor."

Irma, on the chair, was wiping her own face with a towel.

"Tell us about it," said Emil.

"Not yet, Irma." Lena stood up. She looked lost, touching

everything. "First, yes. First, a doctor." She reminded Emil of shell-shocked soldiers—he'd heard about this from veterans. The bounciness just before their explosions.

But he looked at Irma instead. He had his window—it would soon close. "Now," he insisted. "If you can."

Lena's brief hysteria passed, and she sank, cross-legged, to the floor. She was still in her dirty raincoat, her bare feet thick with mud.

Irma talked out of the side of her mouth, as though the right side were filled with pebbles. The man had come soon after Lena went to meet Emil. He wore sunglasses and knocked at the front door. He had been caught by the rain, he said, and had lost a tire on the main road. "But he didn't look so wet," said Irma. "I should have seen that."

"And you let him in?" Lena asked.

She shook her head. "I remembered what you'd told me. I asked him to wait, but he didn't wait." The man shouldered his way inside and began rifling through Lena's cabinets and drawers. Irma followed him, explaining that he would have to leave, that her mistress would return soon with a policeman. The intruder finished with the drawers and moved on to the bookshelves.

They looked around. Half the books from the shelves covering the wall lay scattered on the floor.

"I put a hand here." Irma placed her fingers on her own shoulder. "He slapped me then. He had white gloves. Soft. And he asked me where it was."

"It?" said Lena. "*It?*"

Irma nodded as vigorously as her blood-puffed face would allow. She didn't know what *it* was. She told the man as much, but he began beating her, and as his fists struck he repeated the question: *Where is it?* Finally, he gave up and returned to the shelves. He took each book and flipped through it very quickly, as though speed-reading, catching any slip of paper that fell out and looking at it before going on to the next title. He shouted sometimes out of frustration: *It's here, isn't it?*

Lena looked at Emil, then at her maid. "And he never said—"

"Never." Irma's grainy voice had acquired an edge of impatience.

There was little more to the story. When Emil's Mercedes rolled up the drive, she had tried to make it to the door, but the intruder was on her again. He beat her face and chest until she collapsed on the stairs. Then he ran to the rear of the house, where he had parked his car.

"Can you describe him?" asked Emil.

"Tall," she said resolutely. "Light hair, old eyes."

"Old eyes?"

"Wrinkled. Dark." She closed her own eyes. "His face was thin. He had—I think—a German accent."

"German?"

She looked at him again with wet, red eyes. "I'm sure. German."

Emil took out one of the nine photographs still in his pocket. He showed it to her. He pointed at the man who was not Smerdyakov, the one who had said: *Comrade Emil Brod?*

"Oh God." Her bruised head nodded with conviction.

"Go," Emil said. "Both of you pack some clothes." He felt himself sinking.

CHAPTER SEVENTEEN

****

In the car, he finally admitted to his gunshot wounds. A few words, nothing more. Lena was beside him, and her face quickly exposed her feelings—it felt good to see the deep concern that she finally controlled by speaking: "Christ, Emil. You almost died."

He shrugged, but even that movement hurt.

He was given three stitches to reclose his wound, and Irma was given, for a substantial bribe to the Unity Medical head nurse, a private bed. He drove Lena to the Brod apartment. They said nothing the whole way, but the silence was a warm, easy thing. Despite the cane, he was able to carry her small leather suitcase, and he set it down just inside the door.

"She's staying here, maybe a few days," he told Grandfather, who was grinning in his chair, wet-mouthing an unlit, frayed cigar.

Lena tried to hide her disappointment as she looked around the meager home. Grandmother was still out.

"A girlfriend?" Grandfather asked when Lena was in the bathroom washing up.

"A widow," said Emil. "A case."

"Some widow." He stuck the cigar back in his mouth. "You look like hell."

He was leaving stains on everything he touched. "I tried to run down a car."

"A motor car?"

Emil nodded.

"You're a goddamn dog, that's what you are."

By the time she emerged from the bathroom, Lena's disappointment had become a buoyancy he could see in her step, in her smile, as if she had decided this was not to be a sacrifice, but an adventure.

"Do you have anything to drink?" she asked the room.

"Girl after my own heart," said Grandfather as he grunted out of his chair and went for the liquor cabinet.

It took an hour to heat his bathwater, and by the time he emerged, bruised but clean, toweled dry and in fresh clothes, Grandmother had returned and made dinner. She gazed over her plate at Lena. When she spoke, her voice was thick with admiration: "Who else *lives* out there? Near you."

Both Lena and Grandfather were tipsy by now. She smiled slyly at her drinking partner before answering. "No one, not *really*. A lot of *bores*." She choked down more cabbage soup, which, for an instant, made her easy demeanor stumble: She looked as though she had discovered new teeth. Then she swallowed. "Rich people are as dull as proles, I can promise you that."

"You're kidding me," said Grandfather, and it took a moment before Emil realized he was being sarcastic. "But aren't they all filled with charm? With *poise*?" He sipped from his spoon daintily and stared at Lena. He was plainly charmed, head over heels.

Lena settled her gaze on him. "Comrade Avram Brod," she said in a suitable Russian accent, "the wealthy are butter in our churn. *Delicious.*"

Grandfather burst out laughing, suddenly red-faced, healthy again. Spittle shot across the table, and Lena laughed too, winking at Emil, the brandy and laughter flushing her cheeks. The old man pointed at Lena, and between gasps said, "This one. *This one.*"

****

He slept on the sofa—or, he tried to sleep. It was difficult, knowing she was only a couple yards away, in his bed. He was distracted, horny, and had to throw off his sheet; he was sweating. He ached everywhere. If he went to her, he could do nothing anyway. Not in his condition. He sat on the balcony, looking out to where a lone woman stood at the water spigots. A dog circled nearby, sniffing the ground around her.

Blackmail. It was the only thing that made sense. Janos Crowder had blackmailed Jerzy Michalec with something that could fit in a book: a document, or a photograph, like the ones he had found. Aleksander Tudor became mixed up in it at some point. There was a German working with Michalec. Maybe he was the deliveryman, bringing the boxes of cash to Janos's door. But at some point Michalec decided he would no longer pay, and instead liquidated Janos.

One pail was full, and she set it down with a thump on the cobblestones, then started filling another.

He tried to think through what he was going to do. There were rational options. Put Lena into protective custody, or keep her here. File a report on the German assailant; he had the man's photograph, after all. He could ask the other inspectors for help, or even advice. They had decades of experience between them.

The dog was circling closer, sniffing out dinner on the woman's dirty skirt.

Lena was spread under his sheets in his room. The rational solutions left him. He still didn't trust those homicide inspectors, no matter how many cakes and coffees they brought him. That would take a long time. Maybe he could get advice from them, nothing more.

A few streets away some dogs began barking in an uneven chorus, and the mutt down below stopped sniffing, raised his head, and barked back. Then more dogs joined in, from streets further out, and soon it was all he could hear. The woman down by the spigot was running as best she could with her heavy pails into an alley, and the dog in the square was walking in a circle, backward, barking frightfully at canine armies he heard but could not see. It was a city of dogs.

He knew, all of a sudden, that he couldn't do it. This was too important. He couldn't protect Lena on his own.

"Tell me about the shooting," said Emil. "The one who shot me."

Leonek sat down, and they faced each other over Emil's typewriter. He shrugged. "What's to tell? Tall guy in an overcoat. A hat. You saw him. Right?"

"Briefly."

Leonek pulled an ankle up over his knee. "He shot you three times and drove away."

"Did you get the plates?"

"No license. But it was dark blue. One of those Czech models. Streamlined. A Tatra, I think."

Emil hesitated, remembering. "Was *he* driving the car? Or someone else?"

"Yes. Just him." He glanced over at Brano Sev working away in his corner, then let his foot drop to the ground again. He leaned forward, voice lowered. "But listen, Brod: This is done. It's finished. These aren't the kind of men you want to chase after. You understand?"

Emil noticed a dead roach on his desk and flicked it away.

"You attacked him, and he attacked you," said Leonek. "It's over."

"Listen."

Leonek held up a warning hand and glanced back at Sev, who still faced the wall, then nodded at the door. "Come on, let's get a drink."

This bar was a few streets away, hidden beneath a flat-faced, between-the-wars post office, reached by a door recessed in the sidewalk. Despite the early morning hour, it was filled with the law-enforcement community. He saw judges and prosecutors and even overdressed members of state security, looking much more distinguished and put-together than their own department's famous-but-sloppy security inspector. The bar was the longest Emil had ever seen, its clean brass fixtures shining. A stiff, white-shirted bartender asked very formally what they would have to drink.

"Two beers," said Leonek as he tossed coins on the counter.

He helped Emil to a table in the corner, pushing through fat men in suits. They sank into a plush, velvet booth. "*You* come here?"

Leonek shrugged. "Not usually. Tell me what's going on."

So Emil did. He sipped his lukewarm beer and related all the details. The man who searched Lena Crowder's house was the same man who had shot him, a German, and a German was seen around Janos Crowder's apartment before he died. All roads led to the German. The German led to Smerdyakov.

"How's that?"

Emil took out the small photos again—worn now, a little damp—and handed them over.

"Where did you get these?"

"Behind Aleks Tudor's icebox. You recognize them?"

Leonek held one close to his face, then the next, one at a time until he had seen them all. "Smerdyakov," he whispered, then nodded. "And your killer." He laid a hand over the photographs, covering them. "Lena Crowder doesn't know what *it* is? This thing?"

"No."

"That's her story."

"She doesn't know." Four Central Committee members made a loud circle near the bar, singing some rowdy song from their youth.

Leonek dropped the photos by his beer and shook his head.

"You know you can't touch him, right? He's not a full member of the Politburo yet, but he's almost there. He'll be one of a select twenty. People like you and I can't do anything."

"Obviously some people can, or he wouldn't be murdering them."

A pause, as Leonek rethought his approach. When he spoke he whispered. "Listen. Jerzy Michalec started *off* as the top man in the Central Committee, back in 'forty-five. His best friends are the minister of international affairs, the chairman of Party control, and the head of regional secretaries. He eats lunch with Mihai himself. Do you see what I'm saying?"

"He's connected."

"No, you goddamn idiot. Michalec *is* the connection. Once he's a full member of the Politburo, it's just a few years until he's nestled beside Mihai, waiting to receive the General Secretaryship." Leonek leaned back, his voice severe: "When that happens, when Michalec becomes General Secretary, you, my friend, are a dead man."

They looked at each other across the table. Emil had listened to so little before—he'd understood everything like a child. His cold fingers tapped distractedly on his glass, then stopped. When Jerzy Michalec became General Secretary, there would be no place in the entire country to hide.

"You remember when we brought in Liv Popescu?"

Emil nodded.

"You asked what was wrong, and I lied. I said it was nothing." Leonek looked down and gathered himself before continuing. "But the case—Cornelius Yoskovich in particular—made me think of my informer, Dora." He stopped again, drank some beer.

"The bastard who lied about me?"

Leonek nodded morosely. "I first knew Dora years ago. He was a banker—it's hard to imagine. He had a wife and a daughter. This was a little before the war—summer of 'thirty-eight—and I was as new to the Militia as you are now. Back then we weren't relegated to just homicides. It was a peaceful town; we didn't need a homicide department."

He paused again, and Emil wanted to ask him how old he was, because to Emil he looked so young, but he had the kind of face that would hide its age until he was a very old man.

Leonek said, "There were accusations at his daughter's school. Apparently, Dora had been spending his lunch hours there, and he would talk to his daughter's friends. They were ten and eleven, pretty young. After a while, he invited them out of the schoolyard and talked them into coming with him to a hotel room. He did this with many of the girls. Finally, the girls started telling their families."

Emil started to speak, but realized he had no question to ask.

"It's a short story," said Leonek. "I brought him in on multiple charges of molestation. It was a simple, straightforward case. I hated this man, and I was happy to put him away. It was a good day for me." He drank some more and squinted into the gloom. "But Dora convinced the royal prosecutor's office that he had information on illegal financial transactions, some major scandals, lots of them, and they made a deal. He was free."

"They let him go?" Emil finally asked. "Just like *that*?"

"Sure," said Leonek, shrugging. "Dora's wife took their girl and left the country—she had family in Switzerland. And the bank, once they learned about the confidential information he'd given out, fired him. His life was fixed from that point. A permanent criminal, a pimp. He lures little girls just in from the countryside. Information is his protection. But he works by habit: I'm the only one he'll talk to. He's my curse." His glass was empty, but he upended it regardless, then set it down. Laughter came from the front. "Sometimes Dora makes the difference between solving a case or giving up."

"This man is shit."

Leonek nodded his agreement. "But this is life, my friend. You make it the best way you can. You compromise, and you know when you are beat. But one day, Dora will run out of information, and I'll be standing over him, with a gun to his head."

Emil pressed his fingers against his closed eyes until he saw stars. Then he blinked, focusing. "Tell me, then."

"Tell you what?"

"What you would do now. You've been in this for years. A veteran."

Leonek had a pack of cigarettes that he rotated in his fingers, hammered lightly on the tabletop, then began to open. "Drop it," he said finally. "It's a dead case anyway. The chief won't let you touch it; he takes orders too. He's a good soldier, but he won't break any rules for you."

"I see."

"Don't look so down." He offered Emil a cigarette. "This is too big for you. You're a cripple, you'll end up dead. Throw your dear Comrade Lady Crowder to the wolves, and come get drunk with me."

They lit their cigarettes. The slurred sounds of wasted politicians washed over them.

CHAPTER EIGHTEEN

****

Grandfather opened the door before Emil's hand could touch the knob. He looked confused. "A call," he said feebly. "Yes."

"There was a call?"

Emil heard banging sounds from inside. Grandfather's confusion melted into shame. "How was I to know?"

In the bedroom, Lena threw clothes into her bag. She stopped only to shout: "Your *grand*father has been advertising me!"

He was shuffling around the living room, shrugging helplessly. "How was I to know?" He stopped and said to Emil, "The man asked, *Is Lena Crowder staying with you?* What was I to say?"

"You *lie*," barked Lena, slamming her valise shut.

Emil held up his hands as though his command for calm might be heeded. Lena ripped up the bedsheets angrily, searching for something. Grandmother appeared from her bedroom with a fistful of scarves in dusty, muted colors. She presented them to Lena. "Will these do?"

Lena's voice dropped an octave. "You've been very kind, Mrs. Brod."

"*Comrade* Brod to you," warned Grandfather.

"You wouldn't know a comrade if he shoved *Das Kapital*—"

"I was in *Moscow*!"

"*Now,*" said Emil as he put his arms around his grandparents' shoulders and led them into their bedroom. Once inside, they looked at him questioningly. "Wait here," he said, and closed the door.

He squatted to pick up the cane, then returned to his bedroom. Lena stood up from the bed, arms crossed. She was in a ladies' suit, narrow at the waist, wide mustard lapels. He lowered himself into a rickety chair, grunting. The beer had ruined his stomach.

"I'm leaving, Inspector Brod. You won't stop me."

"I don't want to stop you," he said. "Do you have a cigarette?"

She took out her pack, but didn't have matches. While she went to the kitchen to find some, he wondered whom he knew in the city that she could stay with; Leonek was a choice anyone would figure out. But he knew very few people—solitude had never before been a problem. Those few he could dredge up—Filia, perhaps, and her soldier husband—he didn't know if he could trust.

Lena squatted beside his knees, lit a cigarette and passed it to him. He took a drag and looked at the box in her hand: American. "We're both leaving town."

She picked tobacco off her tongue and waited for more.

"Do you have money?"

She nodded.

"A lot?"

She shrugged, then nodded again.

"No one can know where we're going, all right?"

"No one except me?"

"Not yet," he said, and took another drag. "I won't tell my family, and I won't tell you. Not until we're on our way."

She seemed all right not knowing. She settled on the corner of his bed and finished her cigarette without speaking. She looked at the narrow window and the short shelf of books he'd brought with him when everything with Filia had ended. And then she looked at him, her delicate features betraying nothing, yet hiding nothing. He wondered how she could do that.

****

Grandfather didn't like the sound of it. "But *where?*" Emil told him that what he didn't know, he couldn't tell. Grandmother raised a fat hand in farewell. When Emil looked back at them standing in the doorway, Grandfather, in his shame, looked feeble and old and alone.

By eleven-thirty, they arrived at the hospital. He asked her for some money. She reached into her handbag, then looked at him. "What for?"

"Irma."

She handed over too much. He counted off enough and gave the rest back. Inside, he found the nurse in charge of Irma's floor. She was a big woman, with a white coat that was stained with old soup. "How long is Irma . . ." He realized he didn't know her last name. "A woman," he tried again, and held a hand at shoulder height. "About this tall. Southerner. Dark hair. Bruised face?"

The nurse let the silence hang between them a moment. "Bobia. Irma Bobia."

"Exactly," he said. "Bobia. How much longer are you keeping her?"

She looked through files for a while, and Emil leaned against the counter, watching invalids maneuver slowly through the corridors. He thought of the Uzbek and his bodies a few floors below this one.

"Tomorrow," she said flatly, and looked back at him.

It was Tuesday. "Can she stay until the end of the week?"

"This is not a hotel."

The bills were on the counter now, visible under his hand. She noticed. "But it's a difficult situation," he said. "She can't go home now. Not yet."

The koronas were hypnotizing her. "Not yet," she mumbled, then: "Friday?"

"Friday would be good." He slid his hand forward until the money dropped over the edge of the counter and onto her desk.

He went by the room. Yesterday's bribe had bought a tiny private room with an old, flat bed and a deflated pillow. Irma was asleep. Her blackened, puffy face no longer looked like her. The nose was fatter, the cheeks lumpy, and a few stitches sutured together the flesh around one eye.

Lena was scared and impatient. She asked how Irma was doing.

"She was asleep."

"Then let me see her."

He started the car and drove out of the Unity Medical Complex lot. "There's no need to involve her anymore."

Lena remained silent until the train station appeared in front of them. Then: "Well?"

He parked near a row of horses with knotted legs and chests. "Well?"

"Wait," he said.

The station was a dark, stone monstrosity that sucked up the morning light. Eyes followed Lena—soldiers and beggars. They heard her heels against the cobblestones. Emil shook off a beggar at the door who clutched at his jacket. Peering from above, the sculpted stone hawk sat on a ledge, at rest, wings tight to its sides. Then they were inside the cool, airy station, swallowed by its shadows.

They sat in the first-class waiting area, drinking something that claimed to be coffee. It was terrible stuff, the black, ground-acorn muck that had come with wartime and still lingered in public places.

"How long?"

"What?" He had leaned as far back as possible on the wooden bench to reduce the strain on his back.

"When does the train leave?"

The station clock said twelve-thirty. "Half an hour."

"We're going to Cluj? Romania?"

She had memorized the departures schedule, he realized. "Not the whole way."

She sank into quiet speculation, marking up the map in her

head. Through the windows he watched young Russian soldiers toss a wooden ball back and forth on the platform. There were five of them in their ragged uniforms, laughing whenever someone dropped the ball.

"I feel sorry for them," said Lena.

He watched them play a little more. "You should feel sorry for the rest of us."

They gave themselves a little cheer, raising hands over their heads.

She looked for a cigarette. There were a few others in the waiting room—a wealthy couple looked at them from the far gray wall, and a boy slept on a chair. She lit up and whispered, "How old do you think those soldiers are?"

"Seventeen, eighteen," he said.

"And they're peasants. You can tell by the way they walk and how they wear their uniforms. You think they want to be here?"

They were kicking the ball now, as if it were a soccer ball. Content enough, he thought.

"They want to be at home," she said. "They want their mamas and their little farm girlfriends. They want their Mother Russia. They go crazy here."

Emil straightened and looked at her gazing at the soldiers. Her face fell sadly into softer features. Her cheeks, her lips, her eyes.

The platform was crowded with farmers who had sold their vegetables early and had already begun drinking. They smelled like rotted meat and sweat. They held milk bottles filled with homemade brandies that they moved aside when Lena marched through them. Emil carried her bag with general success, and helped her up the steps. In the train corridor, men in earth-toned jackets clogged the small space with their smoke, and the least-full compartment they found contained a mother and her boy, curled together against the window, snoring. Emil put their bags in the overhead netting and sat beside the door's curtain. He watched her adjust her stockings beneath her skirt, then take a small mirror out of her bag and stare into it.

The conductor whistled down the platform. They felt the brakes releasing, the pull and counterpull, then the grind of the train moving southward.

"Ruscova," he said to her.

"*What?*"

He tried to keep his voice quiet, but it was almost drowned by the laboring engines and laughter from the corridor. "It's near the Romanian border."

She snapped her mirror shut. "It's your home village, isn't it?"

He nodded. "But I grew up in the Capital."

She looked over the sleepers' heads at the city thinning into farmland. "Why does everyone think their home village is the best place in the world? I'd never force anyone to go to Stryy. That's unmitigated torture."

She was looking at him again, and he didn't know what to answer.

"What's this Ruscova like?"

He told her the details that came to him.

When she repeated his words, her voice was full of mockery: "Peasants and *beautiful* hills and *big* wooden gates." She shook her head. "You haven't been there in a while, have you?"

"Four years."

"And you're . . . twenty-five?"

"Two," he said. "Twenty-two."

Her mouth slid down her face, and she turned the purse over in her lap, then opened it and closed it. She closed her eyes. She opened them.

"It's quiet and safe," he said quickly, hopefully. "You can stay until I've figured this out."

"Until you figure it out?" She was herself again. "*That's* reassuring." She sighed. "Twenty-*two*?"

When the conductor arrived, he bought tickets for them both. The mother and her child were still asleep, but the conductor shook them awake. He looked over their tickets a moment, considered something, then told them to go back to second class.

She dozed a while, and he, after finding a position that did not hurt too much, rested his eyes. The hills dimmed as the low sun elongated their shadows, and after they had stopped in and left Béréhové, Lena opened her eyes and smiled sleepily. "Is all this really about little Janos?"

"You tell me." He opened his own eyes.

She wiped her face hard enough to stretch the lids over her skull sockets. "Nothing to tell, my Comrade Inspector. I swear." A little yawn escaped her. "Janos leaves me, then he comes back. Then he's dead. Take that as a warning." She winked.

Emil smiled. "What did he do for money? Other than song-writing."

"I don't know what he did for money." She fell to picking at the hem of her skirt.

"You never asked?"

"You've never been in a failed marriage." There was a trace of scorn in her voice. "Have you."

The early, fall dusk had begun without them noticing. They were nearing the outskirts of Vynohradiv, where light poles along the tracks flashed into the compartment. Her face was descending into thought like a woman in the moving pictures: the soft pulse of frames and light.

"He went to Berlin, you said. Six months ago?"

She nodded, pulsing. "Yes. Back in February."

"Why Berlin?"

She reached her arms over her head to stretch them out, then covered a yawn with the back of her hand. "He'd been there before, once a year at least. He told me he was visiting a friend.

But I don't know for sure." She looked at his pale, drawn expression. "What? Do you know?"

He knew nothing, but looking at her made him feel like he was seventeen again, looking at that flickering window to the world.

"Stryy was different than I remembered," she told him after a while.

"How so?"

She shrugged. "The usual. I hadn't been there in years, and it was so small. Nothing going on. Not a decent coffee in the whole town."

"What did you do with your father?" asked Emil.

She looked at him before answering. "The family crypt. My great-grandfather saw one on a trip to Paris, and decided the Hanics needed one too. A small marble house with panels for each of us." She wedged her bag between her cheek and the rattling window, which quieted it. "Maybe someday you'll have to take me to Stryy, Inspector."

"Not for a long time," he whispered.

Her eyes were closed. She said, "You're the only one I've got left, Emil Brod. You took a bullet for me. You're all I've got."

He almost tried to explain that the bullet hadn't been for her, it had been the result of his own stubborn stupidity, but said nothing.

Men in the corridor made loud jokes about stupid policemen and hacked on their laughter. Gray curtains of smoke obscured their red faces, and he saw they were drunk farmers who had snuck up from second class.

Lena was asleep again, her cheek reflected on the window. The city of Hust came and went, and the black plains rose into the southern foothills of the Carpathians. But he could not sleep. It wasn't just the pain. He reached in his pocket for his watch, but it wasn't there. After a few tries he realized it had been stolen. A pickpocket. Somewhere back in the Capital.

CHAPTER NINETEEN

****

They reached Sighet, the provincial capital, after eight. The seven hours in that train had about killed him. Outside the station he moved back and forth and twisted himself gingerly, pressing one hand to the aching small of his back, the other to his stitched stomach.

It was said in the Academy that the last thing an inspector should do is admit frailty to a victim. It would undermine the victim's faith in the organs of administrative justice, and lead to the demise of faith in the administrative systems in general. In a people's democracy, faith was the only power that kept the order from collapsing into anarchy. The professor who said all this had spoken with a dense Russian accent, mauling words like *faith* and *collapse*. The students had all thought it funny; and it was, for a while.

Lena had no faith in the organs of administrative justice—he didn't know where her faith lay—so there was nothing to hide. She watched him bend and twist, and held her bag close to herself. After a few minutes she asked a farmer for a ride into the center of town, and helped Emil into the cart without comment.

They ate omelets in a hotel café, and while she was in the bathroom he approached a table of three farmers who dropped their eyes to their plum brandies and fell quiet. But when he asked about getting to Ruscova, they caught the roll of his slightly affected local accent and smiled broadly. When one suggested a particular friend to drive them, another cut him off, claiming the man was a drunk. He pointed to the window and said to take the train, but the third reminded him that no trains went to Ruscova. The first finally admitted he didn't know Ruscova. "It's small," said Emil. The third told the first that he was an idiot, because Bogdan lived in Ruscova. The second said that a bus went to Viseu de Sus and stopped at the end of the long dirt road that led to Ruscova.

"But the lady's coming?" asked the first one, and shook his head. "Can't ask her to walk all the way down that road."

They nodded in solemn agreement.

"The bus has left, anyway," said the second.

"Talk to Bogdan," said the third, leaning into his cigarette and watching as Lena returned with her handbag folded beneath her arm. They were all watching. Lena settled at her table with smooth self-confidence, not even looking for him. White-skinned. Immaculate.

Bogdan's cart, tied to a massive brown mare with red tassels hanging by her ears, was parked outside a Hungarian bar, across from the park. He was covering a floor of potatoes with burlap. His thin face peered at Emil from under his wide, black hat, but relaxed as they talked. Bogdan remembered the name *Brod* only vaguely, and Emil admitted they seldom visited Ruscova these days.

A little way into the journey, Bogdan began talking politics and did not stop until they had reached the village. He said he could remember when this was Hungary, and, briefly, Romania. He said he didn't know who this General Secretary Mihai was, but he didn't trust anyone who was known only by his first name. "It's impolite, isn't it?" In the thirties he was for the king because no one else said anything that made so much sense, but when the king got them into the war, he was no longer sure. He'd heard all the rumors of the king's mistress, the catty Jewess who dragged him off to Paris and London for their lovemaking, but found it all hard to believe. "I can read well enough," he said. "But how can you believe anything in a paper that uses exclamation points?" Emil admitted he didn't know. Bogdan had a blemish like a dark hole on his cheek. He wiped it with an index finger as he tossed the reins with the other hand. He said the Germans weren't so bad to them, not to the farmers, not even when they used the road to get to Stalingrad. "They left us alone. Why would they bother with Ruscova?" But once the Russians were on their border the Germans became desperate. "I remember a young man on a motorcycle. Blond hair, looked very much like one of them. He drove up and down the main street shooting his pistol. A little thing." A Walther, Emil suggested, and Bogdan nodded. "It was muddy, and his tires became stuck. Do you remember this?"

Emil shook his head, but it was a lie; he remembered that hot day, the shouts and gunshots as he hovered behind a fence, watching it all happen.

"Well, the boy had shot old Harnass and Marta Ieronim. Marta died soon after. The boy had gone off his head. You weren't around then?"

Emil said he didn't remember this as his stomach shook painfully. Behind him, Lena was trying to sleep on a mattress of potatoes.

"Well, he finally couldn't get his motorcycle moving, and by then he'd run out of bullets. He shouted at us. He said we were stupid Slavs and we were going to eat ourselves alive." Bogdan shook his head, smiling into the night. "Imagine that! He had quite a mouth on him." He snapped the reins and *tsk*ed the horse into a trot. "He threw his gun at us, then rocks. *That* was a mistake. Some of our boys threw rocks back at him, then the rest of us started into it. *Tsk-tsk.*" He looked back at Emil, as if he were going to ask a question, then shook his head. "When the German boy realized what was happening, he ran out of the village. It was the middle of the day, and he couldn't hide from us. There aren't too many trees, you know." Emil did. "We surrounded him on a small hill that was thick with big rocks, the size of your fist. I remember his mouth was bloody, and he shouted at us. More of the same. That he wasn't afraid, that we would eat ourselves. Big man. He had a lovely uniform that got all dusty and dirty. Then we threw our rocks." His finger had been back at his mole for a while now, stroking. "I'd never seen a man die like that before. I'd heard about it from the priest, they killed people like that in the Bible. The body," he said, "it falls apart under all that. And the boy, he screamed for a while, a long while, and then he didn't." Bogdan paused, clucking his tongue at the horse. "It's a terrible way; I don't know why anyone would want to kill like that. *Tsk-tsk*. It takes such a long time."

Emil looked off into the night. The breeze off the plains was cool.

He had been there, and he hadn't been there. Through the slats in the fence, he had seen the boy on his motorcycle, skidding around, shouting, shooting. Then running out of gas. He threw his empty Walther at them, some rocks, then sprinted off. The whole town followed, but Emil lingered. He took the pistol from the dust and pocketed it. His grandparents were visiting another village, and, alone, plans formed in his head. Then he heard it, the German shrieking.

"Then the Russians came in," Bogdan said after a while, muttering bitterly. "And this *Mihai* wanted to collectivize us." But they were already on the outskirts of Ruscova.

He left them at the door of the village's one bar—really the extra, candlelit room of a village widow—and Emil forced him to take some koronas for his trouble. It was a long fight, but Emil finally won. Lena hovered in the background, looking uncomfortably at the small wooden houses surrounded by weathered fences and the few villagers passing with burlap sacks and pails.

Emil didn't know the widow who served them tea. She stood near the wall with crossed arms in the flickering light, and stared.

So did two small, sturdy men nursing brandies at another table. Lena sipped her tea. She was plainly uncomfortable.

"Ma'am," Emil said loudly. Everyone looked up. "Do you know Irina Kula? I'm looking for her."

The widow frowned deeply. "Of course I know Irina. Who are you?"

"From the Capital," said the farmer with the mustache.

"I'm Emil Brod."

The second, smooth-faced farmer stood up, and Emil thought his face was familiar. "Valentin Brod's son!"

The others looked at the grinning farmer, then back at Emil. The widow began to laugh.

Irina Kula's two-room house was as near as everything in Ruscova—a few houses down, then back through someone's garden—and Irina glowed when she saw Emil. She pulled them both inside with her hands on their backs and called for her friend Greta, who was waiting in the kitchen. They were two fat, aproned women with sunburnt smiles. Their short hair had gone frizzy and useless years ago. Irina served plates of baked apples, one after the other.

"Tell me," she said, watching them eat. "Your grandmother—how is she?"

"She works now, in a factory. Textiles."

"Shirts?" asked Greta.

"Slacks and jackets."

"Factory pants," Greta muttered disapprovingly. "And that red husband of hers?"

"Still red."

He told them about his travels in the north, the cold Arctic, the cold Finns, and admitted to the massive beauty of Helsinki. Lena, he noticed, listened closely to all of it.

"But you came back," Irina said, smiling.

"Where would I go?"

Greta slid a soft mound of apple from her wrinkled fingers into her mouth. "You came back and married." She smiled at Lena as she chewed, and, after a moment, Lena smiled back.

Emil avoided as many details as possible, only enough to make them understand the severity and secrecy of his request for a room. "Just a few days. For her safety."

Irina glowed. "She'll live here forever if she likes—such a beautiful girl! Don't you think?"

"*Indeed,*" said Greta, nodding.

Irina gave a wide smile that was short on teeth. "She can be my daughter."

"I thought I was your daughter," said Greta haughtily, and both women laughed.

After a late dinner of pork-stuffed cabbage, Emil smoked on the front porch, watching two shadowy horse-forms grazing in a black field across the road. They moved in increments, holding their bowed heads to the crabgrass, unaware. There were other small homes farther along, some with high fences blocking them from sight. Irina's home and a few others had no fences, and he could see straight through to the low beginnings of the Carpathians.

The door groaned, and Lena squatted beside him. She blinked, adjusting to the darkness. "You've got a nice little town."

"Not mine," he said. "Not much, either." He pointed. "Some houses, fences and mountains, like I told you. The occasional horse." He wondered how long she'd be able to take living in the sticks without her scotches and American cigarettes, in a hard bed, surrounded by the clumsy handcrafts of the peasantry. "Is Irina still up?"

"She's listening to the radio," whispered Lena, and Emil realized they had both been whispering all along.

As if on cue, tinny voices drifted through the window, sub-merged in hisses, then rose again like a swimmer struggling in the middle of an ocean.

"Only one station, she told me. And only sometimes."

Emil pressed his palms against his knees. He reached for his cane. "A walk?"

They made it to the road without speaking, then crossed into the field where the horses cantered nervously away. Lena twisted long grass into a knot. "When I was in Stryy again, I was reminded what it means to be alone. It's not good."

Emil knew, and said as much.

"It's hard to find someone," she said. "To trust, I mean. It's rare."

He didn't know how to answer that. The breeze was chilling him, but he hardly noticed.

She looked at the mountains, then back at the village. There were no lights. "How long are you going to be gone?"

"A week. If I take longer, I'll send someone to get you."

"You're going to Berlin?"

He squatted, trying to get rid of the ache in his stomach that had pestered him since the train. Lena Crowder was no fool.

"You'll fly?"

"I've never been on a plane," he admitted. "I'm terrified."

"You shouldn't go. You could get killed."

He wondered, amid her innuendoes and his own mounting confusion, if she understood how much danger *she* was in. Two old women could do nothing to protect her.

When she walked, her skirt moved with the breeze. "I'll write you a check. You can't afford the trip."

"I'll find a way."

He heard her exhale a soft, weary laugh in the darkness, but couldn't see her smile. "Not the People's Militia. They won't pay a single korona." She was a little ahead of him in the grass, standing with her legs apart. She was so quiet he could hardly hear her, even this close. "You're not sure about any of this, are you?"

He squatted again as the pain shot through him, and when he looked up she was right there, standing over him, shaking. The airy smell of her perspiration filled him. From the sound of her breaths, he knew she was crying. He stood up quickly, unsure, and held her shoulders. He slid his small, flat hand across her back and felt her ribs shaking against his chest. His cheeks were wet from her tears, and her short, hot gasps warmed them. His cane slipped from his grasp, and now both hands were on her.

"I'm sorry," she whispered.

She kissed him first, lightly on the neck, and when he kissed her salty lips it felt as if they had done this all their lives. There was no Janos Crowder, no People's Militia, no one. His legs gave out, and she fell with him into the grass. It had been such a long day.

CHAPTER TWENTY

****

O n the train he tried to ignore both his aching back and stomach, and his fears for Lena. He tried to focus on the facts.

February 1948, Janos Crowder made a trip to Berlin. This was before the present Russian blockade and Allied airlift.

Soon after Janos returned to the Capital, he had enough money to take an apartment in town and leave his wealthy wife.

(*His wife,* Emil thought. In the field last night, she kissed his scars.)

Six months later, in early August 1948, Janos made a half-hearted attempt to get back together with Lena, and after a week was kicked out.

One week after *that*—August 18—Janos was killed.

Then his building supervisor was killed in the same way.

Emil had few doubts: Jerzy Michalec, alias Smerdyakov, was his man, and Smerdyakov used an unknown German to do his work. For Emil it was not a question of who murdered these men, but *why.* Presumably, they were killed over an object that Janos Crowder and Aleks Tudor had in their possessions. Something that could fit into the pages of a book.

(He felt the blades of grass cutting into his palms as he held himself over her moist face.)

He again looked over the photograph of Jerzy Michalec and the tall German who had shot him three times. Certainly *these*

photos couldn't be the objects that had killed two men? A meeting at an automobile. Nighttime, talking. They proved nothing.

Another photograph, he thought.

When they called her that first time to tell her Janos was dead,
she felt as if she were being watched. *You know the feeling.*

Maybe they were watching her, waiting for her to run after the
photograph. But she didn't, because she knew nothing.

(When he closed his eyes, he was back in that field, at the foot
of the Carpathians.)

It was three in the afternoon when he dropped by the state bank,
cashed Lena's exorbitant check, and then made it to the station.
Big Ferenc was getting ready to leave with Stefan, but they
stopped when they saw him clicking along with his cane. Leonek
sat up in his chair, waking. "Brod! What the hell?"

Emil went straight to Brano Sev, who was sliding his file
drawer closed, watching him approach. Emil dragged over a spare
chair and settled into it.

"Comrade Brod," said Sev—round, flat face, tiny eyes.

Everyone in the station was watching them.

"I need some help," said Emil. He neither whispered nor raised
his voice, so the others had to lean to listen. "Information."

Brano Sev gave a minimal shrug and brought his fingers
together on the impeccably clean desktop.

"There's a man who went to Berlin last February. I want to
know who he visited."

The small mole on his cheek didn't move when he spoke.
"Depends on the man."

"Janos Crowder."

"Ah ha."

Emil lowered his voice—just a little, but enough. "Can you
contact the Berlin MVD?"

Sev looked at his hands, then at the buttons on his leather coat.
The hardly visible shrug again. "Maybe."

"Can I know by tomorrow?"

The security inspector gave a sharp, economical nod.

Leonek was waiting at Emil's desk. His eyes shifted back and forth between Emil and Sev, as if he couldn't make them match. "What's *this*?"

Emil laid his cane beside the typewriter. "Can you get me a visa?"

"A what?"

"I need travel papers. Berlin. Here's my passport." He grunted and withdrew from his inside pocket the hard, maroon booklet.

"*Berlin?*"

"Spare me the surprise."

"And this?" He touched some koronas sticking out of the passport.

"Bribes, I suppose."

Leonek rubbed the bills between his thumb and forefinger. "I'm coming with you."

"No, you're not."

"You'll get killed."

"I need you elsewhere," said Emil.

"Where?"

"First, the visa."

Leonek frowned and handed back the money. He held the passport beside his face. "Come on."

Roberto did a fine job acting overjoyed to see Emil. He scrambled up and over the counter and patted his shoulders violently. "A ghost! It's the curse of Sergei—that accursed typewriter!"

"Shut up," said Leonek, though Emil smiled.

Roberto patted Leonek on the cheek, his lazy eye observing the far wall, and spoke reverently. "I'm sorry, my sensitive comrade." Then he turned back to Emil, loud again: "So what can I do for my most abused customer? Typewriter ribbon? Blotters? Lamps? Erasers? Picture frames?"

Emil nodded at Leonek. "Tell him."

"Travel visa."

Roberto's smile slid away. "Now *that*, my friends, is highly complicated. Do you realize?"

"But not impossible," said Emil.

"*Nothing*," Roberto explained, "is impossible these days. The only issue is *how*."

"And tomorrow," said Leonek.

Roberto looked as though he had just witnessed a murder. "My *God*! Friends! How can I?"

"And for free," said Leonek, his stony face making no suggestion of flexibility.

Roberto emitted more sounds of protest—whimpers and shouts—and pulled at his hair, but in the end took the passport. "For you," he said to Leonek. "And that's *done*."

In the corridor, Leonek explained that, a year ago, Roberto was caught selling surplus Militia pistols in the Canal District. Leonek saved him from being sent to the labor camps. He had milked that favor for as long as possible, and Emil's visa constituted the final payment.

"You're a good man to know," said Emil.

Leonek shoved his hands into his pockets. "Take a walk?"

They left the station house, and Leonek guided him through a couple turns, stopping often for Emil to catch up. They were soon in a busy market—loud voices, hands shoving vegetables in their faces.

"I've been asking around," Leonek said, nodding an old woman and her wooden spoons away. "Like a real inspector."

"A real one, huh?" Emil tried to keep up.

"About your Michalec. He's up for a vote in one week."

Emil started to ask for clarification, but quickly understood. "Politburo?"

Leonek stopped just past a butcher with gutted lambs hung up to dry. "You think he's untouchable now? Just *wait*."

Emil remembered Smerdyakov's explanation: *We, as members of the Political Section, have very specific duties. And these duties confer upon us specific* rights.

"How did you learn this?"

Leonek smiled and leaned close to his ear. "Your favorite informer, Dora with the girl's name."

That name brought back everything—the suspicion and abuse of his first week in Homicide, the shooting and the two dead children in Republic Park. He hated this man he had never met, who had nearly killed him without even knowing who Emil Brod was. "Can you trust him?"

Leonek shrugged. "Eighty percent of the time."

Emil started moving again, and finally told him what he'd done with Lena. "She's safe for now," he said, but felt the doubt swell in his gut. "If something happens you'll have to get her. I'll give you directions."

Leonek smiled broadly. "I can vacation in the provinces while you're vacationing in Berlin." They were out of the market and in the narrow, winding alleys. "Bring an umbrella. I hear things are dropping from the sky." He nodded at a Russian soldier who passed them. The soldier, surprised, smiled and nodded back.

He gave his grandparents silence for their concern, and the next morning the chief gave him an angry frown. He called Emil into his office and closed the door. "Sit." Emil did. Moska walked around him, looking down, and settled on the edge of the desk. His form arched over Emil. "I hear you're working on a dead case."

"A dead case?" He spoke with measured stupidity.

"Maybe you've forgotten," Moska began again. "In the hospital—you certainly weren't yourself, were you?"

"Hardly."

"I specifically told you the Janos Crowder case was closed."

"Yes," Emil nodded. "Of course that's a closed case. You told me."

The chief pursed his lips and looked at the thick, barklike nail on his right thumb. He spoke quietly. "You've been with the Crowder woman, Inspector Brod. She called here and left a message, and you met with her."

"That's true."

"And now she's apparently gone missing."

"Who reported her missing?"

"None of your concern," said Moska, "because the Crowder case is closed."

"Agreed," said Emil, nodding. "Janos Crowder's case. But Lena Crowder has been the victim of burglary and threats."

"Until she's dead, it's no concern of yours." The chief stopped looking at his nail. "Tell her to call the district police, Brod. Burglaries are their jurisdiction."

Perhaps it was only Emil's hereditary hopefulness, but it sounded like the chief was reading reluctantly from a script that had been prepared in other offices, in the Central Committee back rooms. His words came out stiffly and without proper conviction. Emil shifted to take pressure off his stomach. "You're right, Comrade Chief. I'll drop the case right this minute." The lie was a breeze.

"What about this?" He lifted a maroon passport from his desk and held it between his thumb and forefinger.

Emil didn't know what to say.

"I'm not an absolute fool," said the chief. He opened the passport, turning pages until he had reached the German visa. He shook his head. "You do realize, don't you, that outside our border, your badge is worth nothing?"

Emil nodded.

Chief Moska closed it again and stared at the cover, thinking. Then he handed it to Emil. "Brod?"

"Yes, Chief?" He stood.

Moska looked at him. "Sympathy will only take you so far."

****

The others were arriving, clutching coffees and blinking tired eyes. Brano Sev was already at work in the corner, speaking into his phone. His whole body tilted toward the wall in a position of urgency.

Emil waded through some clutter that had built up over the last couple days—an informative proclamation on the tense situation in Berlin (*When all nations allow Germany to be a nation again, all nations will deserve their annihilation*), two notes from yesterday asking that he return his grandparents' calls, and a sealed envelope marked by typed capitals: BROD. The words cut into the thin paper.

7 October 1948, Thursday

Comrade Inspector Brod,

Regarding our exchange of last evening, the following facts have been ascertained from Berlin:

1. On 10 February 1948, J. Crowder arrived in Berlin by Aeroflot #34B. From Schonefeld, he took a taxi to Wilhelm Strasse 14, the residence of Konrad Messer, owner of a nightclub called "Die Letze Katze"—or "The Last Cat." Messer is originally from Heidelberg.

2. Comrade Crowder stayed overnight and in the morning crossed into the American sector at the Brandenburg Gate. Our Berlin comrades followed him as far as the end of the Tiergarten, but for various reasons lost track of him.

3. At 20:30, Comrade Crowder returned to the Soviet sector and took a room in the Hotel Warsaw. In the evening he had drinks in the lounge, and a search of his belongings came up with nothing of interest.

4. He was allowed to leave Berlin without questioning. He returned on 12 February, Aeroflot #29.

It is my sincere wish that this information is of service to your investigations.

Respectfully,

It ended with a scrawled flourish of signature.

"Still here?" asked Leonek. He was crossing the room, feeling his pockets for change. "Get some coffee?"

But Emil didn't look up. This was exactly what he had wanted from Brano Sev, but now that he had it in his hands, the intricacy of the details disturbed him. They kept names upon names in the Russian MVD files, and he suspected his own—since he had traveled outside the country—was relatively thick.

"Emil?" Leonek said.

Brano Sev had hung up the telephone and was staring at him. Emil nodded his recognition. The security inspector turned his simple, peasant's face back to the paperwork on his desk.

"Some coffee?"

He blinked at Leonek and knew, finally, that he had made a mistake. He had suspected it before, ever since they sat in the station waiting for the Sighet train, but now it was undeniable. There was no place to hide in this country; there was no place out of reach. He had left her in a little village, unprotected, and anyone with his file would be able to figure it out in five minutes. Michalec had a whole universe of files at his fingertips. He could send any number of shadows into the countryside to close in on Lena Crowder.

"Leonek," he said, deciding everything as the words came out. "You have to get her for me. Forget everything else. You have to protect her."

Leonek began to make a joke about only wanting coffee, but changed his mind when he saw Emil's face.

CHAPTER TWENTY-ONE

****

T he rain-wet blacktop stretched unnervingly into the darkness—this midnight flight had been the earliest available. He
imagined slick rubber tires skidding forward, then the explosion
amid the pine trees at the far end of the runway. The Soviet stewardess, a pretty Georgian in a long, straight skirt, told him to
hurry. He turned back to the fat Aeroflot plane and mounted the
steps. His feet were numb.

Through the window he saw the propellers kick and begin to
spin. The vibration shook the whole cabin. Businessmen and
government men—all the shades of Slav—cracked jokes among
themselves. The stewardess made sure he was strapped in, and he
noticed her hair was tied tight beneath a blue cap that reminded
him of his nurse, Katka, in her medical cap. Hospitals.

Again, violent deaths. Explosions.

She smiled very close to his face—some musky scent from
Moscow department stores—and he tried to relax, thinking of
the field in Ruscova, of Lena, but he only saw men in tall grass,
converging on Irina Kula's fenceless house.

The takeoff was shaky and insecure, but no one else seemed concerned.

He could tell the government bureaucrats by the smug way
they called the stewardess over and tapped her ass to send her on
her way. The businessmen were the ones who laughed loudly; the

bureaucrats supplied the jokes. He'd heard there was big business to be done in Berlin—supplying a decimated city always took work. And these days, with all supply trucks cut off from the western half of the city, some westerners migrated east during the day to buy the goods the Americans and British hadn't yet dropped from their planes.

He'd only seen pictures of Berlin: flattened residential buildings and fire-gutted churches. Some newer news clips showed women and children wrapped in gray blankets, crowds huddling around military transports full of bread. Three years after the defeat, and Berlin was still crippled and hungry.

When he felt flush he waved at the stewardess and she brought a paper cup of tepid water. She held it to his lips and whispered something he could not hear above the whine of the engines.

Then the cabin became very cold. For those without heavy coats, she retrieved blankets, and, covered by his, Emil turned to the window, where black clouds merged into black, starless sky. He wondered what the pilots could be using for navigation. He felt like a peasant facing a locomotive. Everything was beyond him.

Emil was astonished by how solid the chilly earth at Schonefeld felt. The Russian customs officer, a severe young soldier, looked him up and down and jotted his name in a notebook. A second guard stamped passports between yawns. It was three-thirty in the morning.

A taxi driver approached him, and Emil shared the ride with a fat bureaucrat he thought he recognized as one of the famous "thick Muscovites," but wasn't sure. He had a dramatic mane of wavy hair rising from his forehead. "Hell of a town," he said, nodding at the shadowy ruins passing them by. "Been here before?"

Emil shook his head.

He stuck a thumbnail between his lips and picked at his front teeth. "But you can't sleep here anymore. This trash with the

Allies. Blockade, airlift, *Christ*—planes all hours of the night!" He cracked his window and let the cold hiss inside. "The Germans are remarkable people. Like slow-witted insects who don't get it. They just turn up the jukeboxes and dance!"

He laughed at his own observation, and Emil noticed the taxi driver looking at them in the rearview. He was a thick-jowled man who steered with one arm. The other sleeve was pinned flat. A veteran, maybe. A one-armed veteran forced to listen to foreigners' views on his people. The bureaucrat opened the window the rest of the way, and they could now hear the far-off murmur of airplanes.

The Hotel Warsaw was one of the few comfortable places in the Soviet sector. Half the buildings on the street were shells of rubble. He had seen this kind of damage on that train ride back from Helsinki, in Poland and Czechoslovakia, tall buildings compressed until they came up to your nose. It made him wonder how much space the Capital would take up if all the air were sucked out of it. A home was always smaller than you thought.

The Warsaw was generally filled to capacity, but when Emil tried out his German on the morose desk clerk, he learned that a small, cold room—just big enough for the bed frame and a sink—had recently been cleaned. He took it. His head lay near the windowpane, and through it came the whine of engines. It was like flies buzzing in his ear, and he wished he had a bottle of plum brandy to put himself out. He wished he had a stomach that could take that much liquor. He wished he could stop thinking of Lena. He would have to lie here until sleep, at its leisure, claimed him. Then, from the exhaustion of his anxiety and the low, dull pain of his wounds, it did.

The airplanes had not ceased.

After a shower down the hall, he bought the sector's cur-

rency—Ostmarks—at a bad rate from the front desk, and break-
fasted in the hotel café. The bureaucrat from last night sat with a
young brunette who looked like she had weathered a storm. She
sipped at her coffee and stared straight ahead, while the bureaucrat shoveled fluffy eggs into his mouth.

It was a cool, brisk morning. There were a lot of pedestrians
out, going to work, which was strange against the backdrop of a
demolished city. It brought him back to that first year when he
returned to the Capital, after the Arctic. Women in thick heels
stepped carefully over broken bricks and stood outside shops
waiting for work and busses. There were few men—German
men, at least—except the very young and the very old. Russian
soldiers with rifles walked in pairs, watching over everything
under a sun that gave no warmth. It was all too familiar.

The rubble of broken buildings had been collected at some
corners, and children scrambled up the little mountains, laughing. Some workers in coveralls held hammers and long, discolored boards cannibalized from exploded homes. Now and then
his cane slipped, and he grew accustomed to watching the broken sidewalks. Ahead, a crowd descended into a metro station.

Always, the backdrop of planes. Buzzing.

It took a while, maybe an hour, before he picked them out. Ever
since arriving, he had been paying close attention to faces. Maybe
too much attention. He hadn't seen a thing. When eyes met his he
paused a moment to give them a once-over, or stopped now and
then to look around, playing the lost tourist. Then, while looking
at a store window stocked with ten colors of fabric, he noticed a
man pause at a display of children's clothes. Low-slung fedora. A
leather overcoat.

He couldn't know for sure, so he crossed to the other side of
the street, took the corner, and waited in the blackened doorway
of a firebombed restaurant. The man appeared soon, hands in his

coat, and was followed by a partner. Fedora, leather coat and, for distinction, thick prescription glasses. The first was wide-faced, fat, while the one with glasses was thin. They both had serene, unsmiling faces.

Russian Intelligence. MVD. He was expected.

He left the doorway and took some streets at random. His shadows held back as he made his way up streets; then, just before he took a corner, they began jogging after him. Near an uprooted park, he found a sidewalk café and sat in the shade. By the time his coffee had arrived, the two men were at the edge of the park, waiting. They sometimes came together and talked, nodding and shrugging, and once a third man recognized them and shook their hands before leaving. Emil paid for his coffee, but did not leave. He gazed at the other customers, some pretty girls and an old man. He tried to clear his mind, to look utterly at ease, but when he did that, Lena came inevitably to him, and worry thickened his throat.

Finally, the shadow with the glasses spoke to his partner (who gave an unexpected, broad smile) and walked away.

Emil waited. Once the man was out of sight—looking for a telephone, perhaps, or a car—Emil got up and left the café.

The abandoned partner hesitated, unsure and again unsmiling, then followed.

Emil took quick turns, hobbling along, and dove into small, unlabeled streets. He was getting himself lost, he knew, but that wasn't his worry now. In some dark alleys, men slept among trash cans, and in others, plump prostitutes muttered at him. Then he appeared in an empty, bomb-damaged courtyard with three possible avenues of escape. It was lined with trashcans on one side and a high pile of discarded clothing on the other. Emil crouched behind the clothes, as low as the pain would allow. The soiled clothes stank of death.

In no time the fat Russian appeared, gasping. He looked up

each alley, considering the possibilities. Then he chose the middle way, and rushed forward.

Emil waited for his breath to return and his heart to slow. Then he backtracked, leaning more heavily on his cane. His stomach was troubling him again. A prostitute recognized him and smiled. "Change your mind, sweetheart?"

He offered a few coins and asked the fastest way to Wilhelm Strasse.

CHAPTER TWENTY–TWO

****

Wilhelm Strasse 14 was one of four buildings that survived on its block. It rose three floors, noticeably tall and skinny amid the ruins scattered around it. On the steps, three children blocked Emil's way.

"Pay the toll," said the tallest one, maybe twelve.

"Yes yes," said a smaller one. Eight, or nine. "Money."

Emil considered their grimy, open hands a moment. "Listen," he said. Their faces wrinkled as they tried to place his accent. "You clean these steps, and I'll pay you. I mean it—will you look at them? They're filthy."

The tall boy cocked a head that had been shaved bald to rid him of lice. "You're Russian?"

"Close enough." He stepped past them into the foyer, where the mailboxes placed a K. MESSER on the second floor. He looked back at the children and made a swirling motion with his index finger. "Clean!"

Hardly any light leaked into the stairwell, only the buzz of planes, and he had to feel his way up. There was something foul-smelling here, turpentine or urine; he couldn't place which. On the landing, he had two doors to choose from. One had been struck repeatedly until the wood around the handle had shattered. When he pushed it open, dusty sunlight from the empty apartment illuminated the other door behind him. He knocked and waited.

"Yes?" came a thin voice.

Emil knocked again. "Konrad Messer?"

The door opened a few inches. A tall man with dark hair swept over his brow stared at him. "The very same. Who the hell are you?"

"Emil Brod. I'm a homicide inspector."

Konrad Messer nodded. "Do you know what time it is?"

"Noon," said Emil.

"Smartest Slav I ever met." Konrad showed straight, clean teeth when he smiled, then licked his lips, and at first Emil thought from these gestures that the man was scared, really terrified, then he wasn't sure.

"I need to ask some questions." Emil took off his hat. "I've come a long way."

Konrad opened the door. He wore a short, rose-colored silk robe and Oriental slippers. "Do I look *ready* to answer your questions?"

Emil was out of words. He shrugged.

"Where are you from, then?"

Emil told him. "I'm here about Janos Crowder."

Konrad judged him a moment more. His thin, arched brows were almost sculpted, and his skin looked soft. But his thick nose was as bent as a boxer's. He sighed finally. "Then come *on*. I need to get ready for work anyhow."

The bright apartment was fully furnished. Konrad pointed beside the sofa to a large radio set.

"Put something on. And don't touch *anything*." He disappeared behind a door.

When the radio warmed and the dial glowed, Emil heard a voice speaking in German with a heavy American accent. "*Operation Vittles, the goodwill of the Allies toward the German people.*"

"Something *lighter*?" came Konrad's annoyed voice.

There was big band music on another station, Duke Ellington, and Emil tapped his foot, remembering the music he'd heard in Helsinki. It was fast music, good for dancing, but when he returned home there was none of that business anymore. Stravinski, Shostakovich, Tchaikovsky. No Ellington, no Mercer, no Basie. He'd almost forgotten the world could produce such fine music.

At the window, Emil hummed beneath his breath and looked out over the field of rubble that surrounded them. Red Army trucks navigated the crumbled hills, and Berliners waited at corners for busses he didn't see. To the west he could just make out Allied planes descending through the haze.

"Quite a view," said Konrad, dressed now in tan slacks and a red cravat folded inside his open collar.

"Janos Crowder came here in February, didn't he?"

"All business." Konrad sat down and took out a cigarette. "Just don't start talking ill of the dead."

Emil pulled up a small cushioned chair and opened his own cigarettes. Despite a fine covering of white powder, he could make out the thick black follicles on Konrad's jaw line. Konrad lit both their cigarettes with a heavy glass lighter.

"Are you working for the Russians?"

Emil shook his head. "I'm just trying to find out why Janos was killed."

"How's that wife of his? Liza?" Konrad picked tobacco from his lip.

"Lena."

"Yeah, I know."

"Someone's after her."

"Someone?"

"To kill her."

Konrad bit the nail on his little finger, and thought. "Fair enough," he said finally, as though something had been decided. He held Emil's gaze. "Janos Crowder was a beautiful man, you know that? Intense eyes, statuesque. Did you ever see him?"

"Only in the morgue."

Konrad's mouth hung open a moment, then closed. "Janos Crowder was a genius. A real one. You've heard his songs?"

Emil nodded.

"Then you know. He wasn't the kind of man who can keep track of the mundane side of life. Money, taxes, friendships. He kept losing it all. It wasn't his fault. No one understood him. Do you follow?"

Emil said he did.

"But I understood him," he said, settling back in the chair. "I think Janos knew that. We were what you would call *very* close."

It was in the enunciation of "close"—*intim*. That, and the robe and all the dramatic sighs. Emil understood completely. He cleared his throat, and knew he was blushing.

Konrad smiled at his discomfort. "This is not so strange. Difficult to prance around in public, maybe, but always a large, unspoken clan. Before the Kristallnacht it was different. We *ran* Berlin. But like everyone, we learned to shut up. Or go join our Jewish friends."

Emil nodded brusquely. "This is why he visited you? You were . . ."

"This is how we knew each other," said Konrad. "We saw each other when we could, usually once a year or so. Keep the fire burning, and so forth. Does that surprise you?" He sculpted the edge of his cigarette ash, rotating it in the ashtray. "But this is not why Janos Crowder visited me in February." He tapped his forehead and smiled. "This time he loved me for my mind."

Emil waited. Duke Ellington had ended, and someone he didn't know played a sappy waltz.

Konrad crossed his legs at the knee. "We'd been in contact for weeks before he came to Berlin. Telephone. A friend of his was in trouble. Was being blackmailed for a lot of money. And the incriminating evidence, it seemed, was here in Berlin. He didn't know what the evidence was, or where. But, knowing of my *extensive* contacts, he asked for my help." Konrad frowned. "I could never say no to him."

Both their cigarettes had gone out, and each offered the other his own. Emil accepted the American tobacco, but Konrad shook his head. "No offense," he said as he lit another one.

He described how he talked with Soviet colonels and lieutenants who frequented his nightclub. "Even the Slavic soul has room for liberal love," he said, toying with Emil. "They come for the stage shows, and stay. All rather wonderful."

Emil realized his arms were clenched uncomfortably, so he crossed them over his stomach. "Go on."

In the mist of their blissful intoxication, the Soviet officers listened to Konrad's subtle inquiries and smiled, clapped their hands, and told him everything. "Janos's friend, it turned out, was very well known to all of them."

"Jerzy Michalec?" Emil tried.

Konrad's eyes swelled. "You really are exceptionally bright for a Slav. You should be proud."

"I am," he said.

"Well, the Russians had no real dirt on this Michalec character—some war hero, they said. But they didn't call him Michalec. Something like—Smerrykov?"

"Smerdyakov. It's from Dostoyevsky," said Emil.

Konrad winked, ever more impressed. "Exactly. So I talked more to my friends—my *German* friends, of which I still have a considerable number. This Michalec—or Smerdyakov—apparently has even a *third* name. Do you know this one as well?"

Emil shook his head.

"Graz."

"Like the city?"

"It's where they first made contact with him."

"The Russians?"

Konrad leaned so close that Emil could feel his warm, moist breath cross the distance between them. "The Gestapo."

Emil blinked.

Konrad waved his surprise aside and leaned back again. "This is long before we marched on Stalingrad. Back when Uncle Josef was still a friend to the Reich. Jerzy Michalec was a Hungarian clerk or something-or-other working out of Vienna, and after we marched into that impeccably tidy country in 'thirty-eight, his

Jewish wife became a problem for him." He raised an eyebrow, and stopped.

The dramatic pause was driving Emil crazy. "Well? What happened?"

"The details are hazy. One friend says he spied in Budapest before we marched in, another says he went as deep as Stalingrad, just before that debacle. The only agreed-upon story is that he was one of the Gestapo's men in the East."

"Do the Russians know this?"

Konrad stubbed out his cigarette. "If the Russians made him into your country's war hero for the Great Red Cause, do you think they'll want to hear the opposite is true?" He smiled and tapped Emil's cheek with a hand, like a mother. "Not without evidence they won't."

Emil inhaled when he realized he hadn't breathed for a while. It cleared his head. "Is this what Janos was looking for in Berlin? Evidence?"

Konrad looked very pleased with himself. He had Emil's complete attention. He leaned back, glanced at a wall clock, and said, "I've got a job to see to. Why don't you come along?"

The children had put considerable effort into brushing off the steps, so Emil dropped some change into the eldest one's dirty hand and spoke loud enough for the others to hear. "Share, Comrade. You're running your very own soviet." This brought a look of nausea to Konrad's face.

They walked back into the city in silence. Emil began to understand just how much Janos had betrayed his friend and sometime-lover. In order to collect blackmail material, he had sent Konrad into what could have been a fatal investigation. And Konrad, made stupid by love, couldn't see any of it. He remembered Lena: *Women get stupid for the men they've married, it's a fact.* Not only women.

Around them, a couple new buildings were ringed by shells of old homes and a few unscathed ones. They passed through many black markets, Konrad pausing long enough to consider some used shoes. "Makes me shiver to think where they got those," he muttered, then bought a carton of Lucky Strikes. He knew half the old men standing around, opening their trench coats like flashers. Russian soldiers stood on the sidelines, charging sellers for the right to sell, and pawning off their excess rations and ammunition. Emil used his cane to keep up.

"How long have you been in Berlin?" Konrad asked once they had left a square.

"Since last night."

"It's an amazing bit of fortune you came across me so quickly, don't you think?"

Emil lowered his voice as they passed more soldiers. "There's a file on Janos. The Russians watched him come to your house, then go into the American sector. Where did he go in the American sector?"

Konrad's smile disappeared, and his lips formed a vague sneer. "They saw him?" he said finally. "Come to me?" He was wide-eyed as the implications became clear. "And that warranted a *file?*"

"Everything warrants a file," Emil said and, perhaps for the first time, realized that Michalec had access to all the same files he did. All it took was the inclination, and he would know everything Emil knew.

Around another corner Germans stood in a loose crowd by a building with two hissing speakers blasting news at them. The Soviet sector was prospering despite all the westerners' efforts. Next week in the Tiergarten, on the western side, the Socialist Unity Party would hold a rally against the opportunist mayor, Ernst Reuter. General Sokolovsky promised that the hugely successful Moscow dance troupes would return regularly for the Berliners' enjoyment.

A motorcycle buzzed by, and when its noise faded it was replaced by far-off planes.

"Hurry up," said Konrad. He grabbed Emil by the elbow.

****

Die Letze Katze was on a pockmarked block, and Konrad used one of ten keys on a ring to open the door to the basement level. Two more locks on the inner steel door. The club smelled of sour liquor. Konrad used a key to open his office—no more than a closet, a table covered with a telephone and slips of paper, photos taped to a mirror on the far wall that gave the illusion of space—and another key on the liquor cabinet behind the bar. Emil climbed onto a stool and grunted.

Konrad filled two glasses with tonic water and held his up. "Janos."

Emil drank. It was sticky in his mouth.

Konrad nodded at the cane lying across the next stool. "So what happened to you?"

"Bullets."

"The war?"

"At home. Recently."

"Nothing to do with Janos?"

Emil shrugged.

The room was long and narrow and a lot like Helsinki cellar bars, where dingy workers chain-smoked and fought and broke bottles. At the far end was a small stage framed by cheap satin curtains tied up with yellow rope. Stale smoke was in everything—the carpet, the chairs, the walls—and only lighting a fresh cigarette helped dispel it. "Your place is nice." He didn't know what else to say.

"My place? I own nothing. *Manage* is the word."

"The Russians think you own it."

"Well, they do me an *honor*," he said, and raised his glass to toast again.

"Tell me," said Emil.

Konrad set his glass down.

"Where did Janos go? Who did he see in the American sector?"

Konrad held up an index finger, then pointed at the front door. "Outside again? You mind?"

They walked the length of the block, slowly, as though they were in another Berlin, one where they could admire the flowers. In the middle of the street, two very clean children pushed a rusty, rattling baby carriage filled with coal. "I'm sure of my own apartment," said Konrad. "But the bar? I don't know. People I don't know are in there all the time. A friend of mine says I'm paranoid, but he was arrested last week."

"What about me?"

Konrad stuck his hands deep into his pockets. "I think we have some solidarity, you and I. Janos was beautiful, a poet, he understood solidarity. I think you do too. People from your country know about living under the boot of another nation. Am I wrong?"

Emil said he wasn't.

Konrad cleared his throat and stroked his boxer's nose. "On the telephone—on a friend's secure line—I told Janos everything. Everything I'd learned. It seemed to me that this friend of his, this Michalec, as an employee of the Reich, would have had a file. The Gestapo kept files on *everyone*." He thought about that a moment. "Times don't change, do they?"

They didn't.

"Around a year ago, the Americans found a storehouse of records. In Munich, I think. A lot of information—including, of course, files of the Gestapo. Crates and crates. They brought them here to Berlin, then decided to send it all back to Washington. They were going to fly the records out of Tempelhof."

Emil stopped and looked at him. "The airport?"

Konrad nodded. "But nothing ever turns out as we expect, and there was this American lieutenant. Named Mazur. Harry Mazur, an historian. *Harry*, can you imagine?" Konrad laughed—a high, uncontrolled chuckle that he quickly silenced, as though embarrassed by its sound. "So, this American military historian Lieutenant Harry Mazur arrived in Berlin a week before the crates were scheduled to leave us. He found out about them, made some inquiries, and got permission to work on them himself, here in

Berlin. Washington, he was convinced, would leave them to the dust." He paused and, as an aside, cited five sources for this story: two Soviet officers (a captain and a colonel), one de-Nazified liquor vendor, one still fully Nazified policeman and a prostitute who had been a red since birth.

"These files," said Emil. "Where are they now?"

"Still there. A basement room at Tempelhof. Apparently, our admirable Lieutenant Harry has been going at them ever since. Now that all this has started," he said, waving his hand at the buzzing sound they once again noticed, "I'll bet he's had to go it alone. I'll *bet* those are a lot of files for any one man." Konrad stopped for an old woman to pass. She glanced enviously at Emil's cane.

"This is where Janos went? To the airport?"

Konrad shrugged as they turned back toward the nightclub. The breeze shifted, and the sound of planes grew louder.

Emil stopped him with a hand on his shoulder. "How did he get there?"

"Just walk on over, dearest. Nobody will stop you. They might look at your papers, but no more. All they worry about is precious coal making it to the American sector."

"No," said Emil, shaking his head. "*Inside.* Tempelhof Airport."

Konrad shrugged theatrically, palms up. "Back then, you realize, it was a different world. None of these planes, we had plenty American cigarettes and they had their electricity. But now, who knows? Inside?" He reached for the door handle and showed his perfect false teeth as he smiled. "But maybe, dear Comrade Inspector, for the sake of a beloved genius, just maybe I can help you."

CHAPTER TWENTY-THREE

****

Small, shallow bullet holes peppered the Brandenburg Gate. Between chipped columns stood soldiers—Soviet on his side, American on the other—waving people through. A trickle of women stood on the American side with empty shopping bags. In another line, women with full shopping bags returned to the West. Emil stood behind them, looking down at a bag of salamis, wishing he'd eaten.

Janos had stood in this same spot eight months ago, February, single-mindedly focused on breaking free of his wife's support. He had stood near these damaged classical columns, thinking of evidence and blackmail and money. He was already purchasing the apartment in his head, living his new, free life.

And behind Janos, maybe crouching among the blackened shards of the demolished Reichstag, MVD agents had taken notes.

Emil looked back and saw only soldiers with rifles and women with shopping bags. But what he saw didn't matter; they knew whose path he was following.

The Russian soldier smiled at the women. He was a flirt. The women smiled back as necessary when he asked them why they wanted to leave the Soviet sector, where all their needs would be met. Sometimes he asked to see their papers, then, with a wink, flicked them back. *"Nächste!"*

Emil handed over his passport. Close up, the soldier wasn't so young, and he remembered Lena's conviction that these were just peasant boys who wanted their mothers. Lost children. The boy-man looked him up and down and spoke in Russian. "A long way from home, Comrade?"

Emil took out his green Militia certificate, which was half in Russian, and handed it over. "Yes, Comrade."

The soldier shifted his rifle so that the barrel no longer pointed at the ground. "What kind of business do you have with the Americans?"

The badge was useless, but the soldier might not know this. "Just visiting the enemy, Comrade. Taking a *look.*"

The soldier pursed his lips as he read the certificate carefully, then handed it back. "Not much to see over there," he said. "Sta-lingrad, *that's* a city."

Emil folded the Militia certificate back into his jacket.

"They're different here," said the soldier confidentially. "They don't understand the value of *gifts.*"

Emil understood. He put his hand in his pocket and spoke loudly. "Thank you very much, Comrade! Your assistance is appreciated."

He held out his hand to shake, and the soldier, uncertain, took it. When he felt the Ostmarks slide into his palm, his features relaxed. He stood straight, at attention. "May your business long serve the interests of the victorious proletariat!"

"That's my aim, Comrade," said Emil, and after five long steps he passed a sign that told him he was in the American sector.

A thick boned GI asked in clotted German what his business was.

He had an impulse to bribe again, but he'd heard about the Americans. They were fat, rich people for whom a bribe was no temptation. Certainly whatever meager bribe he could afford.

"Tourism."

The GI nodded at the soldier he'd just left. "What did you show him? That green thing."

Emil looked back at the Russian, who was busy flirting with some more women, then back at the humorless American. He handed his Militia certificate over, and saw, in a flash, prisons and interrogations. His weak stomach trembled, but he forced it to settle. Just a little war tourism. No one could prove otherwise.

The soldier frowned at the cyrillics. He was young, and Emil wondered if the Americans came from farms like the Russians, and if they also felt lost on this side of the Atlantic, buried deep in bomb-scarred Europe. The soldier took Emil's passport and badge to a gray guardhouse and spoke with an officer inside. After a moment, the officer, now holding the IDs, stepped out and waved for Emil to follow him. He had wind-chapped features that Emil attributed to American plains in states he had heard of: Kansas, Missouri.

When he looked back, Emil saw the round-faced Russian boy staring from the other side of the Gate, looking as though he had been had.

Thin, white hair stuck out from beneath the officer's cap. They were beside each other now, approaching a dirty white trailer that, when the door was opened, smelled of scalded coffee. A small iron stove burned in the corner. The officer took off his cap—he was bald on top—and poured coffee from a thermos. He held out a cup, but Emil shook his head. They sat on either side of a small kitchen table covered by a piece of lace.

"Speak English?"

Emil shook his head. "*Deutsch, Russkii.*"

"So you're from the People's Militia," the officer said in unbelievably smooth, fluent Russian as he laid the two IDs on the table. Emil wondered how a farmer had learned such fine Russian. "Does this mean you're investigating something in our sector?"

Emil faltered. His stomach was tearing itself up. The nervousness had come upon him as soon as he had stepped into this room. And now the American officer saw right through him.

But what was he really hiding?

He was hiding everything, because trust was not an option.

"A murder?" the American guessed. "It does say *homicide* here."

He had a kind face, but Emil knew from experience that this was impractical evidence.

Again: What did he have to hide?

"A murder," said Emil. "Yes." He spoke in clipped syllables, trying to hide his sudden despair.

The farmer-officer pressed his lips together as he nodded. "Are you an agent of Soviet Intelligence? MVD? MGB?"

"What?"

"You heard me." The kindness had slipped from his features.

"I'm not. I'm neither."

The officer sipped gingerly and considered Emil a moment. The iron stove kept the trailer very warm. "Tell me about your case."

His stomach was furious, tumultuous. "I'm afraid I can't."

"Why not?"

Emil raised his palms helplessly. "I don't know much myself. And what I do know is questionable." He rubbed his face, the adrenaline now exhausting him. Maybe it was the fatigue making him say so much. "This is my dilemma," he told the American. "What I do know may be of more value than I realize. But not necessarily of value to my case. So I can't share any of it. Do you understand?"

The officer did, Emil could see this. He leaned back in his chair, nodding, spreading his feet as wide as they would go in the cramped quarters, but said, "Please explain."

He shifted so his stomach could expel the gasses building inside it, then felt the sharp old wounds. "If I tell you something that is of more value than I realize," said Emil, "I could be in trouble with my own government. Or with the Russians. As soon as I step back over that line, I could be shot."

"Nothing would leave this room," said the American officer. "You can trust that."

Emil leveled a cool gaze on him, but his empty stomach was a writhing acid pit. "I can't trust that."

The officer licked the inside of his mouth, rapped his knuckles on the tabletop, then glanced out the window. "What about them, then?"

"Who?"

"The Soviets." He leaned forward. "You can't be too happy with them, now can you? They marched into your country and set up a puppet dictatorship. You *do* know this, right? They rewrite history like it's their own goddamn Tolstoy novel." He paused to let it sink in. "You're not a fool, I can tell that. You don't think that Mihai of yours is doing anything other than listening to his Moscow phone for orders—do you?"

Emil heard his grandfather muttering in his skull, but shrugged it off. "No country's perfect."

The officer almost shouted: "That's what drives me crazy about you people! You've got the lowest standards in the world."

"We're never disappointed."

He laughed a big, American laugh, and patted his big hand on the shaking table. Outside, a dented green Opel pulled up. "All right, Emil Brod of the People's Militia," he said as he handed back the passport and certificate. "Have a good stay in the American sector. Excuse our lack of electricity. Another gift from your Soviet friends." He smiled. "And remember. You hurt anyone under our care, and you'll have the United States up your ass."

A man got out of the Opel's passenger's side and stood waiting.

Emil's stomach cleared suddenly, then sank. He was so slow. He took too much at face value. The officer had been holding him here, waiting.

"Are they taking me away?" asked Emil.

"What? *Them?*"

Emil waited for an answer.

"Maybe in your country, kid, but not in ours." He handed Emil his cane. "Just some eyes to make sure you stay out of trouble." He held out his hand, and Emil took it.

"Thank you, Comrade."

That word brought a sudden frown to the officer's cheery face.

Konrad had given him a name and address—Birgit Schlieger, Friedrichstrasse 36—with a small, hand-drawn map. Emil stopped at a corner to try and orient himself. The demolished Tiergarten was to his right. Upturned trees had been cleared, and someone had planted a few twigs to mark their passing. Along the far end, army blankets held up by sticks formed tents. The Opel hummed on the corner behind him. It was quickly becoming dark, and no lights appeared in the houses, only the faint waver of candlelight. He turned the little map ninety degrees and held it to his nose before finding where he was. Friedrichstrasse was on the opposite side of town.

He took a long tram ride to the street—another demolished wreck—but before searching for the apartment, he stopped at a café that had a candle on each of its five tables and mildewed, yellow wallpaper peeling in the corners. He settled near the door. The Opel was nowhere to be seen, but in the corner there was a well-fed American Negro with a round face. He wore a brown overcoat and drank his coffee as if it were water. Emil stared— he'd never seen a Negro in the flesh before, skin that dark, absorbing the light like that. The American nodded pleasantly enough at Emil's stare, then went back to the candlelit paperback novel in his hand.

On the cover: a lurid painting of a terrified woman under a knife. The decadence, Emil supposed, of capitalism.

He ordered coffee and a breadstick. The waitress didn't notice his accent, or maybe by now she was all too familiar with Slavs. A couple of thin, coal-blackened men sauntered in and began drinking beer.

He wondered if Leonek had found Lena yet. Alive, safe. He hoped. He remembered the field, Lena stretched whitely in the grass, then that white, bloodstained rug.

The bread was dry and the coffee too watery. But finally being off his feet was something. The coffee made his stomach burn, then the bread bloated it. The two Germans were talking coal: load sizes and quotas. They talked about American C-4s flying from Hanover.

The men worked at Tempelhof Airport, he realized, part of the gangs of Germans hired to unload the planes. He wished he could simply sneak into the compound with them, but Konrad had been clear: *Trust Birgit. Absolutely. She's devoted to the Great Red Cause.* What about you? Emil had asked. *Friends,* he said, *that's what I'm devoted to. That, and the longest path to the grave.*

He put his money down as the waitress collected his plate. She stopped, one hand on the edge of the table, and stared at it.

"Isn't it enough?" asked Emil.

She looked from the money to him, and straightened her black skirt. She spoke bitterly: "*Ost*marks?"

Emil looked down at the bills. He had known this, of course, but it hadn't occurred to him. The German workers stared; the American read his thriller. "I apologize," said Emil. "Can I exchange here? Whatever rate you like."

Her eyes had narrowed to slits, and she chewed the inside of her mouth. "Just leave," she muttered. She took his plate away.

In the cool darkness, the whine came from everywhere. Laboring plane engines were echoed and redirected by the blasted walls and valleys of rubble. Beneath the sound, though, he could hear footsteps. Very close. Two pairs.

The black shells of Berlin rose all around him. He couldn't go directly to Konrad's friend, not when he was being followed, yet as he turned he was less and less sure where he was, but he pressed forward, using his cane for leverage against the uneven concrete. He heard water running and women's voices from dark homes and children squealing. He turned onto a busy street cut down the middle by tram tracks. Berliners on foot squinted into dark shop windows. He didn't look back, only dove into a crowd and emerged on the other side of the street, behind a sparking, packed tram, and into an alley. Deep in the blackness someone was coughing, hacking, but he turned back to face the street, waiting for the Tempelhof workers.

"A single Mark," came the whisper, then more coughing.

Emil held his breath, listening to the voices from the crowded, dark street, then the heavy breaths behind. But no one came after him. He glanced back at the old man emerging from the dark. His face was splotched by lumps, some disease taking hold, and his breath was poisonous. Wiry gray hair twisted over his brow, and he started to speak again. Emil slipped back into the street.

He found his way through the crowd again. The Germans held their thin coats tight to themselves, their eyes encircled in darkness. Planes buzzed in the distance. He couldn't imagine how anyone slept over here.

The Opel seemed to have vanished.

He heard the truck before he saw it: an urgent voice calling in German. Then it was on their street, weaving around pedestrians: a truck topped by bullhorns, with *Rias* painted on its door. The voice shouted, "*Berlinern und Berlinerin,* your city is in danger!" Then it took the next corner.

The Friedrichstrasse third-floor walk-up was a long railroad apartment with large windows on either end and none along its length. Birgit—stout, with a white bun atop her head and deflated bags for cheeks—didn't smile much. After she introduced Emil to her fat but grinning husband, Dado, she ordered her happier, sweating half into the kitchen, where he knew to close the door.

"Here," she said, pointing at a scratched dining table. It was an order, so he settled down quickly. "What's wrong with your leg?" she demanded as she sat opposite him.

"It's not my leg. I was shot in the stomach."

She nodded, unfazed. "Americans?"

It took him a moment to understand. "No, no. Back home."

"Counterrevolutionaries." She spoke as if she knew all.

The apartment was cluttered like a grandmother's—lace on the end tables, lace covering the sofa, lace on the shelves. He wondered how her poor grandchildren would fare. On the mottled wall was a portrait of the Comrade Chairman, his thick brown mustache like a roach on his lip. "Konrad Messer sent me."

"Of course he did," she said. "Would you like some tea?"

He shrugged.

"Dado!" she called, her mouth stretching at the edges. "Tea!"

He could hear Dado grunting behind the kitchen door as he stood up. Birgit smiled at him, but only briefly.

"Konrad did this before, you know. Sent me someone from your liberated nation. I was of some small assistance. Tell me. Do you know . . ." She paused, touching her lower lip in thought. "Mihai, yes. General Secretary Mihai? You know him?"

He shook his head.

"You have friends that do."

"No," he said. "The General Secretary keeps to himself."

This seemed to displease her. She tapped her lip, nodding absently until her eyes snapped back to him. "Do you want to get to the Tempelhof air field basement as well?"

"Yes," he said. "As soon as possible."

"It's a simple thing for the children, you know. They're always cutting through the fence and running wild. The Americans spend half their time rounding up little German boys."

He smiled obligatorily and nodded.

She brushed some dirt from the corner of her eye. "What for?"

"Excuse me?"

"Why, then, do you want to go to Tempelhof?"

Konrad had told him she would ask this question. He had given Emil the answer, just as he had given it to Janos months before. "For the interests of world socialism."

She closed her eyes and nodded sharply. This was what she had suspected; the one reason worth her efforts. Dado stumbled out of the kitchen with a metal tray and two glasses filled with hot, brackish water. His blue worker's shirt was stained by tea drippings, and his thick hands were motor-oil black. He set out the glasses with the efficiency of a drunk headwaiter, then departed.

"Tonight?" she asked.

The tea was unsweetened and bitter. "What?"

"You want to get into the Tempelhof basement tonight?"

"Oh God, yes," he said automatically.

She frowned at his invocation of the deity, but slowly told him what he needed to know.

Tempelhof Airport was shaped like a parenthesis, the planes collecting on the inside of the curve. She drew it on a piece of butcher's paper. It was a vast complex, she said, much larger than the Americans needed for their airlift, and many sections, particularly in the seven-level basement, remained unused. At the end of the war, German soldiers—boys, probably, the only ones left— laid bombs that destroyed the lowest two layers, but the remaining five were still too vast for the Americans. "This is to your advantage," she pointed out, hovering over the pencil drawing he was barely able to make out in the candlelight. She drew five Xs for planes, then an angular line around the whole thing. "The fence. Here," she said, marking, "is the main gate, simple enough. But your concern is the basement, the third floor down. Right here." She drew another X at the bottom of the parenthesis, on the outside of the curve.

Tempelhof had its own generators, so he would not be left in the dark, not like the rest of the city. "I can get you an ID and a ration card, and that will put you inside. Unlike the little boys, you'll have to go in the front gate." She used her chubby finger like a teacher's pointer. "This is where you will enter the gates. With the other workers. This is where you will separate from the workers. This is where you will enter the building. Here is your storeroom. What are you looking for?"

After all the commands, the question was unexpected. He stalled.

"Why are you sneaking into this place?"

"I'm looking for something," he said finally. "A file."

She nodded. "You won't tell me what."

"I just did."

She looked as if she didn't believe him, and moved her teacup away from herself.

"Did Janos Crowder go through this as well?" he asked.

She shook her head. "Comrade Crowder came before the blockade. Any fool could get onto Tempelhof. It was just a matter of waiting in a bathroom until the lights were turned off in the evening. Now . . ." She shook her head sadly.

He looked at the sketch in the wavering light. This was all quite crazy. But nothing he had done in the last month had any sanity to it. He would see it through, though, because seeing it through was the only dignity left to him. He looked at her. "How did you learn all this?"

"Nothing's all *that* secret," she confided, and smiled a second and final time. "And anyway, prostitutes know everything, haven't you ever heard that?"

CHAPTER TWENTY-FOUR

****

At the busy, dark street, he boarded an overcrowded tram marked TEMPELHOF. Simple enough. Her directions had been specific and concise, with little possibility for deviation. Emil had one foot inside the car; the other hung out. His bare hands and face froze in the night breeze, and the strain of holding himself up was wrenching his guts. An old man packed inside looked down at Emil's foot, then shrugged helplessly.

They went through all of Berlin, it seemed. In some areas there was solely rubble, while in others the only damage consisted of chipped façades. But most of the bits of Berlin he could see through the darkness were a mix of the two. Jagged walls rose into the air, surrounded by hills of broken stone and intact homes. Occasionally, men in suits rode bicycles alongside the tram, and their car stopped a few times to let convoys of American jeeps pass.

Finally, at the end of a long, bomb-riddled square, beside a gated subway stop, he saw the sign: an arrow beside the words AIR PORT TEMPELHOF. Everyone got off with him.

The whine was continuous here, and deafening.

Workers collected at the high chain-link fence. A few American soldiers stood on either side of the gates and took a look at each man's ration card and ID. Beyond them, the black wall of the airport rose. There were maybe a hundred men here, stuffed tight, and Emil was in the midst of them, their hard jackets scraping his chapped fingers, their stench filling his nose. He wondered if bathing was a luxury here. The old man from the tram noticed him, his white-furred chin shifting as he spoke: "So you held on, did you?"

Emil nodded and smiled.

The old man moved closer, eyes glimmering from the electric lights on poles along the fence. "Usually, I'm the afternoon, but they took me off. How do you get used to these hours?"

Emil shrugged and rubbed his arms for warmth.

The old man nodded with lips pressed tight, and looked around. They all moved up a few feet, then stopped.

Emil's stomach began to act up again. His accent was a badge here.

They moved a few more feet. A plane roared off from the other side of the terminal, and another plane's tires screeched against the runway. The electric lights lit the men from above, casting their faces in long shadow. The old man looked like death. "My daughter-in-law says they're flying in their own prostitutes for the GIs. Direct from Paris." He winked. "I hope we can unload some of *that*."

Some other men growled their agreement, and a short, wiry worker took off his cap. "*Madame, pourrais-je vous aider à descendre de cette échelle?*" He held up a hand and squeezed, as though supporting a woman's ass. The laughter rippled through the crowd, and the little man, pleased, put his cap back on.

They were almost at the front. Three American soldiers, looking very stern in the shadows of their caps, examined each ID closely, twisting it in the light, and then stared deeply into each face. Back to the photo, then the face, again.

· Emil would not get through. He knew this as soon as he looked again at his ID card with *Schlieger, Dado* beneath the picture: dark hair, dark eyes, double chin. Even accounting for weight loss, this could never be him. What was Birgit thinking? What was *he* thinking, letting her talk him into this?

He put away the papers and turned around. The old man put a hand on his shoulder. "We're almost there."

Emil shook it off and didn't look back, but said, "I forgot something."

As soon as the words came out he went numb, but pressed on. There were eyes on him, white eyes against dirty cheeks. Their faces were slack in their momentary surprise, then, when he was nearly out of their mass, shoulders began bumping into his. "*Russian,*" came whispered German voices, hot breath in his ear. White teeth flashed. He pushed forward, just breaking free. Warm spittle hit the side of his neck. He didn't wipe it off. They were yelling at him, hoarse voices in the cold. He walked faster, the cane helping him gallop further into the darkness. He didn't look back until he had crossed the street, and the screaming airplanes obscured their shouting. They raised fists, a cloud of hot words hovered above their heads, and occasionally one broke from the crowd a few paces and spat, but they did not follow. They remained beside the gate, waiting to work for their ration cards. The promise of food held them right where they were.

A cold, black drizzle fell as he hobbled along the outside of the fence. He was cold all the way through. His jacket was thin—worker materials, the Uzbek would say—and when a wind came along, his battered hat blew off, and he had to stumble after it. He reached the other side of the Tempelhof complex, where he could see the activity inside the parenthesis. There were some children up ahead watching a plane touch down—a black silhouette marked by lights and sparks behind the propellers. Trucks burdened with food and coal rolled across the wet runway. From the shadows tiny workers jogged toward a parked truck. A burst of voices shot out—hooting—and the children clung to the chainlinks, shouting with pleasure. Little blond boys dressed as poor adults, or in family lederhosen. They trembled like eager puppies.

The plane taxied, disappearing on the other side of the airport, and another immediately touched down. There were lights in the sky, more planes lining up for the descent. On the ground, figures loaded trucks with the feverish single-mindedness of the hungry. The children whistled. Emil stood at the fence beside them, hands in his pockets fingering the useless ID.

"What kind of plane is that?" he said, and they looked at him. The plane was empty now, moving to the line of those waiting to leave. Another one took off.

There were five of them, feverish with the excitement of big machines, and one with mud on his cheek blurted, "C-47." He seemed very convinced of it.

Emil nodded at the fence. "And this one coming in?"

"I'll bet it's a C-54," said another boy.

"You can't tell," said the first, wiping the mud away with the back of his hand. "You can't *see* it."

"I can see it as well as you," came the bitter reply.

It was, in fact, a C-82—a rare bird, they all agreed. He asked how often they saw the planes up close, and the first boy proudly said, "Whenever we want."

"*Shut up,*" whispered another.

The first boy realized then what he had done. His confused silence endured as he wondered how to talk himself out of his slip, but he finally gave up. "Everyone does it."

"Seen any C-4s?" Emil asked conversationally, as if he hadn't understood the slip. "There were some around earlier."

The rain had stopped, and the boys seemed to want to leave. They retreated a few steps, but one—the smallest, a dark-haired child with perfectly combed hair and immaculate lederhosen—asked if he had a cigarette.

Emil squatted and pulled out his pack. The others approached as he distributed them. When he offered them lights the first boy shook his head. "They'll see us. Want to know how to see them up close?"

The littlest made some sound of discontent, but another gave an unimpressed sigh that shut him up. *"Baby."*

It was another fifty yards farther along the fence. In the darkness one of them tripped, but bounced upright again and ran to catch up. They had marked the spot with two sticks crossed on the ground. At first Emil didn't see anything—it was a fence and two sticks, and on the other side the wet tarmac led toward the planes and, to the left, the Tempelhof building. But then the first boy, with a smile Emil could just make out, touched the fence, demonstrating that the chain links had been cut along a jagged vertical line, about three feet high. The boy bent and pushed through—there was the sound of his shirt tearing—and looked back, beaming. "Come on in!"

Emil came through next, painfully, holding the cane ahead of himself to open the way, and was followed by three boys. The last one, the baby, stood on the other side, watching, frowning. He had his cigarette behind his ear. He muttered something no one could hear.

The first boy crouched and rushed forward. Emil tried to follow his lead, bending and rushing forward, but his damaged body wouldn't bend easily, and could not move that fast. "We should split up," Emil told them. "That way if one of us is caught the others can get away."

They liked the conspiracy in his voice, and were soon running far ahead and to the right, to where the planes were settling down. But Emil waited, then ran to the left. Behind him, he knew, the baby was standing on the other side of the fence, watching, muttering his worries.

CHAPTER TWENTY-FIVE

****

Birgit's scrawled directions were impeccable. They led him down the dark outside of the building's arc, where the planes on the other side were muted by brick. He was to skip the first door, which was locked, and make it to the second, which had been busted two months ago and never fixed. As promised, where its deadbolt should have been there was a perfect hole drilled in the door. He put two fingers through it and pushed.

A generator kept a dull sidelight burning that barely lit the concrete walls, and he had to pause at each turn to make sure the path was clear. Birgit had told him to look for stairs, and had marked where he could find them. The stairwell was completely black, and he had to feel his way. After the noise of outside, the silence made his footsteps elephantine.

First underground level. Then the second. Third. He pushed through the door.

The corridor was lit by a single fluorescent and, at the far end, light spilled from beneath an office door. He waited, sweating. His stomach made noises. He listened. Nothing.

He crept to the door and stopped again. Still, nothing. He turned the knob slowly, hearing the mechanism clicking, then stopped again. This door was not supposed to be unlocked. Birgit had told him he would have to break the lock. But he still heard nothing. He pushed it open.

It was a long office, more like a small warehouse, filled chin-high with brown boxes in all conditions. Ripped, cut, punctured by holes, water damaged. On half of them Emil spotted the small red imprint of flat wings on either side of a circled swastika. A few on the floor were open, revealing files, and more files covered the gunmetal desk in the center of the room, where a single lamp burned. The chair was empty, save a crumpled gray army blanket.

He heard a noise. A door closing.

He scrambled back into the darkness between the towers of boxes, his jacket scraping—loudly, it seemed—on cardboard as he squatted and waited.

A thin man came in and wiped his eyes, pushing round wire-framed glasses up his red nose.

Lieutenant Harry himself. Emil's bubbling stomach threatened to explode.

Harry Mazur went to the desk and closed some files, dropping them into the squeaking desk drawers. He coughed into a thin hand, sniffed and belched. Emil noticed how gaunt the man was, how pale. The office was windowless, subterranean, and he imagined this historian hadn't seen much sun these last months. He was practically wilting. Mazur took his coat and hat from a rack in the corner and turned off the desk lamp. The only light was from the hall. The historian muttered something—a deep, hoarse English Emil couldn't understand—and left, closing and locking the door behind himself. The hall lights went off. Emil sweated and gritted his teeth against the pain in his stomach, but did not move.

Five minutes, maybe ten. He no longer had a watch to judge. He waited in the blackness, wishing he had sent Leonek here instead, Leonek with all his limbs and organs intact. But Leonek would have given up at the front gates; anyone else would have.

Once he was sure Mazur was gone for good, he felt his way to the desk and turned on the lamp.

****

He didn't know where to begin; Birgit's directions were only meant to get him here.

A dullard would pick up these boxes, one at a time, and go through each file, looking for the name Michalec, or Smerdyakov, or Graz. But the boxes were everywhere, stacked in little fascist towers that would take weeks, months to get through. About a third of the boxes, he noticed, had been moved to the front of the room, beside the desk. Maybe a hundred boxes, stacked tight. Each of these had been marked with a black X through its winged swastika, and a number beside it. The one closest to him was numbered 0087. He assumed these boxes had been through Mazur's cataloguing process.

Emil went through the desk.

Beside loose files filled with economic forecasts written in German, there was a thick, hardbound notebook. Inside, grid paper was covered with columns of numbers and English writing. Emil didn't understand a word. Mazur had written RECORDS on the front cover.

It was in here, he knew. There were columns of descriptions, each followed by a number, presumably to one of the boxes. The only way Janos Crowder could have found his evidence, Emil decided, would be to use these boxes, and this chart. He went quickly through the pages, dragging his finger down the lists, looking for anything familiar. But other than the occasional loose word he recognized nothing.

He found a few pages in English that were duplicated in German—a report by Lieutenant Harry Mazur on the history behind the files—but even that didn't go into the contents of the boxes. The files had been taken, it said, from two places: a schoolhouse in Munich and a depot north of Berlin that had been set ablaze by retreating soldiers, then saved by the Red Army (many boxes, he saw, had water stains and running ink). Most of the Munich documents had begun in a warehouse in Oranienburg. When it was bombed, the boxes were moved, inexplicably, all the way to Munich. Even Harry Mazur had no explanation. *It's the madness of war*, he offered in the report.

The rest of the drawers had only pencils, stale fried potatoes wrapped in paper and a full ashtray.

Emil took off his jacket and removed his tie. He would have to be a dullard.

The first box was filled with records of oil shipments from Ploieşti, Romania, and lists of gas usage in five Reich cities between 1942 and 1944. At the height of war the measuring and gauging had gone on unabated. There were letters from a colonel in France requesting extra petroleum rations for trucks that brought cheese shipments of Claqueret from Lyon to Paris.

Emil retrieved the next box and settled at the desk, and by the time he was on the third he had noticed a chill and used the gray blanket to cover his shoulders.

There were boxes of water records and others with troop movements. There were reports on Austrian wheat harvests and predictions for economic activity within Czechoslovakia.

Emil almost fell asleep after the ninth box, but hobbled to the end of the room and back a few times, quickly, to get the blood flowing again, then returned to a box on Dutch black-market activities.

It was late, he suspected, or early. But down here he could hear nothing, not even the planes. For all he knew, there was a war going on up there.

He skimmed over boxes that reported on grain shipments scheduled for the retreating forces on both fronts, and saw their tonnages dwindle. He'd heard stories from men on the seal boat about starving German soldiers raiding homes in a fury. Less verifiable stories had the soldiers eating each other. The one German in their crew, a pink-skinned Bavarian named Jos, sank into silence whenever the stories came up. No one prodded him, not even the Bulgarian. They knew he had seen his future, and it was iron bars, and walls.

A water-stained box contained wrinkled reports on awards given for valor in battle. Lists of men who had received their Iron Crosses posthumously, or those who had killed so many Allies that their lists of commendations went on for many pages. There were reports on brave soldiers of the Reich, and most of the recommendations came from the final months of the war. The soldiers were becoming younger, until they were just children with rifles and sticks, lined up in a ring around Berlin: the Home Guard. Three-quarters were posthumous recommendations. The Luftschutz medal, War Merit Crosses, a few West Wall medals for the builders of the failed D-Day defense on the Siegfried line, and numerous Russian Front medals. Each recipient had his own folder, filled with biographical information and photographs when available.

Then he spotted the folder in the back. Unlike the other orderly files, it was shabby, as if it had been perused by someone unorganized, or excited, or artistic, and then stuffed back into the box with no regard for order.

The label said KONTAKT: "GRAZ."

The first page was an identification sheet. A small photo of Jerzy Michalec: a younger, smooth face. Boyish. Born in Szek-szárd, Hungary, 12 January 1909, to a Polish father and a Magyar mother. Married Agnes Höller in Vienna, 1933. A handwritten note in the margin said that Agnes Michalec had died in 1943 in Mauthausen labor camp, Austria. Jerzy Michalec's association with the Gestapo, said line 26, began on 6 February 1941. Line 31: *For decorations, see attached.*

The attached included typewritten letters that recommended "Graz" for medals of distinction. On 15 March 1942, Michalec had, at peril to himself, used prewar contacts within France to secure the identities of sixteen members of the French Underground. Thirteen of these sixteen had been taken into custody.

Firm block letters at the bottom of the recommendation: NEIN—JUD. Jew.

No—Michalec was not a Jew. It was his wife, Agnes. For that they could not award his work.

During the week of 10 October, that same year, Michalec caught and personally executed three British spies in Prague. Again, NEIN.

Then, in March 1944, he led thirty boys of a mobilized Hitler-jugend regiment into a Soviet garrison in Poland. They returned with the mangled caps of nearly a hundred Russians. Two large, messy letters—JA—in red ink.

Next was a page-sized photograph of Michalec, much older than the young man who had, only three years before, entered the mess of battle. His face was heavy with killing, a blackness lingering beneath the flesh. He wore a loose-fitting black suit, and his smile was weary.

He stood shaking hands with the man Emil had seen twice before in his life: on a series of ten photographs, and stepping out of a blue Tatra with a Walther pistol. A little younger, this man's features were shadowed by his Wehrmacht officer's cap. His dress uniform showed the stripes of a colonel—*Oberst*. He handed Jerzy Michalec a small ribbon, weighted in the center with a cross, and a certificate. Emil could just make out the elaborate Gothic script—*Im Namendes Führers . . .*

It took him a moment. He stared, unbelieving, for a long time.

Then he folded the photograph down the middle, and again, into quarters, then slipped it into the back of his pants, into his underwear. He turned off the lamp, grabbed his cane, unlocked the door and left.

Up three dark flights to the corridors, then out into the shadows. It was still dark, but dawn wasn't far away. He could tell by the increased activity—figures jogging in the distance, workers and soldiers, shifts changing. He followed the curve of the wall to the corner, where the noise of planes grew to a pitch, whining loudly. Across the tarmac, where he and the children had crept onto the base, two American soldiers stood at the fence. One kneeled at the hole with pliers, mending, while the other stood with the lederhosen-clad baby boy. The boy was crying, waving his arms around, telling the soldier everything he knew about the hole in the fence. And, no doubt, the man with the cane, the bad cigarettes and Slav accent who had gone through it. The soldier brought a two-way radio to his face and started speaking.

Half-jogging back along the perimeter of the airport, he was glad, at least, that he hadn't brought the whole file. Lightness was imperative. Speed. The knots in his stomach plagued him, but he pressed the pain down.

He slid his cane into his pant leg until its end hung by his ankle. It made him look awkward, crippled, but everyone in this city was.

Up ahead, a crowd of white, flour-dusted workers, tired and sagging, mumbling to themselves, approached the front gate, about twenty yards away. He didn't know if it could work, and the sharp grind in his stomach was becoming unbearable. He needed to lie down. He needed sleep.

He walked as fast as his stiff leg would allow and joined the men. He hung back, behind them, in case they were from earlier—in case they recognized him. He stuck his hands in his pockets to hide his trembling.

Some GIs smoking by the gate looked casually through the papers of the men lined up to enter.

No one recognized him. The workers were too tired to see who was following them out, and the guards were busy with the newcomers. They didn't care who left Tempelhof.

CHAPTER TWENTY-SIX

****

He urinated in an alley, pulled out the cane, then leaned against a brick wall and vomited a thin stream. He took the tram back to the center of town. The black streets were mostly abandoned, and he even found a seat on the unlit car. His empty stomach bubbled angrily. He wanted to hold the photograph again, to prove to himself what he had seen, but was afraid that if he held it in his hands it would fly away.

Michalec.

A Hungarian who had married a Jew who had been put in an Austrian concentration camp. He had begun working with the Gestapo in 1941. Was his wife in the camp by then? Was this the leverage they had used on him?

But then she died in 1943, and his best work was yet to come. Did he know she was dead? Or was he working under the illusion he was saving his wife's life by all the insidious jobs he did?

Or had he, by that point, become a different person?

Others make the rules, he had said. *We only try to live by them.*

Berlin slid by, and a drunk man in the front of the train gazed at him, squinting.

A war hero twice over: first for the Nazis, then for the Russians. He had turned sides as quickly as the war had shifted. With each shift of history he had relearned the rules. A clerk and then a spy and then a war hero, and now—Jerzy Michalec was a *politicos.* Untouchable. Almost.

****

When he recognized the annihilated Tiergarten, he got out and walked the rest of the way to the Gate, where the gray dawn lit pockmarked columns and loitering soldiers. He held up his passport, but no one looked. He didn't recognize the American GIs who waved him through, nor the Russian peasants in soldiers' uniforms who accepted him back into their sector. He asked one of them the time, and the Russian looked at his left wrist, where he had two watches side by side. "Six o'clock." His other wrist had three watches.

This night had lasted forever.

A gray-haired man noticed him and jogged up. "Taxi? Taxi?" Emil wasn't in the mood to debate prices. The car sat at the beginning of Unter den Linden. Past it, a few brightly lit clubs still tempted westerners with heat and electricity. Beneath the sound of the planes, the low bass of music, bands, voices. Emil climbed into the taxi. *"Die Letze Katze,"* he said. The driver started the engine.

He took it out finally, and unfolded it. He wiped the sweat from the photograph with the corner of his shirt and gazed in the murky light at the two men passing a medal between them.

As Smerdyakov, Michalec had entered a crumbling Berlin and assassinated twenty-three German boys—by then that was all that was left of the Wehrmacht: old men and boys. He handed their bodies over to the Russian peasants, probably with a bag full of the dead soldiers' watches and gold teeth.

The car trembled and shot pain through Emil's side. He gasped.

It was clear, at last. The connection that had been nagging at him. The twenty-three soldiers Michalec had stacked up in a bombed-out living room in Berlin were what was left of the Hitlerjugend regiment he had taken into Poland and used to kill off a hundred Soviet boys.

He understood.

These children had seen their commander again, after months without him, in the midst of the bombs. He would have called them together for a meeting. He would have said, *Let's plan our own defense of the Reich.* They had nothing else; it was their last hope. They were desperate children in an exploding city. He would have had them stand together at one side of the room, him at the other, as if it were a lecture. Their trust must have been immeasurable as they met in the living room with no ceiling, only jagged walls, the planes dropping everything onto their heads. They must have felt a surge of hope as he paced back and forth in front of them, holding his machine pistol like a mother would hold an infant. If they had any suspicions they would have beat them down, because knowing the truth would have been so much worse than those few minutes of delusion and devotion.

He wondered if Michalec had had to reload to finish them all off, or if he'd had two machine guns. Or a partner—the colonel: *Herr Oberst?* Or maybe he had simply been a careful, precise shot.

The taxi groaned up a dusty road, and Emil tried to orient himself. He saw piles of rotting mattresses and bedsprings and shattered wood. This was rubble Berlin, where not even three years of work had made a dent. Not a single building stood. Emil leaned forward, feeling it in his stomach. "Where are we?"

The driver glanced into the rearview, but said nothing. The car bumped over rocks.

"*You,*" said Emil. He folded the photograph into the breast of his blazer. "Turn around. This isn't what I asked for."

But the driver was already parking.

They were surrounded on three sides by rubble, and inside this U stood three men. Two wore threadbare, cold-looking suits, while the third, who raised a hand to shield his face from the headlights, was elegantly dressed. A gray, long coat with white cuffs just visible at the sleeves. When he dropped his hand Emil recognized the *Oberst.* Hard, pale cheeks, wide lips. Very *deutsch.* He squinted.

The driver turned in his seat. "What are you waiting for?" he said. "*Get out.*"

At each door a thug waited. He tried the weaker-looking one on the right, but he wasn't weak at all. His big, sculpted hands wrapped completely around Emil's forearm—a grip like a machine—and led Emil over to the colonel, who was tugging white gloves over his hands. Emil wondered if they were the same ones he wore while crushing Janos Crowder's skull. Cleaned thoroughly, and bleached. Maybe they were what he always put on as a prelude to killing. Executioner's gloves. From across the rubble came the whisper of Allied planes.

"You rose from the dead," he said, and Emil remembered the voice—a little thinner than before, weaker. *Comrade Emil Brod?* "Really quite amazing. Impressed and, in no small way, disturbed." Irma was right: He had old eyes. "I guess we don't need to discuss anything. The photograph, please." He opened a hand to accept it.

Emil only half-heard. He was measuring the distance to the piles of rubble, their height, and how much time it would take him to scramble over and sprint toward the silhouetted buildings in the distance. But it was cold—he had to take that into account. And he didn't know if he could sprint at all. He was still, and always, an invalid.

"I don't have the photograph."

The colonel's face was pink in the cool breeze. He sighed audibly, but it was more a sign of weariness than disappointment. He looked at the thug whose grip was cutting off blood in Emil's tingling arm. The colonel said quietly, "Take care of it," and walked away.

The two men went at it together, laying into him with hard, rock fists. Stomach, chest (they knew his weak points) and face. A steel-toed boot struck his shin, nearly breaking it, and he went down quickly to the damp earth. All the fight in him was concentrated into squirming. His hands fluttered about, swatting uselessly. Rocks cut into his back as they leaned over him and swung, and the numb pain shot through him like the sounds of their voices, saying things in German he had trouble understanding. Then a pair of hands on him—he flinched, but the hands only searched his pockets and removed the photograph.

He closed his eyes to darkness, and when he opened them the two men stood over him, looking at the picture, passing it back and forth. The colonel was shouting. Snatching the picture from them with white gloves.

Then blackness.

Then all three, still standing over him. One pointed a finger down at Emil, then all their hands were moving. Then blackness. A shot rang out.

Then more talking, and *Herr Oberst* was holding a gun. Emil didn't know what kind. It was aimed at Emil's face. He moaned, turning his head. He saw the shadow of the barrel's corridor.

Then a shot, but the gun was aimed elsewhere. One of the other men fell. A flash of light, and the second fell.

The colonel was squatting over him and looking into his face, upside down. He felt the breath on his nose, but the colonel's words were unclear. *Now for yours* or *Off with you* or *This is all yours.* Emil understood nothing because he was sliding again into that warm black river.

Pain. And white, cold sky.

The sun burned overhead. Closing his eyes did nothing to help the grind of his nerves. Sitting up was misery.

He checked himself for holes.

He lay near the front of the taxi. His red-and-purple belly was bruised and aching, but not torn. There was blood on his shirt and jacket, but he didn't know if it was his. In his right hand was a pistol.

He dropped it.

PPK. Walther.

Around him, inside the U of rubble, were two lumps of clothes, filled with two dead men. A face was twisted toward him—one of the thugs. The other—he crawled and checked the face with the hole in its jaw—was the second thug. Flies crawled over their features.

After a while he could stand, but standing was hell, so he threw himself on the fender to help stay up. He shivered from cold and from everything else. He uneasily drew himself up to his full height, and saw the dead driver behind the wheel, head back, the passenger-side of his head blown out by an escaping bullet.

The noise of western planes was suddenly louder, drilling his ear. He tried to be quick about getting to the door and not looking too closely at the corpse as he dragged it out. The seat was covered with dry, sticky blood.

Why am I not dead?

When he sat down he closed his eyes and left his hands on the wheel.

Twice, he thought. I have died twice and twice been reborn.

He held down the nausea.

If this could happen here, if Michalec had found him with so little effort, then Lena was finished. He knew it then, was finally, utterly sure: She was dead. The pain rolled across his skull, pressing him down.

The car started quickly, but was difficult to turn around in the rubble. He worried about crushing the bodies as he backed up and drove forward many times. Once he was turned around completely, he had trouble staying on the path. He had the feeling, and it was overwhelming, that time was moving very quickly while he himself moved in slow motion. Dust shot up as he scraped the concrete blocks and shattered wood that bordered it, and he heard the scrape of baby carriages and bricks. When he came to splits in the path he made intuitive guesses—slow, stupid presumptions. Once, he stopped, opened the door and vomited clear liquid. Finally the rubble ended, and he turned onto a cracked, paved road. A truck filled with Soviet soldiers drove by, their faces tired from late nights out. A few jeeps with stern senior officers followed. No one noticed the bruised, achingly slow man in the scratched taxi, who, every time he shifted, felt the adhesion of blood holding him to the seat.

More guesses. Vague remembrances. He appeared at the far end of Unter den Linden, but could hardly see the peak of the Brandenburg Gate because of speeding delivery trucks that filled the broad avenue. The city was going on as it had yesterday, and the day before. As though everything in Emil's life had not just collapsed. After a few more streets, he was clear enough to find The Last Cat. The bar was closed. The taxi's clock said it was just after noon.

He parked and opened the windows to let out the stink. His hands, his feet, his face—everything shook. When he closed his eyes there were bodies.

Some women with carriages noticed him. They gasped and looked away quickly. Their pace increased. He saw other women, mothers and grandmothers and daughters. Their faces all reminded him of one. Affected faces, faces that have lost their girlhood. A grandmother with long gray hair braided at the neck asked if he needed some food. She seemed to talk so quickly that he had trouble understanding, and when he did understand, he could not make his mouth move fast enough—*"Thank you, no, thank you, I'm waiting for a friend. I'll be all right."*

"The *Americans* did this to you?" It was Konrad Messer, standing a few hesitant feet from the window.

Emil groaned and opened the door. Everything was stuck, then it was unstuck. "Just let me in." He hobble toward Konrad's grimace. "Please?"

The dark and cool, stale air of the club was soothing. He stripped and washed, using the kitchen faucet in the back while Konrad went to move the car away from his club. He came back shaking his head, then went to retrieve a spare suit he kept in the office for emergencies. It was a little large, but better than anything Emil had ever owned. No worker materials here.

Konrad handed him something sweet with gin. "You'll need a few of these."

Emil almost declined, he needed to make a call, but his hands shook too much, and he knew he couldn't make sense yet. He threw the drink back. His stomach would have to take it. He leaned against the bar and began muttering about what had happened. He'd thought he would just tell a little, but when it began he couldn't stop. Konrad nodded continuously to prove he was listening, but his expression never changed as he made gin drinks for them both.

"What are you going to do?"

He blinked into his glass. "Do you have a telephone?"

"In the office."

He took a fourth drink with him. The world was beginning to slow. He talked to three operators in as many languages—their voices sped and slowed with the rhythm of his drinking—and then he waited for the callback. Konrad's office was covered with yellowed photographs from before the war, men on stages. Show-business shots, vaudeville. Men standing next to other men who were dressed up like women. The telephone rang.

It took two more operators to patch him through to the station. He was told by a curt woman that Leonek Terzian, along with the rest of the homicide department, was not in the office. It was Saturday. He asked if there was a home listing for Leonek. "Who are *you*?" she demanded.

He read off his Militia identification number and told her this was an emergency. She made him wait while she conferred with someone else. Finally she returned and unhappily gave him the telephone number.

More operators, another wait for the callback. Then a woman's faint voice: "*Yes?*"

He asked for Leonek Terzian.

The hiss on the line grew louder as he waited. Leonek's voice was difficult to hear. "Emil? It's you?" He was shouting. "Emil, listen." A pause and a whisper directed at his mother to *get out of here.* "Emil?"

"Yes?"

"She wasn't there."

"What? She wasn't—*what?*" He had known it before, had known it in his bones; his premonitions had been astute. But hearing it aloud was entirely different.

"I went to Ruscova," he said. "You didn't tell me I'd have to get there by horse. But I made it. I went to that woman's house. Irina Kula?"

"Yes yes, that's it," said Emil. Everything was being said too slowly.

"She wanted me to tell you it wasn't her. She says it was Greta, her friend. She said you'd know her."

Emil remembered a fat, frizzy-haired woman full of smiles.

"A man came for Lena. That's what she said."

"What?"

"She asked you to forgive her. She feels terrible."

"What man?"

"I don't know. Short, dark hair. That's all I could get. Rude."

Emil couldn't speak. He leaned against the wall and closed his eyes. He could smell Lena's cigarettes and feel the shape of her ribs through the summer dress she wore in Ruscova. She had been crying then.

Something garbled came over the lines, ending with "dead."

"What?"

"That maid. Irma? In the hospital—suffocated!"

Konrad brought Emil another drink and exited discreetly.

"You there?"

Emil wasn't there. He was sitting at the desk, the telephone to his ear, but his body had contracted and convulsed, sending his thoughts elsewhere, to some desperate escape. Part of him wanted to cease right now. To turn off his head and call it quits. This was too much for one young man.

"Emil?"

All he could think to say was "I'm coming home." He hung up.

A pile of twenty-three boys in a shattered Berlin apartment. Three bodies in the rubble. One in a living room, one in the Tisa. A girl in a hospital room, a pillow over her face. God, how they piled up. And Lena—yes, Lena—was just another. *But why not me?* Why was he not dead among the broken bricks?

He clutched his stomach and leaned over the floor, but this time nothing came.

He called the Schonefeld Aeroflot office. A shockingly friendly and perky Russian woman told him the next flight home wasn't until four in the morning. Emil reserved a seat and finished his drink. He floated back to the bar. Konrad looked at him sympathetically and made a joke about his walk. Emil put his empty glass on the counter and asked for another.

CHAPTER TWENTY-SEVEN

****

The bartender arrived around three. Large, burly, peasant stock. He cleaned off the bar and replaced the corks with spouts for easy pouring. He had the look of workers who appeared on posters—strong, Soviet—with sleeves neatly rolled up and a wrench in their hands, bringing forth the future by way of railroads, dams and bridges. Or the worker statue in Victory Square, sharing a stone torch that lights nothing.

Konrad sat across from Emil and started speaking. It was a kind of nervousness. He didn't know what to say, so he touched his broken nose and talked about the bartender's obsessive cleanliness. Like no one he had ever seen. It was the last refuge of civility left in the big man. Konrad slid his glass over to Emil, smiling. "You need this more than I do."

"What about Janos?"

"What about him?"

Maybe it was the drinks, or the despair, or their brutal combination, but Emil was suddenly very sure of himself. "Janos told you Smerdyakov—*Graz*—was a friend. I can't believe Janos lied to you about him. Maybe at first he did, but he couldn't follow through with the deception."

"Why couldn't he, sweet Comrade Inspector?" Konrad's hands were on the table, flat, on each side of his glass.

"Because Janos was in love with you."

It might have been true, but there was no way for Emil to

know. He only knew that the German was holding something back, and flattery was the only way to bring it out.

Konrad let out a long, low sigh, sinking toward the table. He shrugged. "Of course Janos loved me. That is a given. And yes, you clever Slav, Janos could not lie to me for long. I could see right through him. Once Janos was in Berlin, standing in front of me, he could not help but spill the whole story."

It was much as Emil had suspected. Janos went with Lena to Michalec's home for a party. Their shared Hungarian past made them one-night friends, and they were inseparable. Then the *Oberst* arrived. He was a drunk who asked Michalec in loud Hungarian how much all this had cost. Only Janos and a couple others understood the words, and, to Janos, Michalec's angry reaction was shocking. "He grabbed this drunk by the collar and flung him—*literally*—into the garden. The whole time shouting, *What are you doing in my house?*" But the German—a happy drunk— seemed to feel nothing, and murmured joyously that he would go to Berlin, to the files. That's where anyone could learn how much this life had cost.

"God," said Emil, his despair fleeing him in one brief, amnesiac moment. "It was all there from the start!"

Konrad shook his head. "When you're working backwards, Comrade Inspector, yes. But not when that's all you know. We're not all criminal experts."

But Janos's interest was piqued. He took to following Michalec around town, spying on him, photographing him, and once, when he saw Michalec meet again with that German late one night, he decided to get in touch with his own man in Berlin.

Ten photos, thought Emil. The beginning. "So through you and Birgit he located the file and took one of the photographs."

"He made a snapshot of the evidence," Konrad corrected. "Unlike you, he's not a thief."

"But he was an extortionist. Janos blackmailed Michalec for six months. And then it ended. Why, Konrad? Why did Michalec decide it was all over?"

Konrad was sinking, slowly, into his chair. "You tell me, Inspector. After he left in February, I never heard from him." His voice was somber and muted, as if covered by a veil. "It was supposed to set him free. The money was supposed to give him the freedom to leave his wife and come to me."

Emil watched a moment, this man slipping into his own regrets, then put a hand on Konrad's. He told him about the plane ticket receipt he had found in Janos's apartment.

Konrad's eyes lit up. "What?"

"He was killed the day before he was going to fly to Berlin," said Emil, glad for once to make someone happy. "To be with you."

The club was full. There were men dressed immaculately and some women laughing at jokes, and in the corner, on a small stage, a few men wearing women's clothes and wigs prepared for a show. Emil remembered the black garters from Janos's apartment—so long ago—and realized they had probably been his. Cabaret music blared from the jukebox—tinny sounds straining the old speakers—and smoke filled the room. He was surrounded by fur collars and fine hats. His own disarray was painful and obvious. They were watching him, even though their eyes never met his. It was the same trick the homicide inspectors conjured on that first day. He drank to ignore it.

He asked someone at the next table for the time, and the man's milky, German voice almost slipped away before he caught it: 8:15. Still eight hours until his flight. The music swelled and consumed him.

He couldn't remember where Irma had said she was from. He should find out and visit her family. Tell them something kind about her service to the Crowder household. He should not be here.

He dwelled on Irma to avoid thinking of the other one.

234 ★ OLEN STEINHAUER

Konrad sat across from him, looking upset, and tapped Emil's cheek. "You better wake up. There's someone here to see you." His face looked very white and stiff.

Behind Konrad, a tall man in a leather overcoat smiled. His smile was narrow, and he had thick, black-rimmed glasses. Emil recognized him from yesterday morning. "You are Comrade Inspector Emil Brod?" he asked, stepping up. He spoke Russian with a Moscow slur.

Konrad stood aside, whimpering quietly. Emil at first needed help getting up, but once on his feet he could make it all right. Outside, he said, "My cane?" and the Russian nodded to a disheveled-looking teenager standing outside a long Grosser Mercedes. The boy ran into the club. The Russian put a hand on Emil's head to make sure it didn't strike the frame as he got into the backseat. A chubby man with a broad smile was in there already—yes, this was the one he had lost in the alley—and then Emil was between them.

Behind the wheel was the one-armed taxi driver who had driven him and the bureaucrat from the airport. They looked at each other momentarily in the mirror, but Emil saw no recognition in his eyes.

The teenager reappeared with the cane and leapt into the passenger's seat. When the car started moving, he lit a cigarette.

"Can I ask where we're going?" Emil's pulse was so loud he almost shouted his question.

The Russian who had fetched him pushed his glasses up his nose and shrugged. "Somewhere quiet. We'll talk, no problem." He cocked his head. "You want a smoke? Yakov, give the man a smoke. Give me one too."

Emil took one. The Russian lit it for him with a match, but put his own behind an ear. Emil knew from the first drag that he was back in the East. He didn't want his last minutes to taste like this.

The silhouetted shells of nighttime Berlin passed them, and all he could think of were methods of torture. Nothing extravagant, but the simplicity of heat and pressure applied to the tender parts of the body. Shards shoved beneath fingernails. Testicles burned with cigarettes—he gazed, horrified, at his own cigarette—and bones crushed. All the rumors of the MVD rolled over him. Simple visits to answer a few questions became days and weeks and months behind stone walls, iron bars. Became missing persons. Became stutterers and cripples and mutes. Soviet Intelligence had never been known for subtlety.

He wanted to think of Lena. He thought she might give him courage, but in these final moments all he could think of were his own bones, his own organs and flesh.

They finally stopped at a low brick building. A bullet-punctured sign said it was a boy's school. But there were no boys behind the twisted iron gate, and only a few lights in the windows. There were other cars parked along the street. Men leaned against their hoods, smoking. Waiting.

Emil's heart sputtered so loudly he could not be sure of the silence in the street. Then the barking of a dog broke through.

The Russian in glasses, with the cigarette still behind his ear, led him past the gate and inside, down a dim yellow corridor lined by identical, odd-numbered doors: 17, 19, 21, 23. The heavy man with the wide smile followed. Fluorescent ceiling lights buzzed. 33, 35, 37. Their shoes echoed on the floor. He thought he smelled ether.

They opened 47 and let him inside. Somebody hit the light switch. The room was just as he would have imagined: a small desk with two wooden chairs, facing a lone chair in the center of the room. There was a small spotlight on the desk.

"You know where to go," said the one who had fetched him.

He did. He sat in the center of the room without hesitation. As he watched them go to their own seats, he wondered if, had they brought him to the edge of a ditch in a bullet-riddled courtyard and told him to kneel before it, he would follow their orders with the same obedience and wait for the bullet. He nodded at the spotlight, tightening his throat. "You're going to sweat something out of me?"

The wide face looked confused an instant, then understanding overcame him. His smile was huge. "This?" He grabbed the electrical cord and held it up, showing where it ended in a frayed mess. "Hasn't worked for—how long?"

"Months," said the other. But he didn't smile. He left his leather coat on and took some papers from a small bag Emil hadn't noticed before. He flattened them on the desk.

"Months," the smiler repeated, nodding. "It would make this job a lot easier. But for now, the Revolution moves at a snail's pace."

"Is that what this is about?" Emil's voice was beginning to relax, though the rest of him couldn't.

The first one, satisfied with his paperwork, took the cigarette from behind his ear and lit it. "Everything is about the Revolution, Comrade. Some things more than others."

Emil became aware that the walls were filthy. They were speckled by something that looked like brown paint. But it wasn't paint.

"What about it, then?" asked the smiler. "Does your visit to the Americans have a bearing on the course of world revolution?"

"None," he said. "None that I know of."

"Your face," said the other through a cloud of smoke, blinking behind his glasses. "Those bruises."

"I was mugged," said Emil. "I took the wrong taxi." He paused, but they did not help him. "The driver and his friends attacked me."

The wide smile faded, and a look of concern replaced it. "Yes, we know. Berlin is extremely dangerous." He rested his elbows on the table. "Just this afternoon we found three dead men in one of the bombed areas. All three were shot. In their heads." He shook his own head. "Very ugly."

"Ugliest I've seen in a while," said the other. He flicked ash on the floor and looked puzzled. "Wasn't one of them a taxi driver?"

A nod. "I believe he was." He turned to Emil. "I don't suppose he was *your* taxi driver? No." That wide head, shaking again. "The coincidence would be . . . *unbelievable!*"

Emil's tired body tensed from head to toe.

Of course he was still alive, and of course they came to him. The *Oberst* had not shot him, because he knew the authorities would want a simple answer to three dead bodies in the rubble. He had gotten rid of witnesses to the prized photograph, but had learned in the Capital that leaving unexplained bodies around was not wise. So he had placed the murder weapon in Emil's hand and walked away. So easy. Efficient. Herr Oberst gets his picture, and cleans up the mess.

And they all knew he was coming to Berlin—the MVD didn't give out information without wondering who was asking for it, and why.

Emil's mistakes were endless. He had fled the scene without informing the proper authorities. He had left the Walther with his prints all over it. He had driven the blood-soaked taxicab all the way to the club for the whole city to look into. Berlin, for him, had been an extended exercise in stupidity.

Their eyes were red, tired. These Russians had worked quickly, had tracked him down in no time. They would see through him. These intelligence agents were the kind of policemen he would never be. They were efficient and focused and always thinking. He knew this. They were also MVD: militant, brutal and all-knowing.

"Tell me what you want to know."

The tall one put out his cigarette on the floor with his foot. "We want to know what you're doing in Berlin, killing good Germans. It's our responsibility to watch out not only for our Soviet citizens, but also for the defeated Fascist nation that has been entrusted to us."

Emil took only a second to think it through. He told them

everything in a straightforward tone. He was a homicide inspector. He had come to Berlin to look into the death of a well-connected songwriter. "*Proletarian* songwriter." He contacted Comrade Konrad Messer because of information received via their office here in Berlin. They nodded knowledgeably—this was not news. The deceased had apparently been interested in military records at the Tempelhof airbase. He tried not to pause before his one lie: "My search for what he was seeking was fruitless."

He waited for them to ask questions. His body was about to collapse. If they tested him, he would not last any time. But he had to hold his position, if only to have something to give them in case it came to brutality. But they asked nothing. He filled the silence:

"When I returned to the Soviet sector, I was set upon by this taxi driver and his friends. Apparently, they thought I had money. When they discovered how poor I was, they did this to me." He pointed at his face, then shrugged. He tried for casual sincerity, but didn't know if it looked right. "I'm not sure what happened then. I was in and out. A fight, I guess. When I woke up, three of them were dead, and the fourth was gone."

They seemed unmoved by the tragedy.

"I went to Comrade Messer for help, and I made an Aeroflot reservation. To return home. I can't do anything else here."

They nodded in unison. "And Tempelhof?" asked the one with glasses. "You searched the base?"

"I couldn't get inside," he said slowly, evenly. "They turned me away at the gate."

The wide one asked if Emil could describe the fourth man.

He shook his head in an approximation of sadness. "I wish I could. It was dark. I only knew the driver's face."

The other looked down at the papers. "Your prints were on the pistol that killed these men."

"I know." Emil nodded. "I woke with it in my hand. But there was no way I could have done it. You should have seen me last night."

"We see you now." A wide smile. He looked at his partner, then back at Emil. "We'll be right back."

When they were gone, the nausea filled him, a delayed reaction, and he noticed again the speckled dried blood on the wall. It had come out of people who had thought they could outsmart the Soviet secret police.

His stomach seized up—partly nerves, partly the alcohol. He was so stupid.

They knew. They had to know—it was their job to know. He was a liar, and they would soon walk back in here with other, larger men whose job was to beat the truth out of the unfortunate. And when the truth was out, they would continue beating until he admitted to any crime they felt like solving, or inventing. He would admit to killing those three men. He would say he had killed Janos Crowder, that he had been hoping for a shot at Comrade Chairman Stalin. They would open their casebooks and tie him to all the unsolved deaths. Yes, he would admit to anything in the end, because that's how human beings were.

It could have been an hour, or five. He closed his eyes and began, after a while, to drift off. But then the door opened, loudly, and the smiling Russian came rushing up to him. "You have a plane reservation?"

Emil nodded. "In the morning."

"Now," he said, cheeks fat and pink. "It's morning now. I'll give you a lift."

CHAPTER TWENTY-EIGHT

****

Emil expected the Russian to pull over to the side of the road, place a pistol to his temple and shoot. He wouldn't have had the energy to fight it. But then Schonefeld Airfield rose out of the predawn gloom. "You may wonder," the Russian said, smiling as he drove, "and be afraid to ask. Really, you shouldn't be afraid. Just ask."

Emil's voice was hoarse: "Why?"

"Because," he said, "this is not for us. This is for your people. If you want to make trouble with your men, your *politicos*, as you say, then the people's representatives of the Soviet Union would not consider standing in your way. Each of our socialist brothers acts independently, and this is for the good of the whole. You follow?"

Emil nodded, then said that he did understand.

"Your own state security may take some issue with you, but we don't. We are for freedom and international peace."

Emil wanted to laugh, because it sounded like a joke, but didn't. As they drove through the gates, the Russian showed an ID to a guard who waved them on.

"Anyway," he added, "you certainly didn't kill those lowlifes. They're the kind of men you hire to do the kind of thing that was done to them." He parked in a lot and ran around to open the door for Emil. They began walking to the terminal. "I'm Andrei," he said. "From Tblisi, you know? Georgian Republic. Good luck finding your man."

He shook hands with Emil outside the airplane, and held his forearm firmly. A wink and a smile. Ruddy cheeks. All the way up the steps to the plane, Emil waited for the bullet in the back of the head. But it never came.

He searched each face and ignored any taxi driver who approached him. He hobbled to the edge of their crowd and woke an elderly driver dozing beneath the morning's *Spark*. More airplanes covered the front page, more exclamations.

It was Sunday—the Militia station wouldn't be open until tomorrow—so he directed the driver home.

In the Third District they had to wait at an intersection for a parade to pass. Children with red flags held high. Girls with red kerchiefs and boys with red suspenders. Their song sounded familiar. He folded his arms in the backseat as the driver hummed and waved at the children and the portraits of the Great Econo-mists, as a writer in *The Spark* had called them. Emil closed his eyes. He saw nothing but failures.

Janos Crowder, Aleks Tudor, Irma—

God, he had forgotten her family name again.

So many dead, it left him numb.

Lena was the only thing left. Maybe.

A few uniformed Militia followed the marching boys and girls, and waved the taxi through.

Grandfather looked disapprovingly at Konrad's clothes before Emil changed into his own. Grandmother boiled tea. They buzzed and whispered, but did not speak to him. His abused face kept them quiet. He went out to the telephone in the corridor.

As he listened to the ringing on the line, he had a hopeful dream of escape—air or train, no matter—back to Berlin, but with her—find her and drag her along—she packs something small—a few dresses and hats and shoes—he brings nothing but a handful of Ostmarks for the Brandenburg guard, and maybe a joke in Russian. Then they would be through.

Maybe a coffee with the American officer at Brandenburg, whatever he wants to know, then another excruciating flight. To Hanover, or Frankfurt. The West.

Filia had asked him why he didn't stay over there, in the West. The truth was that he didn't know how to live anywhere else.

He hung up when it was plain there was no one home at Leonek's. He had never thought to get Leonek's address, then a word came to him from the back of his mind: *Bobia.*

Swiftly, gratefully. Irma Bobia.

"Who did it?" Grandfather finally asked. He pulled up a blistered balcony chair he'd brought inside. He touched his face to make himself clear. "Those."

"A Nazi," Emil said, and rolled in the sofa to face the ceiling. He wondered what would happen to his grandparents if he left.

"Nazis." He sighed. "They're still around? I thought the Red Army made good meat of them."

Emil closed his eyes. He wondered if they would be put under house arrest. Sometimes that happened to families when traitors ran out on utopia.

"Shut up about your Russians," snapped Grandmother. She almost barked it. She replaced Emil's cold tea with a fresh one. "He doesn't want to listen to your claptrap."

The light was hazy through the windows. Emil blinked toward the sky. "Do you know the time?"

"Seven o'clock," said Grandfather.

He had tried the telephone at least ten times and considered visiting all the bars and cafés in the Capital to find him, but went to bed and tried, again, to focus.

Lena had been taken. Fact.

Unlike the others, she had been dragged out of Ruscova, not

executed where she stood. So maybe she was still alive, somewhere.

He could try to force his way onto the estate, but Michalec
would be prepared for him. He would only join that long list of
dead. Lena's doom would be sealed.

He had nothing. No leverage, no power. Nothing.

Around four he woke from a cold, dreamless sleep to shouting
from the next room. Grandmother's voice quivered at a hysterical
pitch, a sound Emil had never heard from her. Grandfather's
voice was staccato and weakly defiant. Then louder, more angry.
Emil covered his head with the blanket and tried to sleep, but
the walls were like paper. It was as if they were shouting in the
room with him. This was one sleep he needed more than any in
his life; he needed to be unconscious. Words floated through—
Grandfather called her a *whore* and an *ungrateful cunt*, words he'd
never heard him use against anyone. Sharp slaps. Emil was on his
feet then, the cold hardly touching his half-naked form, the
impulse carrying him through the door, where Grandfather's
hand was raised to hit her again. The old man was shouting
hoarsely, his face twisted in pink fury. Emil caught his hand on its
way down, and used a quick fist on his jaw. Grandmother
gasped—she was falling back into the sofa—and Grandfather
tumbled to the floor.

"Are you all right?" he asked her.

But she wasn't listening to him. She was on her feet and then
crouching beside her stunned husband, the trace of blood on her
lip quickly licked away as she whispered and lifted his head into
her lap.

She woke him at eight by sitting on the bed and stroking his hair.
She did this all the time in Ruscova, before the Jews came. He
remembered enjoying how much she enjoyed it.

"I'm sorry," he said groggily, but he wasn't. He would do it again. He hadn't gotten much sleep, thinking of how he would do it again.

She tilted her head from side to side and smiled. The corner of her lip looked a little swollen, but her eyes were sky blue in the light. They had an unreal quality that Grandfather's dark eyes could never have. She picked at her eyebrow. "Your grandfather's a little stupid sometimes."

He nodded into the pillow and slid up against the headboard. "What was it? The argument."

She shook her head. "It's from a long time ago."

He furrowed his brow, and she pressed a warm hand to his cheek.

"It's time for you to get up."

Leonek's mother answered again. "This is Emil Brod. I called the day before yesterday."

"When?"

"Saturday."

Emil waited. Finally a wary male voice said, "Yes?"

"It's me."

"Emil! Thank God it's you. Let's meet."

"Why?" This morning he felt the full, deep knowledge of his powerlessness. It had taken all night to seep into his bones, but now it was there, in his marrow. Leonek was saying something. "What?"

"I said, it's not all bad."

That didn't make any sense. Emil leaned against the railing as some children scurried and laughed on the ground floor. It was utterly bad.

"Emil? You there?"

"Yes."

"Well, listen to me, okay? Last night I went to Lena Crowder's house again. I searched everywhere. Nothing was coming up. Then I remembered those pictures you had. You remember them?"

Emil said he did.

"You found them behind the icebox," he said. "So I went to the kitchen, and there it was. It had been tied up."

"With twine."

"Exactly. A photograph. I recognized Smerdyakov right away. And get this: He's accepting a medal from a *Nazi officer*. Can you believe it? Emil?"

Leonek picked him up in the Mercedes with the smashed headlights, and his face fell when he saw the bruises. *"Christ,"* he said as he drove. "You really are the world's punching bag."

"Let me see the photograph."

It was a large print that had been folded for so long that a white crease cut down between the two men sharing a medal. The difference was that it was a photograph of a photograph that was lying on a floor.

"This is it," said Leonek. "Right?" He squinted at some soldiers crossing the street.

Emil held it up in the sunlight, then returned it to his knee. He began to think clearly again.

She was not dead. Michalec was a killer, but he did not kill without reason. He knew this photograph was still at large. Michalec worked according to the logic of self-preservation. *Others make the rules. We can only try to live by them.*

When they trembled over the tram tracks at Yalta Boulevard, Emil saw what he had to do. A swift, immaculate vision.

"Can you get in touch with Dora?"

"Dora?" Leonek sounded doubtful. "Why do you want that son of a bitch?"

"We need him."

Leonek gazed ahead at nothing in particular. "Did you hear about Liv Popescu?"

Emil shook his head.

"They took her to the holding cells north of town, and she

used her prison clothes to hang herself from the pipes." He turned at the next corner.

A bruise on Emil's cheek was beginning to itch. He scratched it. His organs felt hard and cold. Outside, parade banners were on the ground, and crowds of drunk soldiers were mindlessly trampling political slogans.

CHAPTER TWENTY-NINE

****

They crossed the Georgian Bridge and parked near the arched footbridges leading into the labyrinth. It was quiet here—no farmers shouted out their vegetables, and no engines rumbled—so their footsteps on stone, and the fifth step of Emil's cane, echoed before them. They walked in perpetual shadow. Faces peered through slits in yellowed lace curtains, and some pensioners came out to their stoops to watch Emil and Leonek pass. In place of engines, there was the quiet murmur of water smacking stone. Cats in windowsills kept track of them.

After a few turns, they were in an area of the Canal District Emil had never been to before, not even when he was younger and curious. "We aren't lost," he whispered involuntarily; it was a question.

"You'll get to know this place well," said Leonek. He whispered too.

It was quickly apparent that everyone knew they were Militia. Hesitant glances and mistrusting frowns shot their way. The prostitutes smiled at them, because a single pair of policemen with law enforcement on their minds wouldn't have a chance back here. Emil noticed the young one who had whispered to him before. Her freckles peeked out from beneath powder, and when she whispered to one of the veterans he caught sight of her milk teeth. She moved now with the smooth grace of the broken, as if she had nothing left to lose.

A redheaded, barefoot hooker cut the distance between them

in half. "There's four of us, Comrade Inspectors." Her voice was smoky and rough. "That's a mighty good time."

Leonek smiled and touched her arm lightly. "Maybe we'll come back for that, Beatrice. But this time it's easier money." He took a few bills out of his pocket.

She folded the koronas until they were a tight, tiny package she could slip into her mangled stocking. "How easy?"

"Your brother. Where is he?"

She pouted playfully. "*Inspector*. What kind of sister—"

"Just business, Bea. It's always just business."

Dora's address was in the center of the Canal District, in the grimy back passages where water trickled loudly—Emil heard the occasional high pitch of rats. It was a small courtyard still named after a dead king, and Dora's front door was a soft, waterlogged plank that stank of the sea. There was a worn hole instead of a handle. They climbed the narrow, damp stairs where light came in through a shattered window, and knocked at one of three doors at the top.

There was scurrying inside.

"Dora! It's Terzian. Want to open up?"

The movement stopped, but then they heard a faint *shhh* from someone's lips.

"I just want to talk, Dora. It'll be worth your time."

A lock snapped, and the door opened a few inches. An eye appeared from the gloom, looking at them jerkily, one and then the other. Then the door opened the rest of the way, and a thin, graying man in his forties stood in boxer shorts and an undershirt. He had a thick white scar along the side of his neck. "What is it?" His voice was high like a child's.

"Some help," said Leonek. He showed more bills, but returned them to his pocket. "Can we come in?"

Dora's eyes narrowed. "What kind of help?"

"We need you to set up a meeting. Simple stuff."

Dora retreated into the room, where a fourteen-year-old sat in a corner, her bare, scratched knees pulled to her chin. Her makeup had been smeared by old tears, but she smiled at them.

"Hanna," said Dora. "Get out of here."

She looked at the visitors again, then at him, and went into the next room. When she stood up, Emil noticed the black needle marks on the pale inside of her left thigh, and maybe that was what did it.

Dora sat on the edge of a cracked coffee table, bare feet spread, and stuck a cigarette in his mouth. "Who's your kid?"

"Inspector Brod," said Emil, but he was no longer seeing clearly. What he saw was that first week, the humiliations, the fighting, the gunshots. He saw the unfounded, nearly fatal suspicion all over again, felt it grinding in his gut. The suspicion caused by this one wretch. He saw the abused girl who had just left, saw the freckled hooker who was once a girl and now completely broken, and he saw Liv Popescu and Alana Yoskovich rotting in their graves because of the same kind of sickness. He saw those faceless schoolgirls who now walked the Capital as women who had known more of this man than they ever wanted. Emil's hands were ice cold. "Inspector Emil Brod," he said, making his identity completely clear.

He waited for it. Dora lit a match, but the flame didn't make it to the cigarette. He had no doubt learned what had followed his stab in the dark—*There will be a spy . . .*

His hand lowered again, and his face fell slack.

Emil swung before he could gather himself, fist connecting with bony cheek. Dora's feet lifted from the floor a moment, then he fell back off the coffee table, sprawled across the floor.

Leonek's shock paled him.

Dora propped himself up with a hand and wiped his nose with the other. It came up with blood. "What the fuck *is* this, Leon?"

The urge was all over him now: to jump on Dora and beat him unconscious, to take a blade to him. He couldn't even remember why he hated this man, but the hatred was running him now. For a moment he was sure that if he killed Dora he could get them all back. Janos Crowder, Aleks Tudor, Irma. Lena. Maybe even Filia. Ester.

"*Fuck!*" shouted Dora.

Leonek found his voice, but all it said was "*Emil,*" pleading.

Emil's breaths were shallow and loud as he walked out.

From the mossy square he could hear Dora saying that he wouldn't be treated this way, not by anyone, for no amount of money, and he wasn't going to help a single fucking cop again, it wasn't worth it. Then he was quiet while Leonek counted out koronas and tried to convince him otherwise.

Water dripped from a ledge, and between the stone houses he thought he saw things moving. It was early afternoon, but cold and damp.

Scraping. Their voices again.

Hanna looked down at him from an open window. Her smile was still there—a vacant, bruised one. She had wiped her eyes, but instead of repairing them the makeup had streaked to her temples.

"Is Hanna your real name?" he asked in a high whisper.

The smile deepened into her pale cheeks. When she nodded, her dark, stringy hair bobbed around her ears.

"Where are you from?"

She glanced back into the apartment, then hissed, "*Prešov.*"

"I knew a girl from there," he lied.

She leaned farther out the window, and he saw how thin her shoulders were. She reminded him in some unnamable way of Ester. "Really?"

"A beautiful girl."

"More beautiful than me?"

"Hardly," he said, and a mist of color came into her cheeks. "How long have you been in the Capital?"

"Six weeks," she said. "And three days."

"Are your people here? Your family?"

She shook her head.

The adrenaline had faded, and he was getting a pain in his shoulders from looking up, so he backed against a wall. "My name's Brod. Inspector Emil Brod. Do you think you can remember that?"

"Inspector Emil Brod," she repeated. "I'm very bright."

He wasn't sure if she was making fun of him. "I work in Homicide. Our station is in the First District."

"I've seen it," she said. Very seriously.

"If you need anything, you come to me. Okay?"

She looked at him blankly.

"Hanna? Can you remember that? Anything, whatever. I'll try to help."

She nodded, still very serious. Her brow was stitched tight. Then she looked back into the room and disappeared. Dora took her place. Sadly, there was nothing left on his face of the punch, though Emil's knuckles were still sore. "Get out of here, Inspector!"

Leonek was stepping sheepishly down from the front door.

Emil showed Dora his teeth, then growled.

"Christ, Brod. What the hell is going on?"

Chief Moska glared from his side of the desk. Someone had partly repaired the radiator, and it hissed in the corner, a thin line of steam shooting from a loose bolt. The window had been opened to air the office out.

"Nothing, Chief."

"What's *this*?" He leveled a thick finger at Emil's bruised face.

"A fight, Chief. Happens all the time."

Moska settled on his elbows. He lowered his voice. "What about Berlin? You went?"

Briefly, Emil wasn't sure what to say. "I made a visit." He knew the man wanted to know as little as possible.

"And how was it?"

When Emil spoke it came out as a long exhale: "It's a city that makes you think, Chief."

A smile finally cracked his features, and he leaned back again. He looked ready to laugh. But instead, he scratched his scalp, fingers knuckle-deep in his gray mess. "There's a whole world above you, Brod. You know that, right?" He dropped his hand to the desk. "That's why I'm here. I'm the one who has to listen to their worries. They say, *Why do we have complaints from a politicos about your new inspector?* I have to have an answer. I tell them what I can, and sometimes I even ignore them. But they're not the bad guys, Brod. They're just like me. Someone above *them* is asking questions, wanting answers. So when they come to me I must have answers, or at least promises." The chief paused to look at him, and blinked once, slowly. "They say someone in the Central Committee wants a rookie on this dead songwriter case, don't waste time with good men." He touched his chest. "I say okay. Later, they say the same committeeman wants that rookie off the case, wants the case closed. I promise, because I'm a loyal servant, that this will be done. I haven't lost you in all this, have I, Brod?"

Emil shook his head.

"Good. Because sometimes I make promises for other people. You. I promise you're no longer involved in this case. It's a promise I can keep, isn't it?"

The chief had given him everything he needed—had asked him a question and given him the answer. So Emil nodded soberly. "Yes, that's a promise you can keep."

Moska's tongue rummaged around in his mouth. They did not misunderstand each other. "Go on, Brod. Go do your job."

His job consisted of waiting. Dora would not get back to them until the next day, Tuesday, when they would wait in a café for his phone call. Dora would contact the people he knew, the ones who knew Michalec, and either it would happen or it wouldn't. Emil wasn't sure what he would do if the deal wasn't accepted. He floated through the afternoon indecisively, and during long bouts of silence had the uneasy feeling that he might be near the end of his life. He was a young man, but if Lena was dead he felt an obligation to follow through with certain measures that would certainly be fatal. And he realized then that he had achieved what he had told Leonek he truly wanted: He had achieved devotion.

Leonek brought him home for an early dinner. The house was a low, two-room shack on the edge of the city, just before the farmland, with an outhouse and a well. It had once been a servants' quarters to the large house Emil could just make out on the horizon, beside a black stretch of woods, but after the Liberation the land had been chopped up and redistributed. There were other hovels peppering the field, and a few makeshift tents where families lived until they could build. It reminded Emil of the Tiergarten.

Seyrana Terzian wore her long past on her face. Emil thought he saw the roads of Armenia in her cheeks, and the other countries she'd had to go through to get here. She said only the obligatory greetings to Emil and served them a lentil-and-apricot dish she called *mushosh*, which he ate ravenously. This pleased her, and she finally smiled. She listened as the men talked. Emil told them about Helsinki, the Arctic, and Ruscova. He said his life was not something you could base a movie on, and Leonek said that their life—Emil noticed he never said *my* life—was a movie that couldn't be made. Armenia to Yugoslavia, then Bulgaria, Italy and here. Poverty and violence all along the way. The life of a refugee was not photogenic.

"Then you came here."

Leonek nodded. "After a few more countries, yes. You go where they'll take you. The king was feeling liberal the month we arrived. He even let me go into public service."

Seyrana nodded a steady agreement, occasionally wiping her eyes.

"And here you are," said Emil.

"A simple life."

"Not so simple."

"Extremely," said Leonek. "It's just me and mother." He smiled at her, and she patted his hand on the table with her own shriveled hand. "Look at the others," Leonek said to him. "Ferenc is writing his novel, can you imagine?"

"A book?" Emil had trouble imagining it.

"You didn't know?" Leonek grunted and raised his eyebrows. "Why do you think he's typing all the time? Those aren't reports he's working on. He's been writing that book as long as I can remember. And Stefan is a magician at rebuilding engines. Any time you have trouble with the car, bring it to him. Astounding work. Even the chief."

"The chief?"

"He paints. I guess you couldn't know that. Landscapes. Really very beautiful. But me? All I do is sing. Sometimes. And not very well. And I'm a detective. Not the best, but I make do. And there's you."

Emil didn't answer. He was wondering as well.

"For you, Her Highness."

"Who?"

"Madam Crowder."

Emil smiled, but then there was no energy to sustain it. He looked at his empty plate.

They discussed the case while Seyrana was in the kitchen. Emil told him what he had learned, the details of Janos's blackmail. "This went on for a while. Six months or so. With his money he left his wife and got an apartment in town. But along the way something happened—maybe excess greed, I don't know. Michalec felt he had to kill him."

"It doesn't make any sense," said Leonek, his hand on his rough, dark chin. "You saw how much money they were dealing with. Who's stupid enough to screw that up?"

"Whatever happened, Janos was scared they were going to kill him, so he booked a flight to Berlin." Emil smiled at Seyrana coming back to sit down, and decided to avoid mention of Janos's sexual tendencies. "There is one possibility, though, for what screwed all this up for Janos."

"Aleksander Tudor," said Leonek.

Emil nodded. "Tudor knew about the boxes of money. He was that kind of supervisor. And he could get inside the apartment whenever he wanted. Maybe he had found the picture, or at least those ten pictures Janos had taken of Michalec meeting the German colonel. Maybe he wanted something out of it." He shrugged. "Too many people in on a conspiracy, and it starts to crumble. Janos was killed, and Tudor knew he was next. I thought he was just a nervous man when I met him. But he had reason. He knew he was going to die."

"Please," said Seyrana. Emil enjoyed the heavy sound of her accent. "No more death at the table, okay?"

"You were in Italy?" Emil asked later, remembering.

Leonek shrugged, Seyrana nodded. She set down plates of *sadayif*, syrupy shredded dough. They gave proper attention to the dessert before Emil picked up the thread again.

"Venice. Did you see Venice?"

Leonek smiled and shook his head. "No, but Trieste, yes. It was a gorgeous city."

"But terrible without money," Seyrana said finally.

"*You've* seen Venice?" asked Leonek.

"I've heard of it," said Emil. He described the Bridge of Sighs, trying to tell it as the Croat had, but knowing he couldn't do it justice. "You know when you're on the bridge that all hope is gone, and you're now and forever a prisoner. Behind iron bars."

Leonek leaned back and lit two cigarettes. "I don't think I want to go to Venice; sounds like a sad place." He handed one to his mother, then got up. "Before I forget," he said as he found his leather satchel in the corner and brought it back to the table. He set his fuming cigarette on the edge and took a pistol out of the bag. Not a Walther, but a Marakov 9mm. He set it on the table. "Be careful—it's loaded."

Seyrana raised her weathered hands and muttered something in Armenian, a loud moan of misery.

"Come on, Mama." Leonek frowned at her, and she rattled an angry stream of abuse at him, her brows shifting, hands fluttering about her face. "You better take it before she does something crazy."

Emil held it in his hand. It was heavy.

"Go on," said Leonek, ignoring his mother's shouts. "In your pocket."

Emil dutifully dropped it into his jacket pocket.

Seyrana seemed to quiet a little, but the abuse continued, even as she collected the plates.

"We could go through the paperwork," explained Leonek, "but Christ knows how long that would take. It was faster to go to Roberto for your weapon."

Emil smiled, a sudden, unexplainable joy overcoming his despondency. It was the gift of the gun, the mother, and Leonek's love for the old woman. He put his hand in his pocket, felt the cool barrel.

"Good God," said Leonek. "You're not going to cry, are you?"

He felt like laughing.

Emil went home and took Janos Crowder's 35mm Zorki from the shelf where Grandfather had displayed it beside the books. He walked a few blocks to a photographic studio that was still open, where a man in a white smock with a gold front tooth loaded it for him. He explained some of the details of taking photographs, emphasizing light. "If in doubt, more light!"

He brought their electric lamp from the bedroom. Then he turned on the overhead bulb.

"What the hell?" asked Grandfather when he came out of his

bedroom into the radiant living room. It was almost eight, and the old man had been napping again. The spot on his jaw was pink. He went out to the balcony for a cigarette and watched suspiciously through the door.

Emil used a book at each corner of the photograph to flatten it, shifting until the shadows from the books did not obscure the two men and their Iron Cross. He adjusted the focusing ring to the approximate distance between him and the photo. He raised the camera to his eye. The button the photographer had said to press was stiff, but finally he heard that click.

He adjusted the diaphragm and shot it again. Again.

When the roll was done, he sat down and smiled. This was the first smart thing he had done for as long as he could remember.

Through the door, he saw the back of the old man's head, smoke rising from it. He got up and joined his grandfather on the balcony. There were seven women down by the six spigots, one waiting for her turn. Grandfather passed his cigarette over, and Emil took a drag, but didn't give it back. He blew smoke over the railing, where it formed a loose cloud before sliding away. Grandfather cleared his throat. Emil said, "You're going to have to talk."

Grandfather grunted. Neither acquiescence nor debate.

"This will go on." Emil didn't look at him as he spoke because he didn't want to pressure the old man. "It will get worse, and we'll grow to hate each other. So you have to tell me because I don't want it to come to that."

"It's not your business," Grandfather said finally.

"Everything is my business."

They settled on that for a moment as more women and a thin man showed up with pails and others left. They heard metal striking metal, and water spilling to the cobblestones. Grandfather took out another cigarette and lit it. His voice wavered now and then, but it pushed on, reluctantly, to the end.

"When we came back here from Ruscova, when you were still

up there, abroad, the Capital was mad. You've heard stories," he said. "The starvation, the violence. The Russians."

"I've heard a little."

"It's all true, and you've only heard a fraction. For a while people really were starving. A month, I'd say. They hadn't organized the distribution well, and nothing was getting where it was supposed to go. People were desperate. When they're desperate, when they think they could die at any time, they act differently. Terribly."

The Arctic had been no different. He looked down on the fat women in the square who were the result of wartime starvation—they ate everything now. Grandfather said that on some days they couldn't go out at all. There were gunshots outside, and they had to sit in the dark and wait for them to pass. Then, he would go out looking for food. "It's hard to imagine now, but for a few weeks this is how the Capital was."

"I've never heard this before," he said. "Why haven't I heard about this?"

Grandfather's eyes were almost dry, and his thin lips moved spastically before his voice came: "Why do you think?"

They rewrite history like it's their own goddamn Tolstoy novel.

He shrugged. "I'm sure you know about how the Russians were then. Mara likes to ridicule them, but she's right in some ways. They stole everyone's watches. They were like children listening to their ticking watches. In the street. Wherever. They took them off of dead bodies. And if it was a very nice watch, they might kill for it. They took what they wanted. I can't make excuses for them," he said, shaking his head toward the sky. "I know what they can be, both good and bad. They're a people of extremes, Emil."

He looked out over the city, over the windows and clay roofs and women with pails and the broken fountain and the dogs sniffing around it. His voice was even and quiet, and he told the story to the city, not to his grandson. It involved two Russian soldiers. They came to the apartment when he was gone foraging for food. The soldiers came looking for watches. They banged on the door, and when Mara did not answer they kicked it in.

Grandfather didn't describe them, but Emil imagined the soldiers from the bar outside of town. Loud, scraping fabrics, nervous pistols, acne.

Mara Brod hid her dead son Valentin's watch in the wood stove, and gave the soldiers her husband's broken wristwatch instead. One of them wound it and listened. He shook it and listened again. They were both very drunk. They smelled of cigar smoke. Then they raped her.

The old man was welling up as he stared at the city, and his mouth kept slipping into nervous smiles. He squeezed and released the arms of his chair.

"That's when I came back. They had her on the floor. I saw her there and . . . I don't know how to say it . . . I saw her seeing me seeing *her*. I couldn't move. They were still . . . and I couldn't take my eyes off her face. It was—I could only fall down." He was crying now like he had then, shaking all over, the chair clicking against the balcony, saying, "You have to understand, they had guns. One to her head . . ."

Emil was cold from head to foot.

When they were finished, they gave Avram Brod a pint of vodka. "A thank-you, they told me. Then they were gone." His weeping sounded choked and small, like a child's.

Women's voices came up from the square.

"I just want someone," he began, then shook his head. He looked at the sky. "I just want someone to make it better. Worth living. You see?"

Emil didn't know what to say. He was praying the old man would not ask to see his father's watch.

"We have everything here," said Grandfather. "And we have lost it all. You. You're everything we have left." He was finally looking at his grandson.

He was so old, and Emil was still so young.

CHAPTER THIRTY

****

He locked the Zorki in his desk. He didn't trust himself to unload the film without exposing it, so he left it inside the camera. When he needed the copies, he would have them taken care of. The original was folded inside his jacket, in the pocket opposite his pistol.

It was a little before ten in the morning. Leonek watched as Emil locked the desk. "What's that?"

"Are we going, or not?"

Leonek shrugged, then led the way.

The waitress looked as though she had been in this café, doing this particular job, all her life. Her wavy hair settled over her low brow, and when they asked for coffees, she told them there was no milk.

"It's all right," said Emil. "Just sugar."

"Saccharine tablets," she said.

Leonek winked at her. "Corina, can you tell Max I'm expecting a call?"

Emil thought she was going to spit on them both, but she turned and went to talk with the slight man working the coffee machine. Max gave Leonek a knowing nod.

"You know every café and bar in the Capital, don't you?"

Leonek smiled, pleased.

They sat beside a wide, high window that faced tiny, brick-laid

October Square. They did not speak—they had talked everything out by now—but stared at the busy market and listened to the voices that shot through the thin pane. It was cold, but bright. Vendors called for customers to look at their wares, and colorful Gypsy women lifted fabrics to see clearly while the men behind the tables watched suspiciously. Children appeared from somewhere—quick, hoarse shouts—and ran across the square. Stiff old veterans from the first big war sat on the benches they occupied every day, nodding heads, watching. Some uniformed police stood around eating off a fresh loaf of bread, and a woman with no teeth laughed beside the tallest one, then punched him on the arm. The Capital had always been cosmopolitan despite itself. Romanians and Hungarians and Slovaks and Poles and Ukrainians fell irresistibly into the mix. Fat and round faces, and faces of gradating shades. Emil was unexpectedly overcome.

There was not a single Russian in sight.

"Comrade Inspector!" called Max. Leonek looked up from his own thoughts. The bartender was holding the telephone in his hand, waving it.

They stayed away from the station so that nothing would keep them from their appointment. They drank coffee in the morning, then switched to wine to get rid of the shakes. "This waiting is impossible," said Emil.

"Then think of something to do."

"I will."

But all that came to Emil was food, and once they were in front of their cabbage soups, he had no appetite. His stomach was shrunken and sore.

"I'm getting tired."

Leonek pushed away his bowl. "Then we go back to coffee."

When they finished the coffee, it was time.

They parked in the gravel lot at 8:30, and continued on foot. In the darkness, their slow path along footbridges, through narrow, wet passageways and across steps wrapping around crumbling stone walls brought them to a bridge that had snapped in mid-arch when the far side sank too deep. To span the distance, some-one had laid boards that shifted beneath their feet. They heard fragments of bridge dropping into the canal, and smelled piss.

It was called the Deeps. Here, the silted pilings beneath the stone houses and walkways had begun to crumble, and this cor-ner of the Canal District was slowly sinking. In the thirties, most of the Deeps had been cleared out by the royal police, but during the Occupation, communists and Jews who could not flee to the mountains escaped here, to the higher, dry floors. When the Lib-eration came, German sympathizers disappeared here. Now and then, one emerged and, with great fanfare, was arrested. No one lived here by choice.

The water on the other side was ankle-deep, and they had to maneuver using door stoops and blocks of wood set out like boulders in a pond. The windows were gaping black holes, and from everywhere came the sound of dripping and, sometimes, the labored mew of cats.

Emil wanted to verify again the particulars of what Dora had told Leonek, where the exchange was to take place, what time exactly, but the cold, quiet streets necessitated silence. He had been to the Deeps only once before, during the weeks just after Filia had left him. The water level had been more manageable then, and some prostitutes lived in large attic apartments that had in drier days been home to fashionable bourgeois who had left their murals and bridal beds behind. Emil had met a dark hooker in the squares—not quite as dark as the American he'd seen in Berlin—and she'd led him back to her huge room. She was from Ankara, Turkey, and he never learned how she ended up here.

"What's that *stink*?" hissed Leonek.

Open and collapsed sewers. Rotting vermin. Dead bodies.

The photograph was stiff beside his heart, and the weight of the pistol in his pocket was unfamiliar. It made him fear losing balance.

They turned and emerged into a water-covered courtyard where a church wall hung over them. It was a small square, no bigger than the canals would allow, and the tall church made it seem smaller. In a hollowed alcove stood the broken statue of a saint, without shoulders or head, only the vertical folds of robe. High up, a black, round church window was ringed by glass chips.

He heard a rat swimming nearby, and jumped into a doorway, wavering slightly from the pain that burrowed up his leg and into his stomach. The steps were slick with moss. "This is it?"

Leonek lit a match and squinted at his wristwatch. In the yellow, shifting light his hungry face was kinetic. "Five before nine," he said. He leapt up beside Emil. Despite their efforts, their feet were drenched and cold. Leonek checked the door behind them—soggy double doors—and opened them a crack. Then he wrapped his arms around himself, squatted and rocked on his heels. The flat, chipped walls of the square seemed to slide in as the minutes passed, and in the black pool at their feet Emil thought he saw the ripples of distant movement. They both looked up at the black sky, framed by walls. "You hear something?" whispered Leonek.

Emil did. Then he didn't. Then he did.

The stumble of feet in water, off to the left. Heavy breathing. The hiss of a curse. Leonek held a finger to his lips, then pushed the door behind them open further.

Jerzy Michalec appeared first from the edge of the church, dim, red-faced, straining forward. His left arm was pulling something out of the gloom. A hand, then an arm. Then all of her was visible, fighting each inch.

His whisper jumped out of him: *"Lena!"*

"Emil!" It echoed along the waterways, her head twisting back and forth, then she found him with her eyes.

They were on opposite corners of the little square, the inspectors half-hidden in their doorway, Michalec and Lena just beyond the church. She tried to shake free of him, but he threw her back into the water. A small pistol appeared in his hand.

"You have it?" Michalec's untraceable voice was weary. He was still catching his breath. There was nothing of the control and calm Emil remembered from his house.

Emil unfolded and waved the photograph, though he didn't know if Michalec could see it in the darkness.

Michalec saw. He kept the pistol waist-high. "I'm surprised you mix with men like Dora, Comrade Inspector. That's some lousy company you keep."

"Where's the colonel?" asked Emil.

Michalec made an expression of bafflement.

"Herr Oberst!" Emil shouted.

"Up here," came the familiar accent. The German leaned out of the glass-toothed church window, waving what was no doubt another Walther in his white-gloved hand.

Lena was against the far wall, wet and shivering. "God*damn* it!"

Michalec had caught his breath. "Let's make this simple. Just the photograph, and here she is. No one else needs to die."

Behind Emil, Leonek was saying *shit* beneath his breath, repeatedly, for walking voluntarily into this deathtrap.

"How do I know I can trust you?" Emil asked, his fingers tightening on the photograph, his eyes just past Smerdyakov, on Lena's frantic features.

Michalec's arms dropped to his sides. "What should I tell you, Inspector? That I'm a changed man? That I've grown fond of you through all this? Will that make you feel better?"

"Shut *up*," said Lena. Exasperated.

Leonek was easing into the door behind them, which creaked as it slid open. The German still hovered in the dark window— his pale gloves were like fireflies.

"I want to know we'll get out of here alive," said Emil.

Leonek slipped through the door.

"This photograph is the end," Michalec smiled, opening his hands. "Don't you see? We can get back to the living now." He glanced at Lena, who looked scared against the wall, then stepped back and grabbed her arm. This time she came willingly. *"Now,"* he said to Emil.

The photograph was in one hand, his cane in the other. He stepped down into the water. Trash floated against his freezing ankles. As they approached the center of the square, Lena looked into Emil's face, and when they were close he could see the expression on her face was transparent. There was something behind her fear that made him forget the icy water, and he was suddenly sure that something was going to collapse, and he would lose her. He and Michalec were very close.

"What about the colonel, then?" Emil tilted his head toward the church. "What does he get out of this?"

Michalec's mouth came to Emil's nose. When he whispered, the smell of onions came with the words. "The colonel and I are of use to one another. We have a gentlemen's agreement." He held out a hand; his fingers gripped the air.

When Michalec took the photograph, Emil didn't let go. They held each side. "What if I turn you in?" he asked.

"Without this?" Michalec jerked the photograph away and squinted at it. He gave Emil a smile without warmth. "I know where you live. I know your family, I know everything you love. I've killed you twice already, Inspector Brod. One of these days, it's going to take."

It was cold again, cold right through. That long roll-call of corpses was on him again, with all the pain of this journey.

Lena squeezed his arm while Michalec folded the photograph into his coat, nodding. The gun in Emil's coat was heavy. He could barely hear her whisper *Oh god Emil come on I love you let's go* as he saw those dead boy-soldiers in Berlin, saw soldiers haunting the streets looking for watches, saw skulls crushed by the gears of the world that were run by Michalec's hands. Then a cold deck, the work blade in his hand. He squeezed his eyes shut. *Come with me come on.* She was turning him around, and he felt like crying. Then he was crying, and throwing her off of him. He rushed into Michalec's retreating back, the Marakov in his fist now, the barrel pressed against Michalec's temple.

They were both in the cold water. Michalec squirmed beneath him, shouting "*Oberst!*" weakly.

The Marakov on his ear, on his cheek, on his mouth. Each point of entry was unsatisfactory.

There was shooting up above, and water splashed. Michalec pushed, and they rolled over, struggling, and saw orange flashes in the sky. Michalec tried to punch his stomach, but Emil was on top again, sitting on him. He used the pistol like a club on Smerdyakov's head, twice, then forced the barrel into his mouth. A brief elation sang through him. That face was terrified. Eyes sealed shut, cheeks trembling. He saw the seal blade make work of this man, like the work done on soulless animals. Emil's finger held the trigger.

There was a celebration of gunshots above. Beneath him was an old, crying man with a pistol in his mouth. His fat stomach shook beneath Emil.

Behind him was a voice that he couldn't make out, but he knew before turning that it was Lena calling for him. She was huddled in a far doorway.

The old man was crying terribly now, trying to plead but unable because of the gun, and Emil looked at him for a moment, lightheaded by what he could do, then took the pistol out of his mouth and got up and walked to the door and sat beside Lena. They were both drenched, and holding each other did nothing to make them warmer. The shooting above had stopped. There was only black sky.

The sound of feet running down church steps on the other side of the square, then through water. He knew he should get up, but he couldn't move, couldn't take on the chase. He couldn't even look. Lena's breathing was a rhythm against his chest. The square was empty, old ripples the only sign of Michalec's departure. Then, behind them, Leonek stumbled out of the doorway. One bloody hand gripped his shoulder.

"*Shit, shit,*" Leonek repeated through clenched teeth. He slipped on the lowest step and fell into the water. Groaned. Lena, beneath Emil's arm, was weeping. He turned at the sound of splashing. But it was only the distant noise of running, wet footfalls echoing off the stone walls, becoming quieter by the second.

CHAPTER THIRTY-ONE

****

On the way out of the Canal District, Lena tore off a strip of her skirt and tied it around Leonek's shoulder to slow the bleeding. He grunted when she knotted it, and gave Emil a queer grin. "Crazy bastard. You didn't get hit *once*?"

First, Emil felt only the fatigue—a draining anticlimax, then, once they had reached the drier areas, he put his arm around Lena. She bowed her head into his shoulder. He had gotten her back, alive. He couldn't wipe the smile off his face. He felt her steadying breaths against him, and when he looked down, her soft hair was in his face.

Leonek muttered curses. He was trying to figure out if he'd gotten the *Oberst* at all.

But by the time they reached the parking lot, Emil's joy and self-congratulation was ebbing, and as they drove in silence to the hospital, he became focused on Michalec's Politburo seat, and what lay in their future. In weeks or months, maybe, there would be no place to hide. He felt the Marakov again as he leaned into a turn, and wanted to go back. He still didn't understand why he had let Michalec live.

He touched his bare head. "Anyone seen my hat?"

They both stared at him.

He helped Leonek out of the car and walked him into the crowded hospital corridor. Moaning peasants looked up—they were the same ones, it seemed to Emil, who had been here two months ago when they had gone down to the morgue. As he looked into the glazed eyes of the on-duty nurse he realized he would have to use the photos waiting in Janos Crowder's Zorki camera. Self-preservation demanded it.

The old, stale mess at her house was disheartening. She moved from room to room until she found one—the dining room—that had not been completely demolished by the colonel, Leonek, and whoever else had cut paths through the rubble. She made them both apricot brandies, and apologized for the lack of ice. It had melted. When the icebox, mysteriously, had been knocked over. Then she stood him up, put her arms around him and kissed him very hard on the lips. They stood like that for a while, kissing, their teeth sometimes rubbing together. The whole time it felt like desperation.

He told her about Irma. It came out over the oak dining table, where they sat in stiff chairs with high backs. She didn't cry at first, but her shoulders sank toward her chest, and she shivered as though very cold. The bottle of brandy was near her, so she poured another. She had washed and changed into a long dress made of green, spongy material, and while taking the second drink she spilled some on it. The brandy turned the green to black where it fell.

After a while, Lena said, "She was my friend." She smiled a tight, ironic smile. "It wasn't servitude, not really. Not anymore. She was a sister." Then she shook her head because she knew no one would believe that these days.

Emil was still on his first drink, and his nerves had not calmed. "Can you tell me about it?"

"Irma?"

"Smerdyakov."

She made herself a third drink and swallowed it all without spilling. "This man came to Ruscova two mornings after you left.

A single small man, wiry. A sneerer," she said, and he knew it was Radu, the butler. "He'd been misinformed, I guess, at that little bar, and had already broken into Greta's house. She told him to get out of her house, to go to Irina's, but he must have been afraid of breaking too many doors, so he just knocked. He said it was time for me to go, no arguments." She shrugged. "Irina tried to argue, but what could she do? He dragged me to the car. Some old farmers came out of their houses and yelled at him, it was nice to see. They waved their hands and said God would judge him harshly, but he wasn't fazed. Atheists never are."

It had taken half a day for Radu to drive her, at gunpoint, back to the Capital. Once he stopped and showed his Party card at a house and was given fruits and dried meat from a terrified farm couple. It was twilight when they arrived at Michalec's estate.

She refilled her glass and tilted the bottle toward him.

He shook his head. "Did they hurt you?"

"No," she said, then gripped her glass between her breasts. "He had one of his fits." She spoke quietly, as though Michalec were right there on the floor, convulsing. "The first night. He was arguing with me, and he fell out of his chair. His eyes rolled into his head. It was terrible."

"What were you arguing about?" he asked after a while, but she didn't seem to hear him.

He'd shown her pictures of his wife. Small, ornately framed sepia prints of a dark, beautiful woman in formal white dresses. "He thought I'd understand. Because she was killed in a labor camp."

"Understand what?"

"How it was to lose someone."

He waited.

She loosened her grip on the glass. She took a brief drink, then squinted. "My uncles shot in Austria, that and my father. He said he knew Papa from their social circles, said he was a practical man and that he respected practicality. He said I should understand his position, having lost so many of my family, and being left to fend for myself." She looked at the table, at the glass, then back at Emil. "I told him I didn't know how he felt."

"He was a collaborator," said Emil, suddenly flushed. "He worked for the Gestapo. Did he tell you that?"

She shook her head no.

"And the boys he shot? The ones in Berlin? The ones who loved him?"

She said, "He told me that war makes people like him, that nations did. When he was drunk, he said that after all the wars, natural selection would leave only him and his kind on the earth. But he stopped trying to explain once he saw I'd never understand."

In his dream the boat was made of ice, and the steel bergs floating on the ocean shattered it. Everyone bobbed in the water like ice in a drink. The Bulgarian, Smerdyakov and Lena. And the other faces, Poles and Germans, he recognized from the long ride to Helsinki and back home. Penniless, destitute, weepers and stone-faces, and the whole village of Ruscova, their hands empty. They all swam deeper, but no one drowned. Then he was washed onto a mountain ridge, above where trees grew, and in the high spring grass his mother sat up, smiling. She looked just like her photographs. The soldiers were disappearing behind rocks.

She woke him in the morning with a kiss. He was on the sofa, where he had moved to support his back and then passed out, and she was leaning over him. Sunlight streamed through the ripped curtains. She apologized for waking him so early, then handed him the bulky black telephone from the foyer. "It's your friend."

"Emil? Have you heard?" came Leonek's voice.

"Where are you?" Emil tried to sit up, but his back was stiff and he slid down again.

"The hospital. But listen. Jerzy Michalec."

Lena was stretching by the windows, hands meeting high above her head. He had woken up with her, and though they had not made love, they were lovers. He had trouble paying attention to the phone. "What about him?"

"He's gone. No one knows where. Moska's been looking for you."

He tried again and finally sat up, painfully. "Any details?" Lena looked at him from the window.

"The butler. He says some men broke in last night. Kicked through the door. He heard Michalec calling for help. Squealing, I don't know. I'm just imagining. When the butler came out finally, he was gone."

Emil remembered Radu's adept use of his truncheon. "He didn't help?"

"Would you?"

Lena sat beside him on the sofa, smiled, and stroked his shoulder. "Where is he now? The butler."

"At the station. Moska wants you to call him."

Lena could not be ignored. She drew her fingers over his cheeks and whispered something filthy into his ear.

An hour and a half later he was in the station house. The chief's door was open, but no other investigators had arrived yet. Moska got up when he heard him come in. "Brod, come on. Let's go talk to him."

They took the steps down to the cells. Most were empty because of a recent transferal to the central prison up north, but at the very end Radu sat where Cornelius Yoskovich had sat last week, longing miserably for his daughter. Radu looked just as miserable, but smaller. It was warm down here, and he was only wearing an undershirt and pants. Without a tie he looked like a little boy. He said nothing even when he recognized Emil.

"You want him here?" asked the chief.

"Interview room."

He came without a fight, led by Moska's iron grip. He settled quietly into the interview seat, in a room a lot like Room 47 in Berlin. A table with two chairs, and a single chair in the center of the room. The walls were not quite as dirty as the ones in Berlin, but there were some questionable streaks. Chief Moska stood at the door. "I'll be outside if you need me." He left.

"Let's have it."

"Can I have a cigarette?" Radu asked.

Emil went out, got one from Moska, and after it was lit, Radu told the whole story without a fight.

"I don't want that to happen to me," he said. When he spoke his voice was unusually deep, as though hearing his master being dragged screaming out of his own house had matured him drastically. "I'll cooperate."

Janos Crowder was blackmailing Michalec with the photograph he had acquired in Berlin, but after six months, Janos decided he could not go on with it. "I heard them talking in the foyer. Janos said he was feeling guilty about everything and wasn't going to take any more money."

"Did he threaten to turn Michalec in?"

"No," he said, shaking his head scornfully. "But how can you trust a creep like that? It wasn't *guilt*—he just thought he'd get something from his father-in-law's death. Above-board money. Secure. Who doesn't want that?"

As he talked, Radu's voice raised in pitch until it was almost natural, and he spread his feet on the floor. Aleks Tudor was the wild card, he said. The apartment supervisor had his hand in everyone's business, and during that week when Janos was back with Lena, he went through Janos's apartment and found the ten photos and a box of money. On the strength of these and some telephone conversations he had overheard, Aleks approached Janos when he returned from Lena empty-handed. "Now we had *two* creeps looking for a payoff. What else was Jerzy supposed to do?"

When Emil asked about Lena, he held up his hands. "Listen, I was a *gentleman*. I didn't touch her. Just doing a *job*."

"What about last night, then? Did you turn your own man in?"

"Are you crazy?"

Emil shrugged, as though anything were possible. "You're pretty open now."

Radu crossed his arms, his cheeks going pink. "I don't know who turned him in. Maybe the colonel. Maybe *you*. All I know is I'm not going down with the ship. This is just a job," he said. "It's not some kind of *devotion*."

They returned him to the cell and, back in the office, Moska watched as Emil unlocked his desk. He could bring out the evidence now, it didn't matter. "Would you like to see?" Emil asked, and the chief, indecisive, waited. Emil opened the drawer and reached in. There were a few loose papers in the drawer, some pen tips, a bottle of ink, but no camera. He reached back, sliding his hand around. Nothing.

Under the fluorescents the chief's expectant face had a subdued, greenish tint. Behind him the others were beginning to arrive—Ferenc and Stefan together. Brano Sev was not around yet. The chief looked at Emil's white face. "Something wrong?"

CHAPTER THIRTY-TWO

****

The planes stopped in Berlin. It took months and miles of newsprint, but in May the Comrade Chairman touched his mustache and let the British and American trucks through the barricades. Emil didn't realize how much the whole business had been affecting him until it was done, and when Lena brought him the news he shouted involuntarily. Grandfather shook his head. *We're living through History, and we don't even know it.* Grandmother said that now that there was hope for the world, Emil and Lena should get married and have children. Grandfather claimed to have no opinion on the matter, but advised Emil to eat more garlic with his meals; it would stimulate both virility and fertility.

There were cases. He worked often with Leonek, but when Leonek came down with a debilitating flu that January, he worked with Stefan, who was quicker than he appeared. He joked a lot, said his wife had had it with his eating. He'd been thin before the war, he claimed, but after seeing all those bright young men blown up, and then getting shrapnel in his own leg, his joy at living had been so strong that he couldn't help himself. He ate whatever tasted good.

In March they tried unsuccessfully to investigate the death of a German national named Teodor Schiffen found floating in the

Canal District. He was a tall man, blond, and had been, as an official search of his apartment unearthed, a Wehrmacht colonel.

Someone had gone through the apartment before they arrived, and there was nothing left to tie the colonel to anyone in the Capital, in particular the missing person of Jerzy Michalec. The best they could figure was that Teodor Schiffen, after the war, had ended up on the eastern side of the Iron Curtain. A bad place for any ex-German soldier; a man in that situation, Emil reflected, would need friends—voluntary or coerced. On a hunch, Emil rang Berlin to see if there was more information on him in the Tempelhof files, but Konrad Messer, after making inquiries, informed him that the crates of papers had finally been transported away—maybe to Washington, maybe elsewhere.

The Uzbek had a good laugh when Emil first saw the body, and vomited.

Lena sold the family house in April. She had never hired anyone to take Irma's place. She called distant relatives in Poland and Austria with names other than Hanic, but no one in the extended clan was in a position to take on such an estate—it was the same all over Europe that year. A Central Committee member finally bought the house without much haggling, and after it was gone she heard rumors that it had been purchased for General Secretary Mihai. A privacy fence was put up a month later, so when she drove by, she could not find out if this was true.

In June, Emil suggested they marry. They were by now sharing a large apartment in the Fourth District, near the Tisa, and lived as a couple. She laughed. "You don't have to do that. You don't have to buy the cow."

"But I want to," he insisted.

"No, you don't."

So they lived, as Leonek called it, in sin. Grandfather grandly called it a modern socialist arrangement.

****

The trials started again, in earnest. They were broadcast on the radio just as they had been after the Liberation, filling the airwaves. Titoists on the national scene, like their dangerous Yugoslav model, were trying to lure their People's Republic into the decadence of the West. These conspirators were ferreted out and put on trial. With wobbly voices they asked the forgiveness of the working classes. The bourgeoisie, they admitted, had hypnotized them.

In August 1949, two weeks before the Comrade Chairman tested his first atomic bomb, they heard Jerzy Michalec on the radio. It was a weak voice, marred by coughs and strange hesitations, and hearing him admit to collaboration with Hitlerite forces brought Emil surprise, but no satisfaction. He admitted to murders in both the East and the West, and claimed he had long been a counterrevolutionary agent for the Americans. He was a Titoist, an opportunist, a Fascist, and actively undermining the structures of socialism in the country. Not once did they identify him as Smerdyakov, the Butcher, or a war hero. There were more admissions and presentations of documents and photographs as evidence—they went on for an hour—and when a judge broke in angrily and said he had heard enough, this man should be shot, the eager applause was deafening. Then a confused silence. The accused, apparently, had begun to shake all over like a madman. His eyes had rolled themselves white.

He listened with Leonek and Ferenc and Stefan to the live broadcast from Ferenc's radio in the station house, and even the chief stopped, briefly, halfway to his office, absorbed. It was a miserably hot day—not even the new ceiling fan made much difference.

"Did they want you to witness?" asked Emil.

Leonek shook his head. "No one asked anything."

"Me neither."

Brano Sev came in from the corridor. He nodded at them as he settled at his desk.

Leonek had taken some brandy from his drawer, and they were all drinking. Emil took only a little—his stomach had never quite healed.

The judges returned after ten minutes' deliberation and sentenced Jerzy Michalec to death by firing squad.

"Justice," called Brano Sev from his desk. They all stared as he took off his leather coat. Underneath, he wore a finely tailored dark jacket. Green shirt and brown tie. He picked something off his desk and walked it over. He set the Zorki down on Emil's desk and stuck a cigarette in his mouth.

Leonek looked at the camera, at Emil, then back to the security inspector, confused. Emil had an impulse to rip open the Zorki, but the film, he knew, was no longer there.

Brano Sev nodded at the radio. "Don't worry about him. In a week he'll be commuted to hard labor. He'll be digging in the swamps the rest of his life. This," he said with disdain, "is modern correction."

He lit his cigarette and returned to his desk. Then, with the elegance of those who know they are being watched, he took a file out of his drawer and began to read.